**Their childhood games prepared them for a turbulent future:**

# JACKAL BIRD
a novel in three parts by Michael Barley

**In "Jackal Bird", a story of lost innocence ...**
... We built our mythology by listening to the old tales, and the fortress gradually became a secret headquarters for our own reborn army....

**In "Pangaelene", the dancer dances well ...**
... I had my own plans, my own objectives, not least of which was revenge against that same dreadful creature who had once tried to destroy me. Osseph had annihilated my family, almost the entire Gyrefaeld Addiman....

**And in "Illusions of Grace", life is not what it seems ...**
... "Consider me a new life form. Work with me, not against me."
    I fell more and more under the spell of her superbly modified simulation: she became the almost perfect replication of sister, woman and lover I had known a lifetime before....

# JACKAL BIRD

*Michael Barley*
*24.0695*

# JACKAL BIRD

## Michael Barley

TESSERACT BOOKS
an imprint of
THE BOOKS COLLECTIVE
Edmonton

Published by Tesseract Books, an imprint of The Books
Collective, 214–21 10405 Jasper Avenue, Edmonton,
Alberta, Canada, T5J 3S2.

The publisher gratefully acknowledges The Canada
Council and the Alberta Foundation for the Arts for their
financial assistance.

Edited, designed and typeset by Gerry Truscott.
(Set in Palatino 10/12, with modified Optimum titles.)
Cover art by Mitchell Stuart.
Cover designed by Gerry Dotto.
Jackal bird illustrations by Michael Barley.
Printed in Canada.

**Canadian Cataloguing in Publication Data**

Barley, Michael, 1939 –
  Jackal bird


  ISBN 1-895836-11-5 (bound) — ISBN 1-895836-07-7 (pbk.)
  I. Title.
PS8553.A765J32 1995          C813'.54          C95-910435-6
PR9199.3.B37J32 1995

# CONTENTS

... to my parents, who knew long before I did how unpredictable this world really is ...

... to my wife, whose patience with my typing is remarkable ... thank you ...

... to my children, who never fail to amaze me with their own insights ...

... to friends, who have read proofs and offered endless encouragement ...

... and finally, to ghosts lingering in shadows, their stories yet to tell....

# FOREWORD

So many years ago that I have lost count of them I sat aboard an ancient vessel that rode motionless on the black mirror smoothness of the Southern Ocean. My father, Greghory Addiman, had encouraged me to spend a season with the Port Cray Oceanographers and I was halfway to becoming a sailor. It was early in the day and neither Isurus Prime nor its White Sister had yet risen.

In silence I watched a flock of tern-clones circling in the windless air. They waited for scraps to be thrown overboard from our kitchen. It was all the creatures knew of our business in that ice-cold realm; we were nothing to them but strangers who would on occasion disperse leftovers in their general direction. They were of the newly re-engineered species from the gene banks below Port Cray. We were the intruders. To them, our oceanography meant only rinds and crusts cast overboard.

Small islands dotted the horizon, the southernmost tips of the Long Rim, a drowned impact crater that separates Marn-Cerrit from the Sea of Dreams. First light silhouetted these tiny greened cones as it slowly filled a cloud-streaked sky with its pale, metallic brilliance. Dead smooth, the water gave back its perfect reflection.

An instant passed and I was transported into what seemed like orbital space. Ship, birds, the row of islands, all were suddenly afloat in a surrealist vision where only imaginary boundaries existed between sea and sky, the mirrored planes conveying nothing of up or down or any normal planetary dimensions. It was as if some unknown realm had opened a doorway to its inner court. Had it lasted more than a few moments the vertigo might have suffocated me.

Fighting each other for their meal, the terns howled and screeched like the wild species they are patterned on. A breeze sprang quietly from the east and a surge of black ripples broke past the ship's twin hulls. The entire reflection shattered, its magic vanishing as quickly as it had appeared.

The instant haunts me still, its echo ringing down the years like a reminder of something hidden or lurking behind dark curtains. Of all my memories, this one remains closest to anything remotely spiritual.

The vertigo lingers – the solid ground we walk does not always remain squarely underfoot. When reality seems but the thickness of a shadow away, it is more often than not mere illusion.

Hedre G. Addiman, Translator
21:Mar:15-cy-75

# JACKAL BIRD

Jaeckle Bird, Jaeckle Bird, one, two, three;
Jaeckle Bird a-sleeping in the toplar tree.

Jaeckle Bird, Jaeckle Bird, four, five, six;
Carried him a-home for the Old Men to fix.

Jaeckle Bird, Jaeckle Bird, seven, eight, nine;
Old Men caen't fix him for the Jaeckle Bird was dyin'.

Jaeckle Bird, Jaeckle Bird, ten, eleven, twelve;
Throw him in the river where the bluefish dwell.

Children's Rhyme, New Foster

The following is based on notes made by Cultural Historian, Greghory Addiman, during a series of private conversations with Osseph Tokastevor, Status SRM. At the time of these interviews, Osseph had been released from restricted status for slightly more than a trueyear.

G.A.

# 1

There is a paved square at the southern end of High Street that has staged almost the entire history of our village. It lies where Old Quain Passway once turned west over the river, and where a stone and metal bridge, condemned and derelict, still stretches its rusted lattices across the estuary.

New Quain Passway, which my father and his engineers spent lifetimes building, bisects the township to the north. Between these two routes, the old and the new, our village maintains its somewhat irregular boundaries. The square is like a missing centrepiece in its vague geometry.

When we were children, rows of pale-leafed toplars lined this enormous courtyard. Now, nothing is left of the giant trees but their weather-hardened grey-white skeletons. These lonely sentinels stand guard over mounds of broken masonry and the broad circular pits of ancient cellars, remnants of even earlier times. One of the largest Gillcallian Cathedrals had stood here for centuries until revolution and civil uprising brought about its destruction.

The stony meadow of Cathedral Court with its frost-heaved terraces and weather-stained ruins is like a desolate, unkempt garden. Neglected by the flow of village life for generations before I was born, it always seemed as though some forgotten drama had faltered and paused, waiting for its troupe of vanished actors to re-appear.

When the giant toplars were still alive, we would climb high above the green and black flagstones to perch among the jackal birds' summer nests. Spreading in every direction, the tile-roofed housing compounds were like toys at our feet.

To the north, New Quain Passway marked a severe edge to our village. Coloured peaks of the larger houses stood against it like gypsies' tents. Our own compound was of grey metal and ochre brick. It flanked a narrow sideway at the top of the High Street.

Beyond the passway lay the University with its colonnaded cloisters, its arched galleries and angular towers. Mysterious and remote, its plasteel and glassite domes would shimmer like a mirage in the day's heat and glow with strange fluctuating auras at night. That this world of technologic enchantment was the backbone of our village's existence meant little to us; such things were far beyond our comprehension as children.

To the west was the Quain Estuary, most often resembling a warm, stagnant lake. In winter this broad expanse of water would race and surge against its terraced dikes in the swell of the incoming tides. But in our best times – the gentle and long-drawn days of summer – it was nothing more than a field of bubbling mud.

Down river, the Quain dissipated itself into an endless ocean and the dull haze of sprawling Materossen Peninsula began. The south-western coastline vanished in a maze of marshy inlets and fog-bound bays. Only the packers went beyond that horizon with any degree of confidence.

Moored well above the old bridge, a small part of New Foster's fishing fleet wintered in our harbour, the two-barrelled spinner-ships jostling against each other in their tight rows. Spring would see them geared with nets and spikemen, disappearing for months at a time and returning in early summer with their holds full of bluefish.

Then the decrepit and long-silent processing plants would be started up for their quick season, and the thick smell of flotweed would be constant on the south-west wind, giving the docks all the protection they needed from marauding children such as us. We could only venture that far across the river when the breeze was at our backs.

Inland were the Territories. The gradual restructuring of New Foster's mainland had not then penetrated much beyond the coastal limits of our townships. Breathers still had to be worn in the hills, and the dusty valleys penetrating our continent's western edge held little more than a promise of lung infection for the few souls brave enough to stake homesteads. We never travelled that far east; our world was very much defined by what could be seen from above the square on a clear day.

Sometimes if we climbed high enough we might catch sight of Isurus Station, the original colony ship, its deserted remnants circling endlessly above our heads. The light of Isurus Prime would glimmer briefly from its polished surfaces as the dismantled hull plummeted across our western sky.

And just once when I was alone late at night I witnessed the high trajectory of an outbound shuttle as it lifted all the way to the orbit of one of the few remaining starships.

**2**

We devoted our days to endless skirmishes in and around the ruins of Cathedral Court. For the most part our activities took the form of carefully devised combat. We played wargames.

The great square held no fear for us despite its morbid history; we knew the stories of atrocities and the uncountable dead, of the pathetic endings to so many lives. It all fused into a hazy, careless disregard with which we viewed most of the grownups' concerns. The ghosts they warned us of became a challenge to our imaginations. We tempted these dread spirits to frighten us away as we re-invented their altercations.

Our games were in fact a distorted version of the village history as it was relayed to us by the great-grandfaelders in our gyre. They had endless tales for my brother and me. Despite our father's wishes, they filled our heads with all we wanted to hear about the ill-fated revolution and its bloody ending.

At home the old men kept their treasured souvenirs, handed down from fathers before them: the musty uniforms and medals, the antiquated handguns, the albums of dim holograms with personal letters from those long dead pressed between mildewed pages. These shadows of the village's past were kept well hidden in the backs of secret closets until the long winter evenings. Then, when there was little else to do, the stories would be woven around each artifact as it was produced, examined and stored away again.

Three generations before mine, so the old men claimed, their friends, their cousins, their brothers had carried on a bitter struggle, believing they could change the nature of New Foster's society. To accomplish this they had formed a rebel militia known as the

Yuen-Natal. Most of them had perished, meeting death in battle, or afterwards as Guild prisoners – burned, hanged or impaled in Cathedral Square.

We replayed their roles in our games, our mock wars. We became revolutionaries fighting against the powerful Guild Reserves.

We were the rebel heroes.

My father, Guildmaster Birain Tokastevor, was Chief Engineer and Construction Supervisor for the New Quain Passway, a project that took him from one end of New Foster to the other. His long absences gave us abundant time for the wargames, although he made it quite apparent that he did not approve.

The elders preferred us playing normal childhood games and sent us off to the ragball and fencing courts whenever they could. But, given our choice, we usually ran about the streets and the square, shouting our rebel slogans, carrying on the false war. We were determined soldiers in play uniforms.

Our antics often upset the adults and, of course, we never understood it when some of the children were not allowed to join in. We began to realize why only when it was far too late. And the most patient of them all, my own father, suffered such anguish through our actions that I did not comprehend it fully until many years later. By then, he too was history.


# 3

Being overly curious or perhaps just not as sensible as our father might have wished, we often ventured down into the forbidden ruins of the cathedral. Our largest fortress was buried within its foundations.

There we planned our strategies over poorly lit sketch boards, plotting battles from vaulted chambers long forgotten by the outside world. It was our private sanctum, hollowed and refitted over many long summers. We built our mythology by listening to the old tales, and the fortress gradually became a secret headquarters for our own reborn army.

At dayschool, the tutor-matrix kept us through long, tiresome mornings of language, science, mathematics and the formulas of the Quatrec. This was the time we passed our messages, the coded battle orders for each day's free time. And on most afternoons it was a race from classes to the square.

There were four of us in charge of the games. I devised most of the encounters and my brother, Mihan, directed our infantry. Our young schoolmates were quite content taking my orders, storming garrisons, running blockades or just carrying supplies.

The two other generals in my military hierarchy were twins, brother and sister, belonging to Gyrefaeld Addiman.

Greghory was a dreamer, a strangely humoured boy. He was always the first to appear in his military garb: the ragged head wrap, the dirt-streaked shirt, the skin-tight covettes. He knew how to run a skirmish and I let him take some of the most dangerous missions.

His sister, Iilaria, was a tiny, dark-eyed girl who, in the beginning, looked more like a starveling than a ward of a prominent Gyrefaeld. She became a unique part of the group, gathering and dispersing information vital to the success of our campaigns. She was our reconnaissance expert.

She could scramble invisibly along the shores of the

Quain to count enemy soldiers, recording their positions and equipment. She seemed to operate best when her hair and clothes were thickly crusted with river mud. At the height of summer when our battles raged their fullest, her house staff must have been kept busy just trying to keep her clean.

We plundered "enemy" strongholds throughout the village, capturing their equipment, routing their forces, passing most of our spare time at little else. The four of us lead almost every other child in the village through a relentless series of carefully planned battles and skirmishes.

We might have continued our wars indefinitely, but there came a time when chance dictated otherwise, when the final drama began to unfold and we became players in a far greater game.

# 4

It was Iilaria who first saw the box in the river. We were scouting east of the square and had crossed part of the Old Passway Bridge by crawling along a network of rusted girders beneath its deck. Clambering down into the muddy gravel, we found the exposed end of a tooled saderwood box, its surface glistening with water left by the receding tide.

The rust-coloured wood of the sader tree is almost indestructible. My uncles worked with it in our mill and I knew that a case of that size would have been made only to house delicate tools, or perhaps some type of specialized equipment.

It could have been dropped from one of the river boats, although this seemed unlikely in the shallow side channel. It looked much too heavy to have floated there. Iilaria was certain it had been thrown from the bridge, but when or by whom she could not imagine. It must have lain for years, buried beneath the reeds, until the shifting currents of the Quain had exposed it once more.

As the tide ran its cycle, the container would come into full view again, visible from further upstream and from the river itself when the packers went out next morning. If we were to try digging it out, and I knew quite well we would, there would be only the one opportunity.

If no one else was to discover our treasure, we would have to come back late that same night when the water was at its lowest.

Wanting that buried box was one thing. Excavating and removing it would be quite another.

My brother and I were well practiced at climbing from the windows of our shared rooms above the shop roof. Trellises and a gutter provided ladders to the compound's central courtyard. Escape from our gyre lay through a small rear gate. That cloudless night the dark lanes were our safest route to Cathedral Square.

We skirted the silent houses, passing beneath their slate-edged eaves. We hurried by the few still-lit windows, avoiding passageways that might have concealed enemy spies or late-night wanderers from the public halls. In those simpler days, such adventures were not uncommon to us. We knew our way about the midnight streets as well as any of the gypsies and had often hidden markers for a full day's games under cover of darkness.

Gregh and Iilaria had likewise left their warm toballens and were waiting for us in Cathedral Court near the buried entrance to our headquarters.

Below ground, we tied together ropes, pulleys, shovealls and chemlights borrowed from our shop. We carried a few small tools in our packs as well as slices of dried panaco and sweetcake. And after rubbing greasy blacking onto our hands and faces we looked like oversized holliwoks. But we left behind the usual arsenal of weapons; for once the carefully fabricated guns of painted plastene and wood seemed unimportant.

We wanted no enemy contact. If we met anyone else, we would lose our opportunity. There would be no second chance. We were agents of the Yuen-Natal on a vital mission; our revolution would be won or lost on its outcome. I spun the drama in my mind as we set out.

A direct path to the river would have offered no real cover across the expanse of the square. Instead, we circled east and south in a route that took us along the edges of residential compounds and old packing houses.

South-east of the cathedral was a series of alleyways connecting the square to the river. The one we followed was narrow and steep, having been built in the early days of the Quain's history as a fishing port. In places it was little more than a flight of stone stairs leading down to the water's edge. Overhanging floors and balconies cast deep shadows that concealed us well but made it almost impossible to see. It was here that Mihan dropped one of the wooden shovealls.

Echoes clattered up and down the lane. I knew better than to curse at my brother; I could picture his silly grin even in the dark. All I could hope was that no one would bother to look. We froze against pillars and downspouts certain that someone would burst through a doorway to discover us lurking like reformatory urchins.

Perhaps there was a touch of luck with us that night; only one old woman ventured to look out of her billet. Her eyes were unable to discern our shapes in the darkness. She saw nothing though we stood, tight-lipped and breathless, less than a tenpace from her window.

After a long, agonizing stare she pulled herself back inside. We waited for her shutters to close, her slide bolts to lock. Mihan picked up the shoveall and we moved forward again.

We came finally to the base of the old bridge, our four dark profiles merging with the criss-cross patchwork of dimly reflected girders. Second tide was at seasonal low. After clambering down the stone-faced dike we were able to walk across the river bottom to the pier where our prize lay.

It took us time to relocate the box as we could not risk using our lights unless we were behind the bulk of the stone pillar. For a time I thought the box might have been swallowed again by the river mud, until Gregh tripped over it. In the dim shore-light, its almost invisible bulk seemed far more ominous than it had during the day.

Firmly wedged in river-wash, it could not just be heaved out of its bed. We had decided on our method of attack: two would work below with the shovealls removing the hard packed silt; the others would lift from above with a block and tackle that Iilaria had managed to smuggle from her stepfather's boathouse.

Gregh and I began to dig while Mihan climbed into the bridge frame. Iilaria rigged the pulleys and fitted a sling snugly around the protruding end of the box after we had cleared away the first layer of muddy sediment.

The wood-handled shovealls were short and awkward but they were the best we could find. The longer crolloy-tipped groundblades would have been missed by the house-warden on his nightly rounds.

Mihan and Iilaria pulled up the slack from the top while Gregh and I kept digging in the cold water, but our saderwood container remained firmly and solidly in place. Water surged around our ankles each time a wave crossed the river's central channel washing loose silt back into the hole as fast as we could dig it out. It was only after we had loosened sand and gravel to a depth past my knees that we felt the box move.

There followed a painful struggle which none of us had dreamed possible. One of us would pull and another would push, resulting in almost no progress at all. As the silt washed back into the hole, we removed it again, not once or twice but a tentime, all the while having to brace the box against its tendency to slip back down into the mud.

The difficulty was in trying to work together against the water. It took a long time to discover our mistake – instead of emptying out the hole we should simply have wriggled the box back and forth, letting its own bulk do the work.

We made slow progress. As we heaved and strained, our backs and limbs grew sorer, and the box heavier. But as the ropes tightened, the box gradually began to yield. When finally we realized how much easier it was to lift with the pulleys instead of our backs, we were too tired to enjoy it.

But, like an old tooth, the saderwood block gradually came loose in its socket. And with a final reluctant gurgling pop, it slithered from its bed to swing back and forth, dangling freely at last in the cold night. We hadn't the energy to celebrate; we just quietly groaned to ourselves.

I studied the mud-coated block with one of the miniature lamps, imagining what might be concealed inside. Exotic machinery from research projects in the University up river? Perhaps some long-lost artifact from the Torforatagos ruins? Thick, wet lumps of encrusted residue fell away as we scraped and poked.

Crolloy hinges were visible along one face. They were recessed into a thin groove that ran around one edge of the box. If it was meant to be opened there was no trace of a latch or lock.

Implanted on one end of the lid was a plate bearing the single engraved word, "Dader", which none of us recognized. But it deepened the sense of mystery surrounding our efforts. Whatever or whoever Dader might have been, our container was no longer a lifeless lump of wood.

It now had a name.

Gregh and I tried lifting it; the box was longer than either of us and much heavier. He suggested it might be filled with nothing but stones. I said this would have been a pointless waste of an elaborately made container and that we must have found something of value. We argued with each other while we rested, chewing on blocks of cold sproutcake from our packs.

We had reached a point of exhaustion where we might easily have gone home empty-handed. Time was running out. The tide lapped at our feet. The cold was slowly seeping through our leggings. But Iilaria, always the most energetic when she lacked sleep, nagged us back to work.

Lifting, pushing, hoisting, shoving each other about in the mud, we gradually raised the container in its rope sling. As it rose higher and higher, we continued arguing about what to do next. My plan was to lift the box to the bridge beams and conceal it on top of the pier. We would leave it there for as long as needed before we could move it safely to our underground fortress.

Gregh, tired but impatient, wanted to get it closer to the river bank that night. But the case was far too heavy; Iilaria persuaded him I was right, that we should be satisfied simply with having resurrected it from its burial pit.

From their massive stone supports, the metal bridge frames arched out over the Quain's deep central channel. We had been clambering about in the semi-darkness on a high, stepped abutment. The stones were smooth cut, but the joints between them were deep enough for foot and hand holds. Unfortunately, many of the ledges were covered with a slick layer of dead flotweed.

As we fought to manoeuver the swinging weight over the pier, Mihan slipped off the ledge he was clinging to. With the sudden jarring of the rope, the rest of us lost our grip and it slipped back through its pulleys. Both my brother and the box crashed into the wash with a noise that would have woken half the village had we been any closer to shore.

Mihan hauled himself out of water that had by then risen past the base of the pier. The box was once more in the river, still secure in its harness but with most of the rope coiled on top of it.

None of us said a word.

I thought of the Yuen-Natal. What would they have done a hundred years ago? Would they have blundered in such a clumsy fashion? Never! We would have no second chance. The fate of an entire revolution was at stake. We could not fail! I climbed back down the abutment determined to try again.

Re-threading the rope, we began to lift once more. This time there was no argument or complaint, no jostling in the ribs, no bad jokes. Mihan even managed to control his usually ceaseless flatulence.

We pulled and strained until the box was once more high above our heads, resting in a stone niche between the bridge uprights, well out of sight of both shores.

The tide was then fully turned. Waves broke along the river banks and the water was rapidly getting deeper. After dismantling the tackle and repacking our gear, we climbed into the bridge trusses and up onto the deck. Traces of first light had already bleached the edge of the eastern sky as we crossed the square and made our separate ways home.

Thinking back on it as I have done so often through the many long years that have followed, I wonder that no one heard or saw us that night. If some passerby had come along and interfered, putting an end to that absurd adventure ... if, if, if!

But no one did, and all the rest that followed could have happened no other way.

# 5

Silverday was an annual excuse for public celebration and general inebriation; thankfully, it was also a break from the routine of dayschool. The tutor-matrix did not deliver its usual program of lessons on the holiday and we had several days to ourselves.

"Project Dader" had been neglected for several months while the four of us studied and worked, so when our chance came, we stole the night once more.

The old bridge was closed to heavy traffic since its ancient girders became too rusted for practical repair. A narrow footway ran along one side of the deck. Although condemned, it was used occasionally by those who could not be bothered to walk farther north to the new crossing my father had built some years before. We would have to use this old planked walk to retrieve our container as it was too heavy to carry below on the river bed.

We would use the cover of darkness again, hoping that, as before, no one else would come by. This time we borrowed a wheeled cart from my father's shop with a pliopol cover to conceal its load. With Iilaria's ropes and tackle once more rigged from the bridge's upper railing, we would raise the container to the deck level then wheel it back to our hideaway.

Mihan and Gregh climbed down over the guard rail onto the pier where they fastened the sling. With the pulleys, Iilaria and I lifted the box over the bridge's edge and onto our cart. It was almost too simple.

The darkness of early morning still blanketed our fortress's hidden entrance. Moving back broken paving stones and overhanging bushes, we opened the tunnel we had discovered three summers before. It led horizontally through a weed covered embankment into a series of low, arched vaults, part of a storage cellar buried when the top of the cathedral was levelled. We had managed to clean out three small rooms; this was our military headquarters.

But we had long before decided there should be more space, hidden from the rest of the fortress, a safe retreat known only to ourselves where none of the others could follow.

We had opened two more rooms, concealing them with hinged panels painted to resemble the dull, grey stone of the surrounding walls.

This secondary sanctum was complete with its own laddered entranceway and had tiny slotted windows opening to the scrub-covered terraces above. It was into this doubly concealed series of cellars that we awkwardly wrestled our saderwood relic.

When it was done we sat for a long while, sipping cold callafe from borrowed kitchen mugs. We were silent, not quite knowing the words to describe our feelings. Even Mihan, whose attempts at humour most often kept us gritting our teeth, had nothing to say.

I think we suspected we had somehow changed the order of things. Could we have stopped then? Could we have buried our prize again, or dumped it back into the river? I didn't know the answer. I still don't, having asked myself countless times since.

Iilaria brought us back from our musings with a few simple words. "Now we can begin," she said, walking around the small vaulted room with a curious smile.

Then she kissed each of us on the forehead as if somehow this purely girlish gesture might refocus our strange conspiracy.

"Now we can begin."

# 6

While climbing into our rooms above the shop that night, Mihan dropped one of his boots into the courtyard; I went down to retrieve it. The noise of the pliopol footgear landing on top of a water barrel woke our house-warden, Trevarn. A kitchen lantern went on and he came through the door just in time to see me crawling back through a window two floors above his head.

Had it been his ubine, the nurse Galen, we would have been "deep in the trough" with our uncles. As it was, Trevarn settled for waking us much earlier than he needed the following morning, considering it was still a holiday. I knew by the grin on his leathery face that he suspected something, but he was easily sidetracked and, as well, a good ally when we needed him.

Laughing at us both, he let us know we were at his mercy.

"You'll be needin' baths before the mornin' meal, smellin' quite disagreeable as you do," he said. "An' if I didn't be knowin' better, I'd say it's a smell o' rottin' flotweed about you. Be'en near the river again, ha' we? There's wa'hter in the pump, so get ta it!"

The fusion heaters weren't switched on that early, which meant we would have to bathe cold.

Mihan and I shivered our way through the morning, cleaning the shop, the courtyard and anything else that Trevarn was able to think of to keep us under his watchful eye.

We attempted opening the container with chisels, drivers, even a small spring-powered katsaw; it seemed that nothing would even scratch the impervious outer casing. It was sealed as if it had grown into a single solid piece while lying in the river all those years.

When Mihan tried drilling into the top we learned its first secret. He was using a handbrace with a crolloy punch, trying to cut a hole opposite one of the hinges; he was a half-finger length into the wood when a sudden implosion sucked out the bit. It clanged against something metallic inside. When the hissing rush of air stopped, the top moved by itself. Obviously, it had been vacuum sealed.

Perhaps we expected too much; there was no choral syntheny, no sounding of great panghorns or lutifers, no dazzling aureole. A very dull-looking grey metallic cylinder lay before us secured inside the saderwood box.

Iilaria grabbed a driver and began unfastening the metal straps. The rest of us just stood by watching her, disappointed with the first glimpse of our acquisition.

The straps came away, but there was too little room between the casings to get secure hand-hold. After puzzling over various complicated methods of getting wires or ropes around the cylinder, Iilaria suggested we simply tip the box sideways and roll the tube onto the floor. I think it pleased her immensely to be the one who usually had the better ideas.

Each end was sealed with a plate-like cap, pressed and crimped into place. We worked at undoing the crimping with a small chisel. Thick grease oozed from the cylinder; we scooped it into an empty water barrel. We were soon covered with the shiny, black oil; in the dim light of the subterranean chamber we looked like actors from the Silverday plays.

It soon became apparent that we had something far different than I had expected. Inside was a collection of oddly shaped crolloy pieces, all coated in grease, all finely machined and shining with a deep-orange lustre where we rubbed them clean.

There were tiny threaded cylinders, coils and notched wheels, springs, slotted rings and discs, levers, strangely twisted bars, transparent tubes and blocks.

We found strands of coated wire of all different lengths and sizes. Some pieces were in their own containers, fragile hair-like bristles attached to rods of black plastene. Others, resembling the inside of a small domestic generator, were tied together as if meant to be kept apart from the rest. There was no way to guess what any of it was for. The array of mysterious paraphernalia meant nothing to any of us that first day.

It was to take us until the following summer to determine what it was, who "Dader" had been, and how all those incredible bits of our puzzle fitted together.

# 7

The recollections I keep under the notation "Jackal Bird" are simply the recorded stories of our forefathers. They are much like balls of knotted twine with the ending of one often inseparable from the beginning of another.

The constantly conflicting points of view within my gyrefaeld, between grandsires, uncles and the multitude of other relatives dwelling within our compound on Quain Street made our heritage seem all the more confusing. Coupled with my own developing urge for independence, it generated within my mind such heretical notions that I dared share them with no one. And though it all seemed so contradictory, I still tried to relay the excitement of that mysterious past into our games, to bring it all back to life in the village streets and the great ruined square.

I wanted to keep the others locked inside my carefully planned schemes knowing well enough that I could not hold them forever.

Yet I was desperately willing to try.

The old rebels had abhorred the Quatrec, intending to replace it with some obscure regime of their own. They were not satisfied with defining every aspect of society according to environmental rules, for that was the essence of Quatrec philosophy.

An elaborate collection of formulas for dividing and cultivating, for development and preservation, it was supposedly rooted in ancient scientific principles.

Communities were built, land was utilized, crops were planted and harvested, families were genetically appropriated, all according to a master scheme. It had been engineered by the first colonists and was thought of as the basis for planetary survival. But there were many who thought New Foster could function more efficiently without the imposition of restrictions and quotas.

This dissatisfaction by itself might have led to no more than a few fireside debates or arguments within the University's Guild of Academics. But in places like the Territories, where life was a constant hardship, there were often land feuds, many of them hostile. With the steadily growing population, increasing numbers of settlers refused to accept being told how to live their lives as they were shifted farther and farther into the unclaimed wilds.

Civil unrest was inevitable.

The arguments were as old as my grandfaelders.

Quatrec Law determined where and how people should live; I grew up hearing the endless debates. Their elders before them had gone to war over it, initiating the Yuen-Natal as their own. The stories they told were of their battles with the Quatrec forces.

But the rebels enjoyed only a brief moment in history. They were annihilated because some of those same ancient rules defined action under such circumstances. The original designers of our world had obviously worked through most of the contingencies.

Quatrec-supported guilds quickly raised their own army. They turned every battle into a bloodbath. Like other revolutions that had occurred during the slow process of planet-taming, the Yuen-Natal uprising went nowhere. And, according to the rules, no mercy was shown.

The rebels fled their communes and their towns, leaving behind nothing but desolation and ruin. Thousands of survivors, both troops and civilians, came to the Quain Townships and the surrounding countryside seeking support and sanctuary. Instead, they found an army of well-prepared Guild mercenaries. The Yuen-Natal suffered its greatest single defeat outside our village, being slaughtered almost to the last person.

Their frenzied efforts left Cathedral Square the ruin I knew as a boy. It was here that captured rebel leaders were executed. We learned how the square had been filled for weeks with hanging frames, impaling rods and roasting drums. The stench of death, the bloodshed, the confusion, were never to be forgotten.

The tales were told and retold.

I once found the body of a lone jackal bird hanging head down in its nest high above the square, the leading edges of its wing spines still wrapped tightly around a branch. It smelled like flotweed at low tide.

Its summer skin was hardened and glazed. Where its eye stalks had been there were clusters of small black holes and its breathing horn was twisted into knotty loops. I remember feeling awkward and ashamed, as if somehow I had been responsible for its death.

The corpse seemed a fragile mockery of the living creature. In flight jackal birds are magnificent, glistening red-gold in the air as they plunge through updrafts, their wings wider across than four men's outstretched arms.

Each year, they would come to the village, always at the same time, circling above the clumped groupings of toplars that used to grow abundantly in the region. Selecting individual trees, they would spend days and nights arranging nesting patterns that only they understood.

Of course, jackal birds are not really birds at all but some sort of primordial facsimile flying unwittingly to their extinction. Real birds have never flown on this world, except in children's stories. But I empathized with those poor, flapping creatures who once shared the planet with only their native kin, coming and going with the seasons, mating and migrating as if nothing could ever change for them. There are now less than two hundred left alive in a desolate sanctuary far out along the Northern Rim. They are no longer able to survive the conditions mankind has imposed on their world.

One solitary jackal bird inverted in its nest, blindly waiting for a season that would never arrive; finding it like that upset me more than had the passing of an uncle a year before. I remember holding back tears as I descended to the broken pavement of Cathedral Square.

# 8

On the northern side of the square and terminating the long vista of High Street was another Gillcallian ruin. We had always called it the Turret although my Uncle Erid insisted it had been a clock tower. Standing at halfangle to the cathedral's entrance but a hundred-pace north-west, it had complemented the main building, being circular in plan also. But it was much smaller, consisting of a single, central round chamber about four tenpaces wide, with walls of solid stone at least a twopace thick. The timber floors and roof had long ago burned or rotted away, leaving the sky as its only cover.

Wedged firmly and immoveably in the single, narrow entrance and facing out towards the cathedral were the remains of an ancient armoured vehicle. One of the stories tells that during the last days of the uprisings this great double-tracked dreadnought ventured across the old bridge into the square. It was pursued by four laser-bearing jerrolds, faster and smaller six-wheeled carriers that had the advantage because of their speed and number.

The larger vehicle was vastly more powerful but was vulnerable because of its size. It smashed its way into the tower and spun about to face back through the doorway. As the jerrolds buzzed and fumed around the square, it was able to defend itself for a short while, presenting an impervious front. But foot soldiers managed to enter the tower through a side door to fire explosive projectiles into the side of the monster, destroying its turbines and power system. Thus immobilized, it simply ceased to function.

The wreck was never removed. The toplars cast their long shadows across the hull as its hatches were welded shut to keep children out. It remained there, blocking the original tower entrance, an elegant piece of rusted sculpture with its huge tubular guns pointing downwards to the pavement. A lethal-looking monument to the powers that once battled in our streets, it provided a major part of the stage furniture for our games.

I always attended the forays I devised, usually watching from cover of the many upended stones above our buried fortress. It gave me a chance to observe my strategies first hand.

In the case of the entrapped dreadnought, I had never been convinced that such a machine could have been so easily overcome.

Who had piloted it so recklessly? And how had it managed to end up alone in the base of our Turret? It mocked me with its silence, seeming to challenge my inadequate answers.

I knew there was something wrong with the historical account. But no matter how I replayed it, the battle was always lost.

*A hundred children race into the square from all directions, One group is dressed in dark green covettes and headbands, another in pale yellow. They carry realistically carved and painted weapons: wooden guns, pistols and long, curved fencing blades.*

*Green clambers among the fallen stones along the*

square's western perimeter. Yellow scurries into the Turret and its blocked entranceway; the dreadnought provides them with only limited defensive cover.

Green aggressively divides into three smaller columns and approaches the tower, encircling it on the entry side. They quickly conceal themselves behind weed-grown stairs, tumbled balustrades and the trunks of the great toplars.

One of them, wearing a medallion-covered shirt indicating high rank, climbs into the branches to survey Yellow's position. From his perch in an empty jackal bird's nest he signals a hold to his troops below.

He raises his right arm, two fingers outstretched and pointing skyward. At a precisely chosen moment, he flings his arm back, then forward. Green's right column fans out as a shield, holding its new position while the left column swings around the Turret's south side in a broad, flanking movement.

A small, dark-haired girl in a green smock comes into sight. She carries mock grenades and a loosely-slung rifle so realistically modelled that light glints from its polished barrel. Silently, she leads two others off to the right. They approach a crumbling doorway a thirdportion of the tower's circumference away from the main entry. Yellow has posted a single guard. The girl knows where the hiding place will be and moves to cover it.

From above, the commander waits until the girl is poised, then issues his final signal, a double forward wave of the right arm. He descends the tree, still invisible to the enemy in the Turret.

The girl rushes the rear entrance, ambushing its single guard. By the rules of play, he stays down as if actually dead.

Now the entire troop begins its assault of the dreadnought from all sides. Yellow retreats under the onslaught;

*many fall within the first moments. The children scream their battle shouts at each other, preparing for the final, crucial manoeuver.*

*The three snipers, now inside the rear of the Turret, crouch behind broken archways and fallen beams. They separate, waiting for the first sign of a Yellow rush back into the tower. Before it starts, they advance on the exposed back of the rusted hulk, holding aloft paint-filled canisters made to look like grenades. Well concealed, they wait for the pre-arranged signal.*

*Green and Yellow are now engaged in hand-to-hand combat as the battle moves towards the tower. Green's leader appears, waving his rifle, yelling orders. Again, he signals with hand motions only his soldiers recognize. The three who have remained silent break cover, charging into the centre of the chamber and, in unison, throw well-aimed grenades at the dreadnought's sides and rear.*

*Red and blue dyes smash against the pitted, rust-covered metal of the ancient armour plating, and splash onto several of the unsuspecting Yellow soldiers. Dropping to the ground, groaning in the theatrical anguish of false death, they realize they have been out-manoeuvered by Green's cunning.*

*The battle is over. Survivors are herded out into the square, lined up and shot.*

*No prisoners are taken.*

A hundred years before when the original encounter took place, the captives had been hanged or impaled without a trial. The Quatrec forces were merciless in their victory, hoping to set examples that would dissuade further revolt. We were taught that they could not have done otherwise.

But we could simply reverse sides. Yellow against Green, Green against Blue. Next time, it would be a different colour assuming the rebels' side.

I congratulated the officers. We discussed some of the finer points of the strategy they had just played out. I made suggestions for future deployment of their forces.

The fallen, now resurrected, stood at full attention. As I finished, they saluted, brushed themselves off and began making their way home to well-earned evening meals.

# 9

At the north-eastern end of High Street, New Quain Passway abruptly terminates the clusters of closely structured compounds with its broad, winding ribbons of hardpack gridway. Many of the older warehouses, hostels and residences had been torn down when the throughway was built. A few were left hanging perilously close to its edge.

One of these had been sliced in two, its remaining half supported on slender crolloy columns with black glassite blocks used to fill in the missing walls. This uniquely altered structure became quite famous and master builders would bring their apprentices to our village to study this example of the quaint, local architecture.

The building was refitted as a visary. We were sent there to research most of our school projects. The tutor at the dayschool was linked to the visary's ref-matrix and had records of all the cubes we hooked. It was therefore almost impossible to fool the matrix if we did not complete our assignments properly.

But deceiving the teaching machines was one of my brother's main interests. He would punch in random-access codes and ask for oblique, unrelated information. Mihan was the matrix expert when it came to misleading the sensors and hooking prohibited cubes.

One of his typical tricks was bringing up explicitly detailed reproductions from the Kalanos Pleasure Palaces under the guise of an assigned topic such as "Non-Fosterian Ecology", or perhaps an archaeological report on the "Isurus-Coral Artifact".

Pretending to be researching a school essay, he would hook cubes on old weaponry, getting models for our own arsenal in the games. Once a cube was accessed he could make it reproduce copies of any drawing he wanted. Removing the printouts from the visary was simply a matter of not getting caught. As a result, Mihan had collected details of almost all the military hardware ever used in the colonies.

By going back through the proscribed cubes, he identified "Immin-Dader" as an industrial laboratory operated by the Port Cray Institute and our own University. Later on it became known simply as "Dader". It had originally been established to research high-efficiency laser technology.

My brother and I began spending afternoons in the visary under various pretences so that he could follow through with his discovery. To give him enough time, I volunteered to complete most of his dayschool assignments for him as well as my own. For a brief period, we both submitted work well ahead of schedule, a phenomena as shortlived as it was unexpected.

He eventually found a series of catalogue references for two small laser rifles manufactured by Dader almost two hundred years before we were born. The Yuen-Natal had managed to arm many of its soldiers with these weapons. They were destroyed by the guilds when the civil war ended, placed on a prohibited list and relegated to history. Mihan was convinced we had found either a GF-12, or its more powerful twin version, the field-modified GF-20.

Back in our underground chambers with Mihan's diagrams we continued to clean and sort the delicately machined components. We were putting together our first real weapon, an outlawed laser rifle that had last been used in active battle more than a century before.

Gregh and I built work benches in the back chambers of our buried fortress. It soon began to resemble a machine shop.

Mihan and Iilaria continued the task of sorting. My brother had a sure sense for the technical; where everything fitted and how each of the various sub-assemblies worked was second nature to him. Iilaria kept all the pieces in carefully worked-out patterns that they would modify as new interconnections were discovered.

What I had first presumed to be a rifle barrel turned out to be part of a support tripod; at this point, I was relegated to guard duty and general cleanup.

And we began to realize that we possessed more than one of the rifles when we found that every part was duplicated. It was not just a supply of spare parts – there were two of everything.

Mihan decided we had found a pair of the GF-20s. He showed us how the unmodified GF-12 was identical except for larger pulse and gain chambers, which he pointed out while fitting them precisely over the generating pot. He explained that GF stood for "Generator Focal", the generic term for a class of weapons dating back to pre-colonial times. In these discussions,

Iilaria was the only one who fully understood him. Once she had the basic theory in her mind, she could solve the technical problems just as easily as my brother.

It was, in fact, Iilaria who took the lead. She completed the first major section, a triggering mechanism designed to generate small charges below the firing chamber of the laser, or the "pot" as Mihan called it.

Iilaria rigged batteries to test circuits the rest of us could not even see properly. These were housed in glassite tubes and embedded in many of the components, making positive connections as they slotted together. The pre-circuited assembly kept my brother in awe for days.

Mihan's future engineering genius was beginning to assert itself then. Also, I suspected, he was enjoying the attention of the girl at his side, who seemed every bit as clever as he was.

Mihan worked on Project Dader too long one night. He was caught changing clothes in the compound shop by Aeren, one of the maternal uncles who had come home later and drunker than usual. He hauled my brother into the kitchens by his ear where Old Galen vented her fury on both of them for creating such a disturbance.

To be late for a meal was in her eyes the greatest sin we could have committed. She summoned the paternal uncles, Erid and Osseph, which made things much worse for Mihan – these two did not like being disturbed during their evening arguments.

Their judgement was that he should stay at home for a threeday to study and work, "instead of playing the silly wargames in the square". This pleased Galen, as it usually fell to her to enforce such punishments.

No one in our gyrefaeld suspected that my brother and I were solely responsible for the games, or that we plotted them from beneath the forbidden cathedral ruins. And had any of them known we were reconstructing a prohibited firearm we might have finished our fenyears in a reformatory.

So instead of appealing my brother's threeday detention with Uncle Osseph, I carried on as if nothing were wrong, returning the next day to our fortress without him.

As Military Commander, it was I who decided when and where the games would be played. The others accepted this because I was good at it. I learned very early to delegate duties and to oversee. The result was a well-run army.

We were able to program and control the movements of more than three hundred children. I devised a system of three teams, with only two in action at once. The third group always remained on reserve and would be rotated according to a schedule worked out by Mihan and me. This gave us the best opportunities for competition, with individuals playing by preset rules for points, promotions, medals and other recognition.

An event the troops looked forward to was the parade we held at the beginning of each summer. All the teams would take part in the exercises. They would take stations around the great square in their uniforms of green, yellow or blue, marching back and forth in traditional military patterns.

I would lead an inspection of the entire battalion with Mihan, Gregh and Iilaria. There would be more marching, and a band if we could organize one. A few of the elders would come to watch, frowning and indignant perhaps, but when they saw their children high-stepping to the sound of skins and panghorns they would quietly smile, reacting quite normally to the mood and rhythm of a military display.

We were but a tenday before this event when Mihan was restricted to the gyre. I wanted "Dader" ready for the parade and I was concerned about my brother's absence for those few days.

I worried for nothing. Iilaria not only completed assembling one laser but repacked the remaining parts into the original container. When Mihan returned, she proudly showed him the finished GF-20, then suggested he search our shop for the correctly sized charging cells so we could run calibrations.

Almost a year had passed since we first made our discovery in the river-bed. I had believed all along it would be vital to us.

I finalized my plans for the demonstration.

# 10

From all directions and from every part of the village the children came. They were in full uniform this time, and carried rifles and sabres, pistols and knives, all hand-carved and painted. Polished medallions shone like glystalene in the morning light.

Green troop lived mostly south of the square, Yellow to the north, while Blue crossed the Quain Estuary from north-west to reach our parade ground. Very early in the day, the village awoke to the sounds of laughing youngsters making their way to the ruins.

Not all of them arrived for the start of the ceremony; there were meals and chores to finish. Some were not permitted to participate if their guardians or nurses were inclined against the games. But by the time the toplar's shadows reached mid-morning's halfangle, three battalions of at least a hundred soldiers each had gathered in front of Cathedral Court.

Commander-General Mihan Tokastevor appeared, followed by Commanders Gregh and Iilaria Addiman. They marched with a slow, determined step from the Turret to a wide rectangular platform of dark green paving stones raised several steps above the rest of the courtyard.

Long before the time of the Yuen-Natal, it had been a focus for cathedral processions when the Gillcallians held their festivals in the square. The three officers halted, raising their outstretched arms in traditional salute to the troops, then turned to face the clock tower.

Ranks of soldiers came to attention. Green, Yellow and Blue aligned themselves in a three-sided square formation facing the podium. The leaders faced right, towards me, where I had stationed myself beside the rusted hulk of the ancient dreadnought. I saluted to the battalions, then marched to my usual position on the stairs in front of my fellow officers.

A few adults began to arrive, staying well in the background along the edges of the square. Most were simply and plainly curious. Some actually seemed to enjoy watching their children's parade. I saw Trevarn trying to make himself inconspicuous beside a fallen pillar. Was he there keeping watch over us for our father's sake? I never knew what went through the old man's mind.

Father had never actually seen our ceremonies. I could not visualize it through his eyes; he would most likely have remained unimpressed. I never understood his anger when he learned of our adventures.

The school chestral began playing their version of the Fosteralle, one of our oldest national marches; it added a final military tone to the assembly. They strode about the square, followed by first one proud division, then another. Even though they were merely children in ragged costumes, the feeling of their power was overwhelming; they were keen and excited. Continuing their well-practiced turns and passes, the band went through its small collection of martial music several times.

Iilaria stepped back to a small drapery behind us on the stand. She removed the pliopol cover and slid aside the frame it hung from, revealing our new weapon. Only those closest to the platform saw the GF-20 at first; it was a gradual revelation, spreading slowly from the assembly's centre out to its extremities like slow ripples on water.

Most of our modelled weapons were fashioned from sections of charcoal-painted wood, some of them smooth enough that their polished surfaces glinted dully in daylight. In contrast, the GF-20 was a mirror-textured metallic yellow-orange, its highly machined crolloy components glowing brilliantly as Isurus Prime climbed higher above the cathedral. None of those in the battalions gathered there that day had ever seen such a machine. None of them considered the possibility that it was genuine.

The charging cells had been positioned. I snapped open their cover plates and checked the generator capstock. The plates slid into active position. The clicking of minute relays sounded. There was gradual silence around the platform as suspicion began to grow – our usual model guns did not click and whine, nor did tiny lights flash on and off when chambers were ready for firing.

The sound of the band's tymballines built warm crescendos in the humid air as soldiers continued marching through display manoeuvers. Several of the other officers were making awards, presenting medals to outstanding soldiers from each division. Visitors watched, smiling and chattering among themselves as midday approached.

I counted several jackal birds hanging upside down in the branches overhead. They would be awake before the last leaves had opened, but that morning they were still in their summer skins. Oblivious to the aliens below them in the square, they slumbered through their complex metamorphosis.

# 11

There would have been a crew of at least five inside the dreadnought when it was destroyed. After entrenching themselves in the clock tower, there was time to fire only a few rounds from their cannons before being hit from behind. With both barrels aimed towards the main building, they brought down the entire front face of the cathedral and buckled most of the interior roof supports.

Inadvertently, they destroyed their own people. They could not have known that more than a thousand Yuen-Natal refugees were hiding in the multi-level cellars below. These were injured rebel soldiers who had been given temporary sanctuary by the Gill-callian Society and who might have eventually made an escape through the coastal seaports. And there were women and children, families of rebels uprooted by the civil uprising.

A few managed to struggle out into the square as the structure collapsed into its own foundations. They were cut down instantly by Guild hirelings as they wandered through the dust and debris. The rest were buried under an enormous volume of stone and mortar.

The bodies were never removed. Masses of soil were piled into the hole, filling it to the level of the square. Over many years, gradual settlement lowered the scrub-grown surface until one or two perimeter openings were exposed again, leading into the upper portions of a few basement rooms.

This was Cathedral Court. This was where we had constructed our underground headquarters.

The spirits of those poor unmourned souls might have inspired the final act of our drama. Were they with us then, watching as we strutted their lonely stage?


## 12

The bright disc of Isurus Prime above and behind us cast our shadows towards the Turret. Beside me waited the three other officers of my command.

First was Iilaria, her dark hair wrapped loosely against the pale skin of her neck. Of the three, she looked the most anxious, repeatedly glancing in my direction, waiting for the signal to start.

Beside her stood Greghory, fidgeting with fingers clasped behind his back, large dark eyes fixed abstractly on rooftops across the square as he tried to isolate himself from the tension growing in the crowd around him. This was a trick I had taught him to help smooth moments of panic before battle.

Mihan pulled at the laced front of his covette, trying to tighten it around his thin waist and thighs. He did not seem at all uncertain about our plan and paid little attention to the gleaming rifle he had so recently helped reconstruct.

These were the highest ranking officers of my reborn Yuen-Natal. They stood on their raised stone dais, wooden rifles smartly shouldered, rows of medals and ribbons displayed proudly across shirts and headbands.

Iilaria saluted and turned to face the assembly. A light breeze ruffled her hair. Stepping forward, she spoke quietly to the troops, a short speech I had prepared for her. They strained to listen to each word, as if under some spell. They could feel it as well, a tension building in the air as if something unusual was about to occur.

Gregh gave a series of commands. A tenpoint of soldiers filed into step behind him, his select team who had accompanied him on countless raids and skirmishes through many campaigns. Marching solemnly towards the Turret, they halted before the high stone shafts of its entrance.

The drooping snouts of the dreadnought's rusted cannons hung over them as they about-faced once more. I saluted from the podium and they broke ranks to clear the other soldiers away from the Turret's base, moving the entire assembly closer to the cathedral. There was soon a wide, empty gap between the officers and the old tower. The adults remained in the background; none of them had yet seen the GF-20.

Savouring the moment, I gazed about at the spectators, my troops, my officers. I tried to imagine what it would be to command a real battlefield instead of these games in the now almost too-familiar parade ground.

Where would the enemy appear first? I wondered. In the shadows below the trees at the edge of the courtyard? They would build up their numbers under cover of darkness and try to take us by surprise at first light. But we would be ready for them.

Small groups of grown-ups stood back in the shade, protecting themselves from the increasing heat. I could no longer see old Trevarn but I knew he must be nearby. Slowly, my thoughts returned to the alignment of shadows across the square. It was moments before noon.

The GF-20 stood half my height on three telescopic pistons. Although it had been previously set by Mihan's meticulous calculation, I ran through a check procedure. Levers below the gun's main mounts were locked and the gain chamber showed full charge. We had determined what we believed to be appropriate co-ordinates for a safe, low-level discharge that should simply knock a few stones from the Turret's entrance-way.

Making a few more meaningless adjustments, I scrutinized the new hairs growing on the backs of my hands, the dust on my covette, a leaf fluttering in the slight breeze. I extended my drama to coincide exactly with midday. Iilaria nodded again as if to ask if I had not provoked the audience enough. I checked the gun's alignment once more and, satisfied at last with the stagecraft, reached for the firing mechanism.

I held it firmly, pumping the release.

The GF-20's trigger was designed to be held in a

closed fist, away from the discharger on a flexible tube. The thumb rested on a spring-mounted pin. Once released, a small energy pulse set off a burst from the main pot, or generator, which in turn fired an amplified charge along a pulsating focal beam of red light.

At first it was not as impressive as I had hoped. The firing ended instantaneously. There was no recoil. Residual impulses restarted the cycle; I could have fired again immediately with another squeeze of my thumb, producing a virtually unbroken stream of destructive energy.

What was happening in the Turret deterred me.

I saw only part of it, and that in slow motion, like a hooked cube in the visary running in search mode. A bolt of raw, boiling heat had struck the dreadnought, tearing open its front end. The old cannons seemed to lift themselves from the ground as the rusted vehicle slammed backwards into its tower.

A plume of dust and debris rose above the building's roofless crest. Broken stonework around the entrance collapsed slowly inward. Small fragments of white-hot stone and metal flew in all directions, up and out into the smoke filled air.

Blast-noise echoed about the square for long, terrifying moments. Some of the younger children ran while the older troops held fast. In awe of the explosion, few were aware of the danger.

The first casualties were among those closest to the tower. Flying shrapnel felled a dozen or more unsuspecting youths who had never seen live gunfire. Moments later, lumps of debris began falling in a wider circle. Rock shards from the building landed on at least twenty more children still standing attentively in parade formation.

Panic erupted. In a screaming frenzy, the entire assembly turned and surged towards the river. They crossed the plaza in a horde, racing towards its high, terraced dikes.

The explosion had been directional; its force-cone spread south-west, covering most of the fleeing assembly. Shouting adults raced after them as they gradually realized their children were being hurt. Several of the smallest fell to be trampled by the rest.

Villagers who had heard the thunder of exploding metal and crashing stone began to appear from adjoining streets. It was not long before there were more than a thousand of them. They ran in all directions trying to help those they could and adding yet more confusion to the disrupted afternoon.

My three officers stood by the toplars unhurt by shrapnel or debris. Dust continued to rise above them in a great, grey cloud. They squinted upward into a sky that had been blotted from view.

Iilaria was the first of them to notice me lying beside the still-humming laser, my head in a bloody pool. She was suddenly and harshly aware of what we had done. Bravado vanished. Shock and fear took its place. She howled like a wild banik.

Then the other two spun towards me. Greghory buckled over and turned away. Mihan vomited his breakfast into his lap and collapsed onto the pavement.

An aura of ancient horror permeated the square.

I did not remember any pain. It happened so quickly, as if to someone else, as in a dream. A splinter of burning metal from the dreadnought had penetrated my left eye and torn away part of my cheek. With only one eye, I watched from the noon-warm pavement, my brave soldiers in anguish.

When I tried to lift myself, darkness claimed me.

Overhead, the jackal birds slept on.

# 13

I awoke in the University medlab where Trevarn had rushed me after the disastrous episode in the square. Having no awareness of either time or circumstance, I spent groggy days simply staring at cracks in the plaster ceiling. I waited with a growing fear the punishment that was sure to come. The medictechs told me what happened to my eye and a little about the rest of it, but none of them seemed to know much about the events of that day.

Eventually, after I had suffered a full tenday of self-torture, my father came. I broke down and wailed in front of him, which no self-respecting general should have done. To my surprise, instead of giving the reprimand I expected, he took me in his arms and comforted me. I saw that he too had tears on his cheeks and I felt a little less alone.

He told me of injuries, the many superficial wounds, the more seriously hurt, and of eighteen children killed by falling debris. He was very busy, he said, smoothing rough waters, trying to explain how a long-buried projectile, possibly left over from the Gillcallian rebellion had exploded when it was jarred by falling stones from the Turret's decayed masonry. It was an accident that bereaved parents were long in accepting but which they could understand. It was fortunate, he reminded me, that his high office gave him certain advantages when it came to difficult situations. He never mentioned the laser rifle; for him, it had not existed.

We talked briefly of my disfigurement. I had lost my left eye and the implant could not be installed until parts of my cheekbone had properly mended. My impaired vision would be a life-long reminder of what had happened and it would be sentence enough, he said.

Then he went on to give me a history lesson that none of the old stories had revealed.

It was of the dreadnought in the clock tower and the soldiers who had perished inside it a century before. When the monster was welded shut, it had not been to keep the children out but to keep the surviving crew in. Our firing the laser had exposed the old armored vehicle's inner compartments revealing five skeletons entwined in each other's corrupted limbs. They had, it seemed, died of starvation rather than suffocation.

Three of them were smaller than the others and still retained long, flowing hair attached to the fine parchment of their mummified scalps. It was not well known that many of the Yuen Natal's troops had been women.

"Your games are a travesty," my father proclaimed. "You have no notion of the terror, nor even of the truth. It is part of a history, of our own family history, that we must try to forget.

"It horrifies me – no, it terrifies me to see you assuming the same dreadful conceits of your direct ancestry. I don't think you have any idea of what it means to die as a victim of misdirected beliefs. What you play at is no game.

"You are to stop immediately."

He never told me which of our ancestors had been part of the Yuen-Natal. I presumed they had been members of his paternal grandfaelder's immediate circle. All I had ever seen were the relics hidden away in my uncle's cabinets.

He went on to inform me that the Addiman Gyrefaeld had removed themselves to the Materossen Peninsula where another branch of their family built sailing ships. We would not be seeing Iilaria or Greghory in the near future. My father thought that was, by far, the best thing for my brother and me.

And that was the end of it as far as he was concerned.

Many years after my father's death, I learned that Trevarn had spirited the GF-20 away. I presume he destroyed it, as the weapon was never found. No one quite realized what it had been, or learned how it came to be fired. Labourers had been recruited to fill in the front of our hidden fortress, unaware that they had buried the second laser still in its container.

Our wargames thus came to an end. Two of my commanders were in exile imposed and enforced by my father. The Addiman twins had been blamed for the entire episode while I lay unconscious in the medlab. By the time I could say anything, it was over. They and their family were gone.

The great square remained unchanged except for the toplars. Over the course of several seasons they were stricken with a microcellular disorder known as fools-blight. Nothing was ever done to regenerate them.

Deprived of their usual nesting places amid the silver-orange foliage, the jackal birds ceased their annual flights to our village.

# PANGAELENE

The Pangaelene is an ancient off-world dance said to have originated beyond Viarta prior to the colonization. It is best known here in its casual northern mode. Music and dance structure depend upon improvisation to a basic five-part theme.

Traditionally performed by two women who sought the attentions of the same man, the Gypsies of New Foster still practice variations of the dance during Silverday Festivals.

Also, one who vies for the attention and favours of the powerful, for position, for fortune, is said to "dance the Pangaelene".

The following is based on the written diaries of Iilaria Jacine Addiman. – G.A.

**volume 36, pages 56-60:**

*Looking to the past can be dangerous....*

In quieter moments I return to these journals that I started as a girl. In them I have recorded some of the notions that have flown their overlapping circles in my mind, some of the thoughts, some of the events relating to them.

I do not always enjoy evoking the moods of the past, though that is the price I must pay for sifting through memories. My rational self cries out to leave them where they lie, ghosts lingering in shadows.

But having lived my life tossed back and forth by circumstances too monumental for me to have avoided, I cannot ignore those early remembrances. The danger is in dwelling for too long with the unchangeable; what might have been always presses for recognition.

There were occasions when I thought I might not survive to be as old as I am; I imagined some dramatically early end. I moved with strong men and played in vast arenas. I belonged to times my children do not envy. Ours was a generation of incivility between nations, of harshness between men.

My life was a series of painful awakenings from romanticism; they mark the early volumes of my diaries. And they are the sections I reread most often, as if I must somehow bolster my belief that it has all been worthwhile. A device, perhaps, with which I retain optimism, enthusiasm.

"Silly old woman!", I wrote here today. Well, silly at least; I am by no means an old woman. My face is lined and lean, my flesh whittled, my hair streaked with a fair season's touch of white. But no, I am not by any means old. And I still turn heads when I enter a room.

Today it is the council chambers for me once again. My deputies will notice me. I will walk a little more slowly to the central dias to keep them standing longer. I will wear the emerald robe to entrance the elder members, and flaunt a *little leg to distract the younger.... You see, my diary, that I have not changed much in all these years.*

*I have nothing in mind to add to your ponderous collection at the moment ...*

*... ghosts lingering in shadows....*

*Looking to the past can be dangerous....*

# 1. Denique

The drake-pulled cabriole rolled to a stop in the winding street. Gathering my skirts, I stepped to the cobble.

A warm, light mist floated on the air, almost but not quite a summer rain, its moisture settling onto my skin and clothing. The humidity, thick enough to touch in this season, left its mark in thin, damp trickles that slipped, finger-like, beneath my toplet.

One of Haderan's guards approached, my appointed escort. I followed him through a narrow archway into an overgrown courtyard. Down a long, low flight of stone stairs, a narrow doorway opened into the messalliary.

We had arranged to dine at this particular foodhouse because it was close to the garrison. I was late enough to remind Haderan that my feelings were still bruised – he intended to return to his headquarters, cutting our evening short. It was thus an appointment of convenience, mostly his, with him well aware that I preferred his attentions in more intimate surroundings.

In a low-ceilinged anteroom, the guard took my cape and barrett. At first it was difficult to see across the messalliary. Smoke drifted through its interior in lazy blue, red and green spirals. Huge, slow fans swirled vapours of countless dreamsticks in the thick air; the stim-laden atmosphere could quickly dull the senses with its airborne euphorics.

Dodging our way across the floor, we squeezed between tightly packed tables, avoiding outstretched limbs of a few semi-conscious patrons. These lonely, envious souls, indulging themselves in brief moments of drug-induced pleasure, made their empty gestures as I passed. Most were Haderan's men, ill-paid mercenaries who had little else to do in Denique, the city that had recently become their base.

Haderan was at his private table, near windows that opened onto another exterior court. He had commandeered a raised, partially secluded balcony which gave him a view of the main hall and, as well, a constant supply of sea-scented and reasonably fresh air. Rising as I approached, he dismissed his guard.

A big-boned, brown-skinned man, he stood a head taller than anyone around him. Flinging out his arms, he embraced the entire room, his face gleaming with boyish delight.

I had made myself especially pretty for him; his response dissolved what remained of my anger. He moved towards me with a dancer's grace, embracing me, lifting me easily from the floor. I ran my hand through the triple-striped matt of his close-cropped curls and kissed his nose, smudging the blue line he wore down its narrow ridge. The entire room was this man's audience and I just a player in his personal drama.

"Lovely as ever," he said to me at least three times.

Still grinning, he sat down across from me, his little show over for the moment. Other patrons turned back to their own conversations, to the dancing, the music.

He had brought me a bouquet of pojhon, the tiny blue flowers that grow only on high rocky slopes of

Denique's northernmost islands. "Iilaria, my little parasegino," he said, offering them. As usual, I let him conquer me with his effortless charm.

Smiling, he apologized once more, explaining why he had to return to his garrison early, why he could not spend the entire evening with me. "Necessity borne by command," he insisted. "One of the junior officers has to pay a visit to New Foster."

"New Foster?" I asked. "Why would anyone go to New Foster?"

"A military matter," he replied. "Are you thirsty?"

"If you would, please."

He signalled a passing server, who waved a hand signal to another with an array of wine skins strapped around her torso. She, in turn, disappeared towards the kitchens.

"You're sending a spy?" I asked, though I knew full well that he was. I had learned a twoday before that someone was going but knew none of the details. This was why I had decided to dine with Haderan, though I knew it would be difficult, steering our conversation to the matter of the spy. He was too busy trying to entertain and seduce me.

"What makes you think of spies?" He laughed, easily dismissing my curiosity. "Food should be your concern for the moment."

The server wearing the wine skins arrived at our table with a bottle of ch'ell. Haderan had already selected our meal, and stone trays soon rolled past our table in steady succession. Coned charilfish, kalberries, deretessian mince – the array of heavily spiced appetizers came one upon the other. The main course was shelled bluesteak, the seafood specialty that had made this eating house famous throughout the islands.

We ate, speaking with our eyes, our hands. We sipped ch'ell from tall, crolloy goblets. The messalliary's heady atmosphere slowly absorbed us in its tenuous embrace.

Three musicians ambled between the tables, weaving their lyrical fibres from strands of air. They sang of lost love, of loneliness, casting their mellow sounds about the enormous room.

One sang in a high falsetto, like a soprano, but alternating to a deep, throaty base. I had not heard anything like it on the islands before; dark scars below his larynx suggested vocal surgery. The singer cavorted up and down the scales as another player caressed the panghorn's melancholy reed and occasionally soloed on a sandcast deracco. The third accompanied them on a stringed instrument resembling a delicately pitched tymballine.

Two parasiginos danced a pangaelene in a cleared space below Haderan's balcony. Bare to the waist, skins glistening with scented oil, they circled each other in time to pulsating drums, bending backwards and forwards, their lithe bodies turning faster as the tempo picked up. The crowd echoed the rhythm, drumming with mugs and wooden utensils, beating on tabletops.

One of the dancers threw down her silk scollar as challenge in the traditional gypsy dance. As the soldiers whistled and cheered. The other dancer moved forward until they were touching, breast to breast, stomach to stomach, thigh to thigh. They drew long, coloured bands of silk from above and behind them, weaving round and about each other. Their bright skirts whirled and floated in the air as they swung and twisted about the floor.

The first woman, who had been eyeing Haderan

since she started, swirled towards us, winking up at him, stroking her breasts with quick, upward hand motions, inviting him, daring him, to join her on the floor. She knocked a goblet of ch'ell onto the floor with her flying perricoats – the red-amber liquid splashed across the tiles.

Haderan grinned back at her, turning to me almost apologetically. I teased him, threatening to strip my-self to the waist and join the dancers. He pretended a schoolboy pout, promising to behave, and the dancer moved on to other tables. The entertainers circled away from us, out into the central hall.

Servers brought sproutcake and jellied sweets on polished blackwood, then callafe in iced mugs with drops of freshly brewed holipan. We sipped the steam-ing liqueur, but its euphoric evaded us. As the meal gradually came to its end we found ourselves still in-extricably wound in the webs of our own immediate concerns.

Haderan made apologies once more, and I had yet to ask him my one favour. As we left the dining room and its crowded, hazy loudness, I tried to explain the letter I had written. "It is to an old friend in Materossen. I think he may be in some danger from Osseph if he continues his work. I would like to cau-tion him. It would mean a lot to me if your young man could take it with him. Is there any way you can help me?"

Just as Haderan could be charming and witty when it suited him, so could he be stubborn and unreach-able. "There is no way I can condone the smuggling of illicit messages between countries that are essentially at war," he said. "You should forget, once and for all, the horror you have left behind you in New Foster. Concentrate on your new life here in Denique. For are you not one of the most beautiful women in the Capital? And the mistress of a high-ranking officer in the New Federation Militia? What else do you need? Surely, no woman could ask more?" He tried to dismiss my plea with his flippant conceit and ordered one of his men to summon a drake.

"Haderan, my dear, sweet soldier of fortune, can you not understand my dilemma? Can you not help me get a letter to an acquaintance without making such a fuss? I'm not interested in your war, but I would like to try and help an old friend. That is all I ask."

"I'm afraid it will have to wait, my love," he persisted.

"Wait? Until when? How often do you send someone on such a mission as this?"

"Iilaria. There is nothing I can do."

"I had hoped you might see your way –"

"This is not the time. Now, we must go. I'm due back at the garrison shortly. We must see that you get home comfortably."

We rode in silence. Haderan might have been thinking of the young officer he was sending to probable death in the camp of the one-eyed dictator, Osseph Tokastevor.

I considered this powerful man who sat across from me in the drake's cab, who courted me constantly, demanding my devoted attention like a great banik pup. Like anyone in such a position, he gave back only what suited him.

*It works both ways,* I thought. *We use each other.*

He seemed preoccupied with his coming briefing, and when we reached the archway in front of my domestria, he simply touched my hand and mumbled further apologies for leaving me so early. He signalled the harnessed driver to stand over.

*How easily he commands men, yet how insensitive he is to their lives, their affairs.* I knew he would never change.

At my doorway, I promised a perhaps for the following afternoon. He climbed back into the cabriole after the drake reharnessed, dutifully waving to me as he left. The cab ran faster with its single passenger. I listened as the drake's loping footsteps retreated into the night.

Haderan, I'm sure, was quite confident that he owned me.

I had my own plans, my own objectives, not least of which was revenge against that same dreadful creature who had once tried to destroy me. Osseph had annihilated my family, almost the entire Gyrefaeld Addiman. It was only by chance that I had managed to escape. I was now engaged in running a campaign against him, and Haderan was one of my weapons.

We appeared to be on the same side, both fighting to overthrow the self-proclaimed head of state on New Foster's mainland. Haderan was the highest ranking officer in the Reformist Militia. He took his orders from a Reform Council which had not yet officially declared war on its Mainland counterpart but was rapidly coming to the realization that no permanent peace was possible. They recognized that if they did nothing to oppose Osseph, he would soon try to take over the Island Federation.

But the guilds were not yet willing to separate themselves from the New Foster economy; too much of their livelihood came through trade with the mainland. I found it far more effective, therefore, to work discreetly, behind the scenes. My influence was largely through a well organized underground extending deeply into both Island and Mainland affairs.

I pushed my charming general as hard as I could, but this time he had not bent to me. He rushed away into the night with hardly a backward glance. My inner voice cried out to tread carefully; I listened, but had not yet heard all it wanted to say.

Later, having bathed and cleansed myself of the night's clinging odours, I lay between the silk linings of my toballen. Alone in the deep, circular bed, I cried myself to sleep.

**volume 10, pages 94-96:**

*Haderan has given me an elegant silver yarrenchain for my birthday. It is meant to hold a pendant, which he thinks should be of my own choosing. He has also recommended a guildsmith in the Crystal Plaza. I have delivered the chain with one of the collection of medallions originally given to me by Trevarn when I was a girl in the Quain Townships. At Haderan's insistence, I have commissioned the smith to craft a proper mounting.*

*The pendant I have chosen is embossed with small notations encircling a bearded man's profile:*

E PLURIBUS UNUM    UNITED STATES OF AMERICA

*On the reverse face is an imprint of a colonnaded building and more notations:*

ONE DOLLAR - ANNO DOMINI 2044

*Other symbols are too worn to be legible but they appear to resemble an ancient version of our own printed alphabet.*

*I have identified the piece as pre-colonial, only because there are references in our matrix to similar notations on artifacts preserved in vaults at the Port Cray Institute. These objects originated in the colony ship which was, of course, dismantled in orbit.*

*Meanings of most of the words are unknown. "DOMINI" are numbered tiles in a game similar to rucque. "2044" is a numeric, most likely denoting value.*

*I thought this medallion to be one of the least conspicuous of my collection. The rest remain concealed near Kalanos Separ where I maintain a hostel for travellers in my employ.*

**volume 10, pages 98-99:**
*A tenday later and I have claimed my gift from Genter's shop. Haderan is so impressed with the completed necklace that he has again started calling me his "gypsy" or his "little wanderer". He flatters me. The gypsies wear a lot of elaborate hand-made jewellery and I have always imagined myself kin to the travellers.*

*Most important to me, the medal I wear at my breast is a simple reminder of what has passed. I have surrounded myself with the trappings of a new life, but I am so often heartsick for the old! The slender chain may be a lover's gift, but the medallion it carries remains a talisman from my childhood.*

*Dare I admit to you, my diary, that I secretly believe it will help bring me full circle to a reckoning with the forces that have so completely shattered my life?*

## 2. Denique

Two men were following me, very obvious in their manner, not making any effort to prevent me from knowing they were there. They appeared coarse and ill-groomed, as if their fortunes were not at the best.

I had left the house early after my morning meal and walked the short distance along Ambassador Row, having intended meeting Haderan near the Science Institute. But he was not there and I did not wish to stand alone outside the museum. I entered, acting as if I had planned to view the exhibits.

I followed a tour through the building, presuming the pair would be gone when I came out, close to the half-day. I was wrong – whatever they wanted of me, they were determined about it. They still idled in shadows across the road.

I hurried away, heading diagonally across the civic square and its crowded intersection of streets. They kept behind me as before, making it very apparent it was me they were pursuing. Rushing along a boulevard I did not recognize I found a small dress-maker's shop with its racks of clothing fluttering outside. I entered through the low-arched doorway.

A girl approached me, anxious that I should buy from her and not the other yardser slouching fatly against a serving counter. I asked if there was a rear door.

"A door?" She did not understand my urgency. Not waiting to explain, I pushed my way past her to the back of the shop. "The courtyard, matalin. Just the courtyard out there."

The shorter of the men entered through the front door and stared at the fat girl, who still just leaned. He signalled his companion as I fled the rear of the shop.

I noticed he was missing one or more fingers of his left hand.

I found myself in a deeply shaded courtyard. There were trees and pathways winding between artificial hills and waterways. I momentarily recalled the garden my mother had kept behind our compound in the Quain Townships. In front of me, the dense tropical growth of the Ten Thousand Islands crowded every passageway. I imagined instead the tall, silent toplars of our home coastline. My racing heart gave tangible dimension to the noon-warm air – I felt as though I was in a distorted, frightful waking dream. "Haderan," I desperately whispered. "Why didn't you come? Where are you when I so need you?"

A vise gripped my wrist from behind; without thinking, I jabbed my other elbow straight backwards, kicking out at the same time. By luck, I must have hit the man's vitals. He let out a grunt; I was free and running.

"*e-Grinn a! Mas e-Grinn a di bhekk!*" His muffled voice slurred as if he were in pain and trying to catch his breath.

Short of wind, I slowed and glanced back from a narrow stone bridge. The taller of the pair was slightly built and wore a thick blond beard. He stood at the doorway clutching his groin. The one with missing fingers, dark haired and stocky, was shouting at his companion to move quickly. He pointed in my direction and to the rear of the garden court where I could see the eaves of a small stone shed. I ran towards it hoping to find a hiding place.

I saw no other gates or throughways in the high stone wall enclosing the garden. I had little choice but the shed. Reaching it, I pushed on the wide boarded doorway and almost fell through. It closed behind me and I fastened the wooden cross bar. I didn't stop to think that it could also be operated from the outside.

I was in a storeroom full of tools: rakes, shovealls, cutters, groundblades, hoes, mowers – all the implements necessary to keep up this enormous estate. As I caught my breath, I looked about for something to protect myself with. I picked up a short hoe and backed into a dusty corner.

The short man arrived first, peering through the panes of a dirty window and shouting back to the other. "We've found her now, haven't we?" he jeered, moving towards the door.

The blond joined him. I heard them laughing outside. "Locked herself in, huh? Locked herself away. Try the handle. She might be surprised."

I realized then that the bar could be lifted by simply turning a lever outside. There was nothing I could do. They opened the door, crowding the opening so that very little light came in. "This time, you're not going anywhere, slough."

"Who are you? What do you want?" The hoe shook as I held it in front of me.

"Want? What do we want? Agan, tell the slough what we want." The dark haired man leered at me like an animal.

"*?e-Bragha ret e-Fellish quaam sodni!*"

"Agan says we take the medal and you go free. I say we take it and break your pretty little neck for what you did to him back there. Besides, you know his name and we can't have that, can we?" The dark one had translated the Viranti not realizing I understood it well enough to know that the blond had actually asked if I was the right one. "Grab her. Get that hoe away from her."

"*?e-Dokni ret desann uyullu!*" Yellowbeard wanted

to know what we were going to do with this "wild woman". They laughed as they moved towards me.

I had dropped my sleevepouch to the floor and raised the hoe with both arms, slashing at them as viciously as I could. "Leave me alone! Leave me alone, you sons of baniks!"

The tall man lunged at me. I brought the hoe down towards his head. His arm flew up, deflecting my blow and throwing me off balance. He grabbed my weapon, wrenching it from my grip and throwing it across the room. The other's face twisted into a grotesque leer. The vise-like grip clamped my wrists again as yellowbeard pulled me up towards him. His breath smelled a tenday stale.

He spun me around and twisted my arms behind me. Holding me firmly with one hand, he pulled a cord from his ragged coat pocket and tied my wrists. The dark one just stood watching. "Fasten her good. We don't want her running off any more, do we, Agan?"

Yellowbeard pushed me against the wall with my bound hands lifted behind my shoulders. There was a hook projecting from the stonework supporting three or four rusted metal shovealls. These were thrown to the floor and I was hoisted up to dangle in their place. My arms felt as if they would pull out of their sockets. My feet were off the floor and I could barely breathe with the pain that tore through my chest.

"Uncomfortable, are we? Never mind. It won't be for long. Now then. Where do you suppose the medal might be? That's all we want. The one you took to Genter's shop."

"*e-Haggarran raglam. Noni pa trebbi!*" Yellowbeard muttered. Let me find it! It must be on her!

"Genter said it would be on a necklace," the smaller

one stated.

Rough hands went to the collar of my toplace. With a violent tug it was torn away from my neck and shoulders. I felt as though my arms were about to snap. I was nauseous and I thought I might vomit all over this beast.

"Well, now! Between her sweet little breasts! That's it, then, Agan? Will it come off?" The necklace was fastened with a small threaded couplet. The chain itself was quite short. "Can't get it over her head? Well then, how do suppose we are going to get it off? What do you think, Agan?"

The tall one chuckled, his deep voice sounding as though it were bubbling through thick oil. He picked up a rake with long, thin wooden tines and with a quick flick of his wrist, broke one of them free.

I thought I might die then; I was not afraid of dying, only of prolonged pain. I wanted it to stop, my body screaming its hurt. I felt moisture and warmth trickling down my thighs. My bladder gushed its contents into the underlayers of my skirts.

He slid the shaft of wood between the silver chain and my neck, and pulled until it was choking me.

"*e-Gralach sloughlin!*" he hissed. Little mud-slough! "*Fihilli compara mhoi. e-Diss!*" We do this my way!

He began to twist and wind the chain more tightly. My head pounded, I could no longer breathe. I gagged, wanting to vomit, unable to force anything past the taught loop about my throat.

As the necklace wound tighter I had a sudden, stark vision of my brother reaching for me from the cold distance of space. He beckoned from a white doorway that was silhouetted against the blackness of a star-filled sky. I tried to grasp his outstretched hand but as I leaned towards him, his image receded. The farther I reached, the harder I stretched myself out, the more the white door, the stars, my brother diminished. He was finally no more than a fading spot amidst a whirling haze.

"Gregh! Gregh! Gregh!" I cried as he vanished.

My head exploded into blackness, into void.

### volume 34, pages 80-81:

*The vision of Gregh in his cocoon of light speeding away faster than my voice can fly once more echoes down the tunnels of memory.*

*When we last saw each other, we were eighteen. I am told that depending on how far he has gone and at what velocities, he will be between sixteen and twenty-four years older than when he left. I am now sixty-eight true years, and some of the council are trying to retire me. I remind them of my baby brother hurtling towards unknown stars and they laugh.*

*You were my first great disappointment, Greghory Addiman. I put you out of my thoughts: you have been all but dead to me through the years. But there you are now, lingering still in the shadows, another ghostly voice calling my name.*

*If you were to return now I think the shock would destroy me! And I would still not have understood the riddles of your strangely distorted continuum. Nor why you had to leave in the first place!*

*Perhaps you sensed something of the might-have-been, as I surely did. Were you afraid of it as well?*

*Or ... of me? I always suspected that part of the reason you left was because of me. Yet it was only love that I offered you. Only love.*

## 3. Denique

I heard the quiet murmur of voices. I opened my eyes, quickly shutting them again in the brilliant, painful light. I rolled my aching head sideways and opened them more slowly.

I lay on the floor below the window of the old shed. "Are you all right, matalin? Can you hear me?" The fat girl from the shop had tears in her eyes; she was frightened and upset. "Han and I found you here. We followed those men who came into the shop. We waited until they were gone and came in and ... we found you. We thought you were dead." She burst into deep, gasping sobs; the other girl put her arm around her.

"It's all right, Jeva. She's going to be all right." Turning to me, she explained how difficult it had been getting me down, untying me, trying to make me comfortable. They had not wanted to move me from the shed until they knew that I was in one piece, a mercy I could not then fully appreciate. They had waited until I stirred, taking turns at washing my face and neck with cool water, massaging my wrists and feet. I had not remembered the two men tying my feet, but the girls insisted they had struggled with the knots for a long time as I lay on the ground. "We found this beside you," she said, handing me the remains of the yarrenchain.

It was broken and clotted with blood – my own. The coin was gone as well as the mounting it had been suspended in. Had the chain not broken.... I shivered at the thought of my head lying close by, separated from my body. I felt the cuts and bruises on my neck but could not bear touching them.

"You must come with us, matalin. My aunt has salves. Your neck and wrists are swollen. She lives at the back of the shop. She will help you. Can you walk? Here, lean on us. We will hold you." I pulled myself up, falling back several times until I had steadied myself against the pain that throbbed through my entire body. Supported by the two girls, I made my way slowly through the garden. It had taken so little time to run this way before, with the men after me. It was a long and painful walk from the stone shed back to the shop.

The fat girl, Jeva, ran to rouse their old aunt who slept in a room not much bigger than a clothes cupboard. She hobbled out into the daylight, took one quick glance at me and shouted something in Mulao, her north-island dialect.

"She only speaks the Viranti," said Han, "but she will make you well, matalin. Don't worry."

They led me into another tiny room so crowded with odd bits and pieces of chests, benches and shelving that there was hardly space to move. They made me lie on a child-sized couch not long enough for me to stretch out on. My feet hung over an arm rest onto a table while my head was cushioned on pillows at the other end.

There was a sky-window, the only source of light. The old woman busied herself with earthenware flasks and glass bottles, all the while mumbling to herself in the guttural Mulao tongue. She ushered the girls back into the dress shop so that I was alone with the tiny, withered creature.

I could barely speak and she seemed intent on smothering me with her various herbs and remedies. She removed my clothes which was not easy for her and rubbed oils into my skin. She made me sip a spice laden brew and held up some sweetly scented cloth in front of my face. I remember nothing more.

The next thing I recall was waking on the same undersized bed between thick, warm covers and looking up through the sky-window. A brilliant point of white hung in the night above me.

Viarta, the brightest star visible from Denique, marked the constellation Copernica, the Southern Cross. It shone so brightly that I could see the outlines of the furniture about me. I recalled the terrible vision of my brother reaching to help me, then pulling away and vanishing into his sky of stars. Tears welled; I was overwhelmed by a lonely fear that I had thought buried and forgotten, a fear of being deserted by everyone I had ever loved.

"Gregh has been there," I whispered into the pillow as Viarta flickered in the impenetrable distance of empty space. "My little brother, Gregh."

I was afraid of the night, of the strange bed I lay in, of the new threat that had so suddenly been thrust into my life. I felt utterly alone.

I didn't notice then that the pain was gone, that my neck and back were once again comfortable. As tears born of self-pity and physical weariness washed down my cheeks, I drifted into a dreamless sleep and did not move again until the morning.


## 4. Quain Townships

When I was of nine trueyears, I would sometimes dress up in my mother's finest clothes. My breasts were growing, my hips widening. I would parade myself in her dressalliary, reflected in her mirrored walls, thinking that soon we might easily be mistaken for sisters. I would strut in her long hand-woven gowns and silk stockings, stumbling in the high laced boots that were then in fashion. I tried to look as elegant as she did in the tiered wigs and masqued face.

As I indulged my girlhood fancies she would quietly laugh, never thinking me foolish. I was her younger self gliding about the upstairs rooms; she was the ever-indulgent patron.

She wished only for my happiness, believing that it would eventually consist of bonded sirage with a wealthy family, a gyrefaeld similar to our own. She was determined that titles and pedigrees should play a part in our lives for at least one more generation; by carefully selecting my future mate, she thought she could assure the family's position in New Foster's aristocracy. She presumed that I would share this goal.

One man in particular had his eye on a family alliance, a powerful Guildmaster, head of the Gyrefaeld Tokastevor. His son Osseph was the proffered choice.

Tokastevor was an ancient name dating back to the colonization. They grew and harvested forests of wood and had astutely built the transport passways for moving their products the length and width of New Foster. They were involved in most levels of the Management Guild, which comprised the basis of our government. There had been many First-Councillors from the family and my prospective bond-father was himself a candidate for that seat of power.

Addiman was also a well-established house. Our stepfather built ships and ran a world-wide network of ocean transports. It was a logical connection for the two families and might have resulted in a vast economic empire. All this had been worked out when I was a child and I had little to say in the matter. Ingren, my mother, was waiting only to settle the terms of bond when the right time came.

Meanwhile, I enjoyed my fantasies. I was the pretty young wardling trying on all the costumes in her mother's rooms, forever pretending, having no notion of the real world, or least of all, of assuming responsibility.

As we grew older, my brother and I were allowed more free time outside the gyre. We attended lessons at a supervised dayschool and found ourselves in the company of other young children from all parts of the village. Among them were the Tokastevors, Osseph and Mihan.

It was not long before we were invited to their gyre, a large brick compound on the other side of the Quain Townships. We became their most frequent companions, the four of us spending many days together inventing games and adventuring through the village as if it belonged to us.

The young Osseph was obscure in his thinking and curiously unorthodox. He both fascinated and frightened the rest of us. His ideas were far-fetched, extraordinary, though often intriguing.

Among other things, he convinced us to join with most of the other village youths in his incredibly complex wargames. He organized a children's army that most of us were a part of because in those long, playful days it seemed so exciting. For at least five or six years it was the focus of our lives.

But an accident put an end to all this.

My brother and I discovered two laser rifles that had been abandoned a century before, during the Gilcallian uprisings. Together with Osseph and Mihan, we dug them out of the Quain Estuary's gravel bed where they had lain, perfectly preserved in their protective casings. It was as if they had waited for us to stumble upon them as we ran wildly about the village, falling into our hands so that we could play out a final chapter in the Township's history.

It was Mihan who showed us how to put one of the rifles together. But we sadly misjudged the weapon's power. In a demonstration that was meant as no more than a show of prestige, of stylish bravado, several children were killed and an ancient civic monument was destroyed. Osseph was hit by a shard of flying debris and, as a result, lost his left eye.

The senior Tokastevor blamed Gregh and me for the tragedy and wanted us sent to a reformatory, as far away from his family as possible. But my stepfather interceded and a compromise was arranged. He agreed to move our gyre from the village, a halfday's travel south on the Materossen Penninsula, to a district located near one of his ship-building plants.

Thus was Osseph's influence on our lives in those early times, and to the Addiman Gyre he became, even then, somewhat ominously transfigured.

My mother never really recovered from what must have seemed a devastating blow to her social status. She thought herself an outcast, and only barely managed to conceal her frustration and anger. She was forced to discard many of her personal ambitions, among them arrangements for my future bonding. Falling from grace with the Tokastevors made this impossible, though I had no knowledge of it at the time.

She developed a passion for volunteer work and amateur theatre. Gregh and I became her favourite subjects; perhaps this was her way of punishing us. From ages fourteen to seventeen she had us in at least one performance each month in front of various women's organizations and charitable societies.

After the accident, I saw very little of Osseph. He received an eye implant at the university medlabs, regaining most of his sight as far as we knew. He finished his fenyears at the public academy and started a brief apprenticeship in one of his family's mills.

**volume 1, page 65:**

*Uncle Trevarn never laughs at me when I tell him I dream of wearing long silken gowns every day and of having the greatest and most powerful men in the world pay me their respects. He and mother are the only ones who don't! I want to become beautiful, and important. His eyes twinkle, and I know he thinks my dreams are just fine!*

*"Why not?" he chuckles through his moustache. "The world will be yours for the choosin'."*

## 5. Materossen

The relationship that became most important to me was with the Tokastevor's old house-warden, Trevarn. He liked me, perhaps because there were no girl children in the Tokastevor Gyrefaeld. We became friends. He always had gifts for me and he loved to tell us stories of the past.

Sometimes he would take the four of us to antiquaries and museums, pampering us with sweets while he lectured to us. He taught us about the world outside our village in a way that the dayschool's tutor matrix could not.

Trevarn had seen the farthest corners of our planet, from the oxyforests of the Cypol to the silk farms of Torforatagos. He had sailed through the tidal rifts of

Trifan and the mysterious Sea of Dreams and had watched the two Isurian suns set on almost every shore.

He settled in New Foster only when he lost his leg in an accident at sea. Although he had a new limb, it neither grew properly nor meshed fully with his bio-chemics. He walked with a limp, and had lost the strength and limberness he needed to go back to his former life as a shipsman.

He became like a second father to me.

It was Trevarn who kept me informed of Osseph's progress.

Materossen was filled with little galleries and shops and even though we now lived a good distance apart, we occasionally saw each other on outings. The old man knew I was not really to blame for Osseph's mishap and always made a point of being good company.

I wanted to continue our friendship. It was then one of the better parts of my life although it had to remain somewhat secretive for both families' sakes.

Trevarn was a very private person with a mind far more intricate than he ever showed. It was he who suggested I start my diaries. He gave me the first volume of blank pages enclosed in an ancient leather cover that he had bound himself.

By the time I was seventeen I realized that he thought of me more or less as his own daughter. Had he been fifty years younger I suppose I might have suspected him of more obvious intentions.

It was about this time that he gave me the medallions. At first, I didn't understand the significance of his gift, some thirty-seven ancient medals and coins that had been in his family for generations.

Eventually he explained that they were of considerable value and he did not want Osseph appropriating them for his own misguided use. Even then it was becoming obvious that the young Tokastevor was not to be trusted.

Far better, Trevarn believed, for the Matalin Addiman to have the treasure for her purpose, whatever that might turn out to be.

Osseph joined the Civil Militia as soon as he was old enough. These were the reserves kept in training by the guilds, the police that enforced our society's codes and laws. He qualified as an officer because of his education and natural intelligence. Within a year, he obtained a senior position in the c'hele-natal, the elite government security guard responsible for the public safety of high-ranking guild officials.

This, in itself, was no great achievement – there was rarely a need for such protection. But Osseph was ambitious, and he could not have fashioned himself a more self-serving appointment.

A young man of means, close to the most powerful men and women in New Foster, aware of their movements throughout the country. No one stopped to consider what such a devious and calculating individual might do.

With his genius for organization and his family's funds at his disposal, he soon established a private hierarchy within the militia.

His coups are now history. He took over the entire civil operation of Materossen and all the surrounding counties on a cold morning shortly after Silverday. By the time the guilds discovered what he was doing it was far too late to stop him. He controlled the only armed force in New Foster.

Osseph established his military dictatorship with almost no effective opposition.

As head of the Civil Militia he authorized a "general clean up" in the streets of Materossen. Officially, it was meant to rid the city of its malcontents; this met with the approval of the many fickle councillors who supported the young dictator. On the street it meant that anyone could be harassed. It was simply a manoeuvre to allow Osseph's uniformed bullies to threaten whomever they chose.

Arrests and beatings became commonplace and resistance inside Materossen was soon impossible. A few of the serious-minded who were aware of what was happening fled to the sea-coast towns north and south of the Quain Estuary. Here they hoped to form the nucleus of an underground association that could bring about Osseph's downfall.

Marik was one of the first of our small party. He lived aboard his own sailing packer and was able to travel fairly easily between the coastal ports, carrying on his life as a sailor and ferrying endless supplies of equipment as well as people.

Before long, Marik was carrying arms and ammunition. The various groups within our slowly growing alliance quickly realized that civil war was inevitable. Marik enlisted other captains and other crews. He began a network that eventually spread along the entire coast of New Foster.

I found myself developing code systems for transferring information between our groups. It was to become the basis of an elaborate intelligence operation. Using tactics so well learned in Osseph's own wargames years before, I was helping to organize the counter-rebellion.

It was an endeavour that soon came to dominate our lives.

Gregh had left long before we began to feel Osseph's tyranny. For my brother, it was a fateful opportunity when the starship came.

There was little warning of the vessel's arrival except for the bright display of aureole discharges that lit the night sky as it decelerated into the Isurian system. Hasty comnet broadcasts announced the huge black cylinder as it settled into its remote orbit above our heads. Such stopovers were rare events, coming randomly and sometimes centuries apart.

To Gregh, the move from the Quain Townships had been like a prison sentence. He hated Materossen's dusty enclaves and, although it was only half a day's travel by road to our village, he chose never to make the trip. Among other things, he had been an avid rag-ball player and his team had travelled to many of the coastal settlements. But even that lost its appeal when he found himself playing against old team-mates in the tournaments.

When he heard that recruiting officers from the ship were travelling through Materossen, nothing could hold him back. He was interviewed, tested and accepted over many other applicants.

He joined the Viartan Navy.

I never thought I would lose him; he and I had been as close as ... as lovers.

We grew up together and knew everything there was to know about each other. As almost identical twins – he being only slightly taller – we had often been mistaken for each other. Our adolescence granted us the obvious differences of sex, but these too we explored with each other. Our closeness was a delicate balance of intimacy and trust.

Although there might have been little future for us except as occasional companions, it would have been enough.

But Gregh wanted the stars more than he wanted me.

**volume 6, page 107:**

*Greghory has left. I went with him to the transfer station at Pirrit Ennis, the floating island. Ingren refused to go and father was off on one of his long voyages.*

*The Pirrit is not a place I would have chosen for our parting. Completely man-made, it defies all the principles of natural growth and order. It is so large that you cannot feel the wave motion at all. It is a machine devised for the artificial support of artificial life. My little brother will have to get used to that, now that he has joined the Viartan Navy. I cannot imagine living in a space-bound coffin any more than I can understand his wanting to leave New Foster in the first place.*

*Before his shuttle took him, we made love for the last time. The crolloy and plasteel cabin was nothing like our rooms at home. Neither one of us was comfortable. I think he went through with it just for my sake.*

*I was desperate to please him, to make him miss me, to make him change his mind. All he said was that I would find someone eventually, someone with whom I could share bond and start a family. I don't think he understood what it was that we shared through eighteen years of growing up together. There was nothing we didn't know about each other.*

*Well, almost nothing.*
*I didn't know how to keep him with me, did I?*

**volume 24, page 103:**
*I confess this now, having never written or spoken of it be-*
*fore: I tried to conceive his child during those last hours on*
*Pirrit Ennis. I was at the right time in my cycle and I had*
*the notion that I wanted a part of him with me forever.*

*It didn't work. I had my regulars a fiveday late and that*
*was the end of it. Perhaps our twinned chemistry was*
*wrong or our emotions too strained at the time.*

*I wrote that I couldn't feel the waves through the floor of*
*that sterile floating warehouse. I think now it was that we*
*couldn't even feel each other.*

*A cipher came back a threemonth later telling us he had*
*been signed on as an interpreter aboard a Viartan Naval*
*Cruiser.*

*That was the last I ever heard of him.*

## 6. Materossen

Early one morning I was summoned by Osseph to his
military headquarters. An armed escort accompanied
me to a compound in a converted mill on the Quain
waterfront. I was kept waiting for so long that I wondered if he was playing some ridiculous joke. When I
finally saw him, I had very little interest in being
sociable and would have happily told him so.

He had not grown much taller in the years since I
had seen him, but he marched into the room like a
much bigger man, swaggering and boisterous. His
uniform was pale grey and not well fitted; tied loosely

about his slender body, it hung from his narrow shoulders in an almost feminine way. He had a thick, blond moustache and long, curled hair. He wore no makeup although his smooth skin looked almost too glossy to be real. It reminded me of burn victims I had seen years before at the university medlabs.

His artificial eye was most unnerving – it stared at me like a glistening bulb of over-ripe flotweed, the tiny lens a patch of luminous gell watching for unwary prey. But this was no sea omnivore; it was a product of medical engineering that could most likely out-perform its organic counterpart. It must have been his choice not to have had it refined cosmetically; it looked fearfully technical, not at all like a human eye. It made him, I thought, a parody of what I had expected. He was a grotesque little mannikin.

"It has been a long time, Iilaria," he stated flatly.

"I suppose it has, Osseph."

"You seem uncomfortable. Can I get you anything? A callafe, perhaps?"

"No. I'm fine. It's just –"

"You weren't expecting this?" he asked, pointing to the left side of his face. "You never came to see me when it happened. My father told me that you had gone."

"Your father sent us away. I wasn't allowed to see you."

"Yet you managed to stay in contact with Trevarn."

"Only by accident," I lied. "We have seen each other a few times at the museum. He told me about you, about what you were doing."

"You could have come to the gyre. I never blamed you for what happened. We didn't know how it would work, did we?" He meant the laser we had fired in the square.

"I think your brother knew. He was the one who put it together."

"It's all history now. I wanted to see you again. This was the only way I could arrange it." Osseph sat down behind his desk on a specially designed chair that elevated him so that his head was level with mine.

"Why would you want to see me? You know I don't approve of what you're doing."

"That is precisely why I wanted to see you. I remember the good times we had as children. I would like to bring them back. For us. For you and me." He looked away as he said this, somewhat hesitantly. He was, perhaps, shy of bringing up personal matters with someone he had known in a different lifetime.

"What do you mean?"

"I mean, I don't want us to be enemies. I would much rather we were ... that it could be as it was ... before this." Again he gestured at the unblinking lens.

"How could it ever be the same when you bully my friends and intimidate anyone who dares speak out against you? How could I possibly ignore what you have become? You're a dictator in a world where there is no room for tyranny."

"Tyranny? I could have you arrested for that, you know."

"I'm certain you could, and if it suits you, you'd better do it. Because I don't like any of this." I shouted at the huge stone room as if the echoes might have some effect on their harshness. "I don't like being dragged here by your soldiers. Are you still playing your wargames, Osseph? Didn't you have enough of it when we were children?"

"These are not games, dear girl. I intend to change things in New Foster. I will succeed where our great-grandfaelders failed. I want to destroy the Quatrec and its ancient rule. That is the tyranny that I see. You are all too blinded by its routine to recognize the facts."

"I happen to believe in the Quatrec, Osseph. We live in a very delicate ecosystem, completely fabricated, imposed on a world that lay dormant for a million years before we came. We don't even know what was here or why the oceans and the atmosphere were so readily transformed by our engineering. The Quatrec was designed to keep it balanced. It's science and logic, not government."

He continued with a quiet fervour that reminded me even more of his boyhood passion for battle games. "It was adequate when New Foster was first colonized. That was over eighteen hundred trueyears ago. We've gone beyond its point of usefulness. This is a real world now with a developed society. You and your friends are all too caught up in the regimen to see beyond it."

"But Osseph, how can you argue with proven theory? How can you disregard centuries of careful measurement, referencing, cross-checking?" I had to say something to him although it seemed futile. "The Science Guild knows far more about these things than you or I ever could! You're the blind one, Osseph, if you believe differently. You're no more a scientist than I am!"

At this he showed anger. "I know scientists who agree with me! Who is to say what is right? I happen to believe in a different set of concepts and rules than you do and I'm not the only one who does!"

"I see there is no point in discussing it with you. You're obviously determined to have things your way." I was beginning to think I was in the presence of a madman.

"Discuss? You won't listen! I was hoping I could persuade you to at least listen!"

"I would gladly listen to you if I could believe that what you were saying was rooted in common sense."

"You are so much a woman, Iilaria! So much a woman! And just like a woman, you judge me emotionally!"

"That's a ridiculous thing to say. If I'm judging you, it's on the basis of what I've seen you doing! The brutality! The domineering attitude! Your overwhelming need to order everyone about! You haven't really changed since we were in dayschool!"

"It's the only way I can accomplish what I wish to. One day you will thank me for it."

"I don't believe so, Osseph. I think you have chosen the wrong path. I want nothing to do with it."

His anger seemed to evaporate as quickly as it had flared. He spoke so quietly that I was again reminded of the boy I had known years ago, the boy who had been a friend. "Then you'll not be interested in what else I have to ask you?"

"I – what else?"

"Our families ... had ideas of full bond ... between us. They obviously don't now, but I must admit I always thought it an excellent prospect. I was going to ask you for permission ... to renew our friendship, and...." He faltered on the words. I could not believe what I thought he meant.

"I ... wanted to ask ... if you would grant me the right ... to court you in the proper manner. Not as a pre-arranged union. More as a personal thing ... between you and me. For the sake of friendship that was fouled by circumstance and the interference of our gyres. You are the only girl – woman – I have ever let into my life. I would very much like ... for that to ... resume." He stopped and looked at me with a strange awkwardness that was out of place within these cold, stone walls.

Was this the same Osseph who paraded his Civil Militia through Materossen each day, intimidating children and old women? Was it the Osseph who had, years before, led us as schoolmates through the intricacies of his contrived battles? I sensed in him a frightened little boy who had no one to turn to in his quieter moments, no one to help him plan anything mellow or pleasurable.

What could I say that would let us both resume our lives without misconceptions? That I hated him for what he had become? That I was deeply involved with many others in formulating plots to destroy him? That I suspected he knew this full well and was simply trying to divert me?

Or, could I tell him that I believed he was a deceitfully complex man who felt guilty about trying to destroy me, a friend from a previous life? For that is what I saw then, his subtle challenge and an inability to face me with direct warning.

He might simply have told me to be careful, that if I continued to oppose him he could easily have me thrown into his prison or worse. Instead, he asked if we could resume our childhood friendship, if he could court me and renew the intention to ally our families by bond.

My intuition screamed warning: *this is a dangerous conversation!* How could I reasonably answer without offending him and without risking some manner of retribution? I did not want to end my days imprisoned in a lightless cellar two storeys below ground.

"I do not see how you can ask this of me when you know I could never accept your ideology. In truth, Osseph, I could not accept you now. It saddens me that we have grown so differently, so far apart, especially when our lives started out together." He sat behind his desk saying nothing.

"Yes, Osseph, I do remember. We had good times, the four of us. But those times are gone, and we are changed. I'm sorry, but it could never work." I was sorry, sorry that it had come to this, and that he had made himself such a pariah. For that is what I secretly thought: not that his power was impressive or even significant, but that he had become as the lowest of creatures.

And I was deathly afraid of him.

"I'm sorry too, Iilaria. I could make you the most powerful woman in New Foster. I hope that it does not turn out ... badly for you."

He turned away from me then and began inspecting a report that lay on his desk in front of him. Was this a reprieve? What he implied was impossible to guess. If he was threatening me, he was alarmingly sly.

Those were the last words he spoke to me until many years later when our paths crossed under much different circumstances. I was dismissed from his attention and from his presence. I was escorted home.

That evening, by his order, our gyre was placed on Osseph's restricted list with our family in "protective custody".

We were under house arrest.

Marik was at sea when I was confined to the Addiman Gyre. When he came back into Tennefoster Harbour, there was no Iilaria running across the docks to greet him. He wandered up the hill late on the afternoon of his return to be confronted by guards in grey uniforms who brusquely warned him away. Unable to signal me, he withdrew to the cabin of his ship and waited, hoping that under the cover of darkness he would somehow be able to attract my attention. He saw me at my window several times but I did not see him in the lane below. Unwilling to risk his own arrest, he stayed well away from the house until by chance he met the houseman who was still allowed in and out with daily supplies. All I was told was that "my sailor was back". I worried for a threeday that Osseph might have him thrown into the basement of the refinery where there were many damp rooms for imprisonment.

But on the morning of the fourth day, after a change of guard, we heard a familiar whistling in our court-yard. It was Marik at the servant's door, dressed as one of Osseph's sentries. He had simply borrowed a uni-form from the clothiers and walked through the back entrance. Two other men stood by attentively while he ordered me to show him the shop and storehouses, which he wished to search for "illegal weaponry".

Instead of firearms, he found only a confused and weary girl who willingly gave herself up to his intense and demanding search. The other soldiers thought it immensely funny and actually stood outside "guard-ing" the closed storehouse door as Marik's "investiga-tion" continued.

We agreed that my family was in real danger as long as Osseph knew I was involved in the under-ground, and that I must flee the house as soon as pos-sible. Marik was my best, my only means of escape. Unfortunately, we underestimated the extent of Os-seph's villainy.

A regular C.M. Officer arrived one evening to inform us that our confinement was at an end and that we would be allowed to move freely again the following day when certain arrangements had been completed. The guards were to be removed as soon as possible.

"Why not now?" Ingren had asked only to be told that Osseph was away and could not sign all the documents that were needed. She accepted this and was grateful. I was suspicious, but she would not listen to me.

"What can you know of such things?" she said. "You are the one who has caused all this." To be blamed by my own mother was extremely unfair. I told myself that she was suffering enormous strain, having to run a household virtually under seige. And, for her own safety, she could know nothing of my active participation in the underground.

My stepfather returned home that night with his own tale of being unwillingly detained by the grey-coats. They brought him back letting him believe that all was well once more. None of the gyrefaeld would listen to my fearful concerns.

I tried to tell them that Osseph's gestures were not to be trusted, that he was mad. The aunts and uncles told me to be silent. They would not wave a noseary if they thought it might offend the young one-eyed dictator. I talked of seeking some sort of defense against him, but they were adamant, even hostile. They sent me to my room on the back of the old stone mansion. Some instinct made me pack the few things I treasured, including the bag containing Trevarn's medallions.

My life lay in a handpouch under my bed.

## 7. Materossen

I remember waking to the crash of collapsing stone and timber; I saw the flickering red-orange of fire beneath my bedroom door. Instinctively, I rolled out of bed, hugging the floor as closely as I could, recalling from somewhere that in a fire the breathable air stayed below the dangerous gasses. I pulled the handpouch from under the toballen where I had been sleeping. Nothing else was within reach except a thin coat hanging near the window.

My room was on the third floor. A steeply pitched roof projected over the servants' units on the back of the compound. I clambered out onto it and crawled along the top courses of stone shingles. Having barely escaped suffocation by smoke and fumes, I feared making the slightest noise. Some inner sense warned me that a cough or a sneeze would give me away, but I did not stop to think to whom.

At the far end of the servaille was a garden of sorts. A thick wall of lowrel divided it from the outside laneway. I heard voices and waited while two uniformed men ran by below. Then I cautiously slid down the edge of the roof to the top of the hedge and, holding my nightskirts tightly around my legs, jumped down onto the hardpack.

I ran downhill towards the river, away from the road that fronted our compound. When I had gone only a short way, a flash of light followed by a roaring explosion made me look back. Where our house had been, a pillar of flame shot skyward illuminating the underside of the low clouds as well as other buildings many streets distant. I saw people running in all directions, vividly silhouetted against the conflagration. There were no dowsers near enough to be of help so I knew what was left of our gyre would have to burn it-self out.

I found my way to the Tennefoster moorages where the packers wintered. Marik lived there aboard his own ship, the *Solyon*. He was the only person I could trust. My running across the top deck disrupted his sleep. Sliding open the hatch, he greeted me blearily.

I can still see the look of disbelief and confusion that crossed his face as I stammered out my story. Gazing up the hill, we could see a reddish glow filling a good portion of the sky. Realizing immediately what must be happening, Marik took me in his arms and led me to the tiny cabin below.

We had joked about running off with each other, particularly after Gregh left home, but we both knew it was only talk. There had been no real impetus for either of us to race away into the unknown. But in the cold winter night, with my home burning behind me and my possessions clutched in a single tattered bag, escape and security were suddenly thrust foremost into my vision. Romance was replaced by terror. Marik understood all this without any of it being spo-ken. And with no second thoughts he prepared to get me away from Materossen.

He had already decided we should leave early in the morning when the tide would add considerably to our speed. I was numb and exhausted and would have agreed with anything he suggested, content to let him take over my immediate future.

He gave me a mug of warm holipan and settled me in his narrow bunk where he watched over me as a fa-ther might his daughter. I drifted into a fitful sleep and dreamed of burning houses.

He woke me late the next day with a quiet kiss on my

cheek and a fresh mug of hot brew from his galley. He made me eat dried panaco to settle my stomach and helped me up so that I could wash myself in the miniature bassette.

The sweeping roll of the ship told me we were no longer anchored in Tennefoster. We had left the delta of the Quain Estuary, Marik explained, and were well beyond Materossen's enormous harbour. He would take me south to a family he knew who would look after me until he could prepare for a much longer trip. Until then I was to stay out of sight where I would be safe.

He had thus hastily contrived my escape from Osseph's Militia. I made silly jokes about the tiny cabin, the awkwardly placed cross beams and bulkheads, the obviously male-oriented facilities. I complained about the dull meals, the hard wooden bunk, the constant motion of the ship at sea.

In short, I was a sufferance that he graciously accepted. His patience was such that I recognized it only much later on in our relationship. He knew that I had not even begun to recognize the depth of my loss.

I owed my life to a heavy masonry wall, originally the outside of the compound until a previous owner had extended the structure beyond. When we had left the Quain Townships and had first moved into the building, I was the only one who wanted to sleep in the back of the house. Above the roof of the servaille, it was considered the less attractive portion of the gyre, but I chose it because it had commanded a broad view of the sea.

My mother and stepfather, her brother and half-sister, my stepfather's two sisters, their bondmates, the nurses, two housemen and most of the servants, some twenty-six people in all, had perished in the fire-bombing.

Except for Gregh who was by then beyond the limits of ordinary space and time, I was the only remaining member of the Gyrefaeld Addiman.

And had it not been for Marik, I would have floundered in a wash of self-pity and remorse. He not only saved me physically, but was the rock to which I clung for my emotional survival as well.

**volume 8, page 36; volume 34, page 20:**
*There is a delacaiceogram that I had carefully translated into the Viranti and copied into my diary sometime before the house was burned. All that is left are its two final phrases. I was never able to locate another copy of the original version, but for me it remains indelibly woven into the fabric of my past, a ghost lingering in shadows.*

> *It was as I had looked across some great river*
> *And seen standing by a ruined tower*
> *Shadowed thoughts of a time-hooded past.*
> *I called; the currents caught my voice.*
> *Obscure it sank, drowned in the roaring passage*
> *Of the tide.*
>
> *I halted, wanting desperately to close that shore,*
> *And saw again the mysterious image,*
> *A next-to-nothing from the world of yesterday.*
> *So far along this road I could not turn;*
> *No bridge behind, only a rubble barricade,*
> *And a great, guarded door.*

*The young matalin no longer played in her mother's finery; the silken trappings had lost their magic. She had discovered a world both grey and cruel, containing more of loneliness than of love.*

## 8. Protec One-Ten: The East Station

Beneath winter's deepening overcast, the cold wind whiplashed spirals of foam along black wave crests, driving icy rain and mist across our bow, numbing our limbs and faces.

We sailed steadily south-west for a sixday on a course clearing the Island of Palang and then taking us east towards the Palos Cerrit. Marik was heading through Gannapes, the canyon-like gash that splits New Foster from its southern continent.

We hugged the canyon's northern shoreline, coming finally to a narrow inlet that threaded it's way gently inland. It widened into a deep passage, a navigable waterway, at the head of which was an ancient power station with its holding reservoir barricading the top of the gorge. Fed by underground rivers and stretching further than the eye could follow, the man-made lagoon drove turbines that supplied power to distant Materossen and its sprawl of satellite communities.

At one time, early in the colonization, it had been a tidal plant with a smaller reservoir filled only by constant movement of the sea. The old stepped dams and pumping stations were still evident, and tucked into a deep stone crevasse above them was a tiny village. Its stone houses clung to the cliffs looking as if they had been cast by the same giant hand that scattered the beach with its grey and white boulders a million years before.

Quays and jetties curved out towards us. I counted at least twenty boats of all sizes at anchor. Like most Power Guild settlements, this was merely a number on a map. Marik had brought me to Protec One-Ten, known by its residents simply as the East Station.

**volume 10, pages 34-36:**

*He would not take me farther, he said. It was too dangerous in the southern ocean at that time of year. But I couldn't listen to his reasons; I couldn't tear myself from his protection, from his arms, knowing that the next months were going to be the most difficult of my life.*

*I think he wanted me just as much as I wanted him, but there was too much else going on around us. We were, by then, inextricably immersed in the underground war against Osseph.*

*"He thinks you're dead. Let it stay that way for a while. When you come back it will be with a solid passion for well-thought vengeance. When I come back to get you in the spring ... well, then we can talk of the future. Right now, you need to heal. These people will help you more than I can."*

*If he loved me then, he kept his counsel. Why did he leave me in that desolate spot when all I wanted was to be with him? I couldn't understand; I hated him, I loved him. He knew I would have gone with him through the ice floes and beyond.*

*He also knew how vulnerable I was, yet he deposited me with little more than a promise to return to me after he had arranged my passage to Denique.*

*I stayed with an elderly couple who had no sympathy for Osseph and his greycoats. But more importantly, Marik trusted them with my life.*

I stayed the winter with them, working as I could around their cottage, cooking and cleaning, more to busy and distract myself than to be of help. I think I was often in their way, but they never complained, leaving me alone for the most part. They probably understood my needs more than I did at the time.

My grief was long in settling. I could no more hide

it away than I could myself in their small house. It flowed and ebbed like the black ocean: sometimes it would smother me and my tears would run in torrents; then it would recede, only to rush back in uncontrollable waves, and I would dash outside no matter what the weather, wanting nothing from anyone. But one of them would always follow to bring a wrap or a covette; without their kindnesses, I might have perished from pneumonia or lung rot.

I took long walks along the beach and up into the rocky cliffs above the station, following narrow pathways carved by the station's first settlers. At the very top were ruins of an old Gillcallian Chapel. I would climb to its roofless but sheltered sanctuary and stare out across the Gannapes. The far side was usually obscured in thick mists, but when its bare, reddish-tinged mountains shone in the distant light, I felt even more alienated in that strange new land.

I struggled to understand why my life had been suddenly destroyed. Slowly I came to think in terms of surviving by myself. If my life was to be new adventure, I was going to have to be very strong to see my way through it.

The memory of my nightmare slowly lost its sharpness; it became as a tale recited by an observer, the details tending to merge with one another. The remembered faces of my family gradually took on the softer contours of worn holograms.

One morning, I walked from the village across the narrow causeway along the top of the dam. There was no wind and I could smell ice in the air. Across the harbour a column of steam rose from the station in perfect symmetry with its white reflection. The only sound was the occasional whistle of the half-tame banik kept chained on the wharf by the resident caretaker.

Halfway across the long, tapered arc of the dam, I climbed down to the water's edge to a block of eroded stone projecting from the coarse shingle. Sitting on its smoothed surface, I was in the center of an enormous natural amphitheater framed by hills and cliffs, by sea and sky. For the first time in the months I had been at the East Station, I felt at peace.

The mirrored shaft of steam disappeared into submerged clouds; the water was a sheet of polished obsidian. Suddenly, there were ripples and the perfect image shattered. Thousands of brightly lit facets raced beneath an early morning breeze. They tumbled into each other, breaking against the stones at the bottom of the beach. I looked up. The masts of a sailing packer were slowly coming into view above a breakwater at the harbour's mouth.

Marik was back.

I would be saying goodbye to the East Station and to New Foster before the day had ended.

**volume 34, page 88:**
*I wrote very little about Marik in the early volumes of these diaries. There was too much of our relationship inside me to make the plain words have any real life. The memories of our times together I trust; they are still warm, clear, untarnished. I can call him back as if everything happened yesterday, as if the long years apart were no more than a few days.*

**volume 12, pages 80-85:**
*The light of Isurus Prime glistens on white sand. Marik runs along the beach ahead of me, his pale blond hair trailing behind him like the tail of a jackal-bird in flight. He stops, turns to shout something, beckons me to hurry. When I catch up, he pulls me along behind him to a shallow, rip-*

pling tidal pool between outcroppings of rock. In the water lies the body of a bluefish, a bachelor, its long dorsal tendrils draped across the sand like ropes of cobalt silk.

Its saucer eyes stare up at us, glazed and unseeing. The carapace has been torn open along one side of the enormous back by some sharp object, possibly a fisherman's spike. Charil-cones poke their pink and amber heads from beneath the wound, not yet aware of their host's death. Injured mortally, the creature had swum landward or been dragged here by the currents.

Marik races about his find like a schoolboy, excited at first, pointing out the features of its alien physiology. I watch and listen, catching his sense of wonder and his concern at this unusual event.

Death has suddenly imposed itself on the pattern of the day, and Marik's heart goes out to the giant. He mourns its passing and frets at the pain it has obviously suffered on its last journey from the Sea of Dreams, where the packers have been hunting.

He finds it hard to accept that any spikeman would leave such a wound, though he knows it happens often. The blues are intelligent, particularly the bachelors whose function it is to herd the other members of their species through the complex mating rituals. They are the most advanced race of living beings native to the planet; by accident of biology, their protein is compatible with our digestive systems. This is why we drag them from the oceans.

Marik's excitement gives way to bitterness as he talks about his profession and about the bluefish. We walk further along the shore, hand in hand, Isurus beating down on our backs from the clear sky.

He tells me about his father who had fished for the great blues when he was a young man, and about how he had learned about these strange Isurian exobrates. His father taught him almost everything he knows about the sea. They *are both fishermen.*

*But Marik will not take the blues, because he believes their behaviour to be that of a cleverly adapted social species. He belongs to a minority that actively promotes this concept of alien intelligence that human society refuses to recognize.*

*We called it the day of the bluefish and I wrote in that early volume of my diary a closing line: "I fear for us; my love speaks more of fishes than of me."*

*But this was my Marik. He filled his existence with purpose and direction, fighting his battles on so many desolate reaches.*

*He and I loved each other very deeply, and that is all I can say, even to myself.*

*It is enough. These memories I trust.*


## 9. Denique

One of my maids informed Haderan that I had still not returned home a twoday later. By the time darkness had fallen on the second night, he had summoned guards from the garrison to conduct a search. It was only by chance that Jeva encountered two of them in the early morning on her way to open the shop. They asked about a missing woman and she brought them back with her.

I was awakened by their boot-steps in the courtyard. By the time they knocked on the wooden door, I was out of bed. The old woman was still asleep on a chair by her stove. The knocking did not wake her and I wasn't about to unlock the door to anyone.

"Matalin, matalin," Jeva called. "It is me. There are two soldiers who say they are looking for a missing woman. They mention the General's name, Haderan. The big boss. They say it is important that they speak with you. Please tell me what to do?"

"All right, Jeva. I'm coming." I struggled with the heavy wooden bars that had been set into slots behind the outer kitchen door.

The two soldiers were apologetic for their intrusion. "We are looking for Matalin Iilaria. Are you –"

"Yes, it's me. Haderan sent you?"

"The young woman brought us here after we described you to her. Haderan has us out searching. Since last night. We will inform him where you are."

One of them left, presumably to find a visport. There had never been many scanners installed in the lower city as they were usually vandalized, so making contact with anyone could sometimes take a long time. I busied myself washing and eating a few slices of cold panaco. The girls brought me new clothes from the shop. When Haderan finally arrived, I was trying on gowns that I fancied. I was pulling a long perricoat over my shoulders with Jeva's help as he burst into the dressing room demanding an explanation. I shouted at him to stay outside until I had finished.

He was totally flustered; his usual charm and self-control deserted him. Poor fat Jeva burst into tears, not knowing which way to turn, so I first had to reassure her. Then I told Haderan about the two men who had left me for dead. He finally understood that, had the two girls not been brave enough to look for me, I would have perished.

He looked closely at the marks and bruises on my throat which were still painful to touch despite the old woman's attentions. He sent the two men out to search the garden and the shed. They soon returned with only the lengths of frayed binding that the girls had left when they untied me.

Haderan gave orders to keep a guard on the shop and sent another pair of his soldiers to watch the jewel merchant's. He said that my attackers might show themselves there, but he did not sound optimistic. He decided to take me home.

I hugged the two girls, and their aging aunt, who by then had wakened, continued a torrent of words in her native tongue. All I could understand was, "Watch out for the Jackal! Watch out for the Jackal!", which she mumbled over and over again. Haderan, anxious to get on with his day, was growing impatient.

At the time, I didn't recall Osseph's self-chosen code name. When we had played out his fanciful combat routines as children, we had all taken secret identifiers, words and numbers known only to each other. His had been "Jackal Bird". We had always referred to him as "the Jackal". There was no way the old woman could have known this. I later put it down to a phrase that I might have misinterpreted, or a coincidence.

Promising to visit them again soon while Haderan dragged me out of the shop, I left the three of them huddled in the doorway I had rushed into a threeday before. Once more, tears were streaming down Jeva's cheeks.

### volume 36, pages 62-66:

*The voices I recall tell me I contradict myself. Or else memory fades. Perhaps it is that simple. The colours overlap, and images merge in time-distorted focus.*

*Haderan was no hero. He was flamboyant, charming, used to having his own way. I was the one that made him take his life a little more seriously, or so I thought. I demanded his attentions, his faithfulness, and to a large extent I was successful. He was convinced that he possessed me* and I was content to let that be.

He fashioned a portion of my life that was essential and it seemed, at the time, appropriate. But just as our relationship was part of a pattern that overwhelmed us both, so too were the events that put him in political focus. He became a hero not because he was remarkably clever, but because those around him demanded it. He was manipulated by the council, by circumstance, and by me.

I was never in love with him. I enjoyed his company; we were good together and he served me well. I was always fair to him so that he would have no just cause to disrespect or disregard me. And in his manner I suppose he treated me as well as any man could have done.

Almost to the last....

I remember him as a tragic hero even though I know better. His best image was his public one. I have a few holos tucked away in my memorabilia; these I resurrect occasionally.

The colours overlap, and images merge in time-distorted focus.

## 10. Denique

I was asked to identify two men found near the waterfront by Haderan's warranters. He sent a drake to fetch me to the garrison; I arrived as the midday shift was changing. A confused young voluntary escorted me to a dark suite of offices on the top floor of one of the old buildings.

The tract of land in the centre of Denique overlooked a park, but during the Gillcallian uprisings over a century before most of the windows had been closed in. The cluster of stone and wood structures might just as well have been underground for all that could be seen of the greenery outside.

Since the Ten-Thousand-Island Federation had become involved in the campaign against New Foster, the almost light-less compound had been made over as an officer's headquarters. Haderan was its council-appointed commander.

I could not help but think of similar quarters I had been taken to years before in Materossen. Haderan's position almost paralleled that of the young Osseph, and old fears reasserted themselves as I waited in the sparsely furnished anteroom. Flags, coats-of-arms, weaponry displays, holograms of dead generals; the walls were the intended focus for anyone unfortunate enough to be delayed in the room for too long. The two guards stood like constipated clothes-maker's dummies as they tried to pretend I wasn't there. By the time Haderan told me to come into his private room, I was thoroughly unsettled. He and his fellow officers must have had some in-built immunity to the effects of the drab decor.

His familiar grinning face greeted me once more. I asked for water, which one of the guards brought to me. Sipping nervously at the glazed flask I was handed, I took the chair in front of his great desk.

"We have the two men. I'd like you to identify them so we can execute them."

Fear surged back. "You're going to execute them?"

"Don't sound so shocked! They left you for dead. If the two girls hadn't come along, you might not have been found for days. They are as guilty of murder as if you had not been rescued. Don't waste sympathy on either one."

"It just seems so brutal. Isn't there another way of handling it?"

"Iilaria, what they did to you was worse than brutal. It was sadistic. As far as we are concerned, they are to be eliminated as soon as possible."

"We? Who is this we?"

He hesitated. I had the impression he did not quite know how to continue. "As of this morning, we have been placed on full emergency alert by the council. We are about to invade New Foster. *We* are their war committee. I am Chief Military Advisor. The object will be to overthrow Osseph before his influence spreads further. It is finally to be an active offensive."

I was speechless. I had hoped this would happen, of course, but I did not believe it was the right time.

The silent war, unofficially sanctioned, had for the most part been a charade. There were too many powerful interests that accepted Osseph's regime because it meant profit. I had worked to influence and persuade, to thwart the dictator's madness from my island base. I had friends with much political strength, but full-scale military action had seemed a long way off to me, and to most of them.

"What has happened to change the council's mind?"

Haderan was once again hesitant. "It would seem that you have happened."

"What is that supposed to mean."

"You are friends with Deretor?"

"The Legal Guildmaster? Yes, I know him."

"Have you ever been his – have you –"

"Slept with him? You foolish man! Are you afraid to ask me, or afraid of my answer?"

"I'm sorry to have to be blunt. At times like this there is no room for ... evasiveness. If you had been close to him in the past, it would be of no concern to me. What has been has been. It's just that – well, my love, he has a very high regard for you and your opinions. He seems more like a lover than simply a friend."

"He is a good friend, and I trust him. If you must know, he owns a part of my stepfather's shipping line. He helped me get back the controlling interest after my gyrefaeld's demise. I had to find good representation. My brother was gone and no one in New Foster thought I was alive. Deretor came with the best credentials and he knew who I was, from before Osseph murdered my family. I actually knew him as a child, only he remembered and I didn't. It's a very long story, but that's how we come by our friendship." I stopped, out of breath, and out of patience with Haderan's self-centred attitude towards me.

"I see," he replied softly. "At any rate, when he and the others on the council heard what had happened to you, they decided that enough was enough. It was a single but timely circumstance that pushed them to a decision that has been hanging over us all for months. So in a way, you are responsible for us being at war."

"That's absurd. What have the two men got to do with any decision the council might make? They are two simple criminals who wanted to steal a medallion. I doubt they are capable of any intrigue much beyond robbery!"

"Those two were assigned by one of Osseph's operatives here in Denique," said Haderan. "They were sent here to kill you and make it look like a robbery. They are dirt. They are the enemy. And we are now at war. We will treat them like any other conspirators."

I suppose I did not fully realize all that Haderan was trying to tell me. It was too much all at once. I had thought myself reasonably safe in Denique. Was I now suddenly a target again?

He went on, ignoring my obvious confusion. "You

are no longer free to be as open with your friends as you have been since you came here. You must realize that it is only because of your relationship with me that you have been allowed so much freedom. There are certain members of council who are much less tolerant than Deretor. I have persuaded them to turn a blind eye to the boat-loads of food, the medicines, the drugs, the arms and ammunition that you have sent to Marik. No, don't interrupt me. Let me finish what I must.

"Don't think that most of us are unsympathetic. After all, Marik is our ally. It's just that until now you have been a like a stone in the mattress to some of the guilds that want to continue trade with Osseph. But it has now become too complex and dangerous for you to continue. Your life is on the *h'kala* board. I must ask for – if not order – your co-operation. I can offer assurances that we will continue to support Marik's operations at sea, but it will be in our own way. We would prefer it if you would help rather than hinder us in our efforts."

"I don't know what to say to you, Haderan. You make me feel ... vulnerable." He had made me extremely angry, but I controlled the urge to tell him so.

"I am trying to show you just how very vulnerable you are. For my own sake, I must make a confession, and please try not to misunderstand me: my actions have been based on my deepest feelings for you and my concern for your safety. I have had you watched for some time now."

"Watched?" He obviously knew about some of my network connections, but I had guessed as much before this. I gave him a look of offended dignity. "Or spied on?"

"A safety measure."

"For whose safety? Mine or yours?"

"Don't be foolish; yours, of course. But I have kept careful track of your comings and goings. Your hide-away on Kalanos is interesting, I must say."

"I make no secret of it. It is my private home."

"Not many of us can afford to build such luxurious accomodation and then leave it closed up."

"It is none of your concern."

"You have never invited me there. Why?"

"If I thought you had the time to go visiting the outer islands...." I could not decide where Haderan was leading our conversation.

"I suppose you're right. But as I was saying, I admire your skill as an operator. Your use of the matrix channels shows audacity, but you must have considered the lack of security? I have had many of your calls relayed to my offices."

"Possibly you overestimate my deviousness?"

"I doubt it, Iilaria. I have even used your connections myself when I needed particularly sensitive information. I apologize for this; I believed it necessary under the circumstances. National interest and military security. But now the situation is changed. I am telling you of my own indiscretions and at the same time asking for your co-operation. We must continue working together."

"I would not have suspected this of you, Haderan. But I don't worry about not trusting you so much as I worry about the thoroughness of your information. Incomplete truths are far more dangerous than ignorance."

"You play with words, Iilaria. War is far too serious to play at half-heartedly."

"I am well aware of the seriousness of what you propose. It's just that, though I thought you would invade Osseph eventually, I admit surprise that it is to be so soon."

"Surprise? You surprise me. Is it only a month since you asked me to smuggle a letter for you? What might have been in that letter? Directives to your underground? New instructions on escape routes? Who would you have been trying to pull out, and why? You knew of our plans, possibly before I did, so don't try to mislead me, my love!" He was being polite. He knew far more than I had suspected.

I continued, as openly as I dared. "That is precisely what I mean by incomplete truths. The letter that I asked you to send with your spy was to Trevarn. He is still Osseph's house-warden, though he is over seventy years old. I wanted him and his wife to leave for their own safety. I don't think he can maintain his security much longer. Even Marik doesn't know about all of Trevarn's activities, or how delicately he treads."

"I have known for some time that you communicate with Trevarn," Haderan replied. "He cannot leave Osseph now. We need him more than ever. Your loyalty to him is admirable but he is a well-spring of vital information. And we need you to continue to pump that well, my gypsy. Above all, we need a combined rather than a fractured effort. And we cannot have you getting yourself murdered by some second-rate operatives. From now on you are to work with me directly. And there is no question that we must execute those animals."

"I suppose I should be angry with you, but I'm not." I desperately tried to cover my rage, lying as I was often forced to by the game I played. "But I am insulted that you should think me no more than simple clay to be moulded.

"Yes, I do attempt to communicate with my friends,

and I am concerned for their safety. But my interests are also in maintaining my business connections. I make my living from trade with New Foster and the rest of the mainland – that is what I wish to protect. Of course I have codes and secrets, but they have little to do with your war. If you were so well informed you would know this.

"As for Marik, he is my senior captain. Of course I send supplies to certain groups who request and pay for them. There is no mystery here, nor any threat to your precious council. Any one of them would do the same thing in my place!"

"And what of Pangaelene? Who is the dancer?"

I was not expecting that. I had to conceal my shock. How could he have known my code name unless he had found his way into the innermost circle of my network? I was more afraid then than I dared show.

"Pangaelene? You know of her?"

"She is one of your spies? I don't know her identity, but I presume she is a councillor's mate?" It seemed he did not realize who I was, but how could I be certain?

"You really don't know?" I laughed, and the faint boyish smile that crossed his face said that he didn't. "Pangaelene was my mother, Ingren Addiman. It was a stage name she used in the village plays. A masque. Trevarn knew. Is that where you picked it up? You have been misled by your own curiousity!" Desperation led me on. Would he swallow my hastily crafted lies?

"I wondered when I read about it. The meaning of the reference wasn't clear to me."

"So you've read my private correspondence. Do I have any secrets left?" The Iilaria buried within me took control once more. She scrutinized Haderan's every reaction.

"A few, I suppose. But I mean what I said. You must be careful. You must not work against us. We are on the same side, you and I. Now, will you come and identify those two creatures?" He was very smooth, very assured.

I breathed a little more easily, reasonably sure he had not yet penetrated too far. My only concern was what he might not be telling me. "Yes, I will come."

"Good. You should be grateful that we discovered who hired them. And that we don't throw you into some forsaken monastery for your own protection. There is a wonderful convent in the Torforatagos...."

He led me down flights of stairs and along an underground corridor to one of the connecting structures behind his garrison. We came up into the light at the edge of long, rectangular courtyard where a muddy path paralleled the high wooden fence. I tried to carry my skirts above the thick, wet clay. Silently cursing this man who seemed absolutely insensitive to the physical problems of being a woman in full dress, I struggled to keep up with him as he strode through a gate into yet another courtyard beyond the first.

This enclosure was little more than a vast pen. Its greenery had long ago given up its fight with the military mind; it was a sea of mud. There were wire cages in rows around a central guard station. We moved towards the far side of a strange array of metal cones. Most of them were empty, but men were chained to posts inside some of them, bedraggled specimens who looked as though they had been out here for days. A few lay inert in the thick slime, dead for all I could tell.

I could not imagine Haderan having anything to do with this dreadful place, yet he marched through the compound as if it were quite familiar to him. One of the guards saluted as we passed. I guessed he was not used to female visitors; he had turned a bright crimson as he saw me approach. He must have wondered what I was doing following his commander through the muck – by then my good shoes, my leggings and the hems of my skirts were soaked and caked in mud. Or perhaps he was embarrassed that I had seen him on such solitary and sorry duty.

We came to the end of the farthest row of cages. Inside one, Yellowbeard squatted awkwardly, his hands and feet chained behind him. He looked up at me, sneered and turned away. His swarthy companion was stubbornly attempting to remove his bonds in the next cage. When he saw me, he rattled them in my direction, mumbling something under his breath that I could not hear. There were two fingers missing from his left hand so I had no doubt who he was.

"We found them in a sail-maker's loft waiting to get onto one of your own assigns," Haderan explained. "They knew you had chartered it, and they were going to try sinking her."

I thought of the irreplaceable cargo in the hold of the small yacht and the risks its captain and crew were taking for me. That these two had been planning to destroy it frightened me more than anything Haderan had told me that day. "So you see, Iilaria, it is much more important that you help us now, so that we can help you."

"What will you do with them?" I noticed fresh cuts and bruises on both prisoners' faces and arms.

"It makes little difference. We've had all we can from these two. Hang them, I think." Yellowbeard stared at Haderan, a defiant hatred in his eyes. "They don't understand what they've got themselves into."

"Isn't there a more humane way of doing it?"

"Humane? I don't consider hanging a woman by her wrists particularly humane! Do you think they were concerned about your pain? Deretor wanted to roast them in metal drums! And he would have fed their coarse flesh to the baniks. Don't think about them. They aren't worth it!"

"Can we go? I'm not feeling well."

"As soon as you've signed the warrants." He handed me a small cypher-block with a stylus. I filled in the blanks where he directed, so condemning the two men to death.

"I know this is difficult for you, but it is the only way." He tried to put his arm around me but I pushed him aside. We started back through the mud.

I heard Yellowbeard's throaty snarl as he yelled a particularly obscene Viranti curse. It was all I could do to keep from vomiting.

## 11. Denique

There was too much that I didn't know. My mind whirled trying to assimilate and clarify what had happened. Haderan had told me just enough to worry me; that he knew this much worried me even more. He was trying to play my game, but he was not as good at it; he had not had the benefit of direct experience with Osseph Tokastevor.

There was a flaw hidden somewhere in Haderan's performance and it agitated me; I could not ignore it.

Why had the two men stolen the coin? Haderan would have me believe they were sent to destroy me, as well as one of my shipments to Marik. He was going to have them hanged without trial. "War criminals," he had said to me. "I am judge and executioner. You will sleep much better tonight."

Or was he afraid of something else? I kept coming back to the coin, to the pendant that had been fashioned to hang on his gift, the silver yarrenchain.

Was Haderan attempting some ploy to keep me under his control? He had virtually ordered me to stop using my underground networks without first consulting him. It was to be a mutual effort from now on, he had said, with him issuing the directives.

The attempt on my life gave him a convenient opportunity to frighten me into his camp. If he wanted Pangaelene working for him, what better way to achieve it? The more I thought about it, the more convinced I became that he was attempting to be clever, deceiving me with some tangled plot.

I needed to determine how far he had penetrated my organization and what he knew about my real objectives. I would start with my friend, Maxilian Deretor.

"I suspect he knows nothing of this, but I must be certain."

"Haderan likes to talk. He bends everyone's ear every chance he gets. Lately, he has spoken a lot about you."

Finding Deretor had not been easy. As Assistant to the First Councillor of the Ten Thousand Islands, he was deeply involved in New Federation politics and was usually off somewhere on one of the islands. Now that war was at hand, he was being rushed from one meeting to another and was in a constant state of exhaustion. But he always had time for me, most likely because I had financed his rise to power along with almost a thirdportion of his fellow councillors.

He was leaving for the Northern Rim when I caught

up with him. I boarded the yacht he used for his longer journeys, promising not to delay his sailing for too long.

"What makes you think he knows anything at all?" he wanted to know.

"He asked about Pangaelene."

"I see. Then it could be serious. We can't allow him to start using our discreet channels. It could give everything away."

"He may be developing his own plans. Like Osseph. I think he admires the man."

"I know for a fact he does. But I would not have thought Haderan capable of such ... self-delusion." Deretor had quickly seen what I feared most, that Haderan's self-serving agenda went far beyond his duties as a Military Commander.

"I may even have been the one who gave him the notion. After all, I have told him many of the details of Osseph's strategies. Haderan soaks up things like that. He stores them away in his mind and out they come much later, turned about and polished in the oddest manner. But he is not clever enough to organize such an undertaking. He would need a lot more than an army behind him."

"He would need someone like you, Iilaria. That is all."

"You flatter me, Deretor. Fortunately, I have other plans."

"We are all slowly discovering that, my dear." His laughter echoed about the cabin. "But what you want me to find out is whether or not Haderan suspects us. I will try. I think I can manage it. He and I have several meetings scheduled when I get back."

"Contact Marik. He's somewhere near the North Rim. Warn him quickly."

"I'll use our new codes. They're going to be changed every night from now on."

"Don't wake up the bachelor fish. Marik will scream so loudly we'll hear him from here."

"All the packers have the latest gear. We're bouncing signals off the old satellites now. You know, New Foster hasn't yet discovered what we're doing."

"I hope you're right. I've never felt comfortable with the matrix channels. Too easy to override or break into. Haderan has made that very clear."

The rest of our business had to do with tallies of shipments and could as easily have waited for another time. We parted as the ship's stays were being removed from their dockside stanchions.

He kissed my cheek and I left him in his sea-going office with its confusion of files and message cubes. My worries about our Military Commander were not resolved, but I was more at ease. I knew if anyone could confirm what I suspected, it would be Deretor.

I went home to continue my delicate scheming.


## 12. Denique

I did not know the exact time my two assailants died. Haderan had them hanged one evening in the filthy courtyard behind his headquarters. Their hasty death was brought about by the simple stealing of an old medal.

That same night, I walked from my house to the Crystal Plaza, intent on losing myself in the crowd. I passed musicians tuning their instruments and young couples wandering arm in arm along the edges of the plaza. Theirs was a gaiety that I could never share.

The plaza is an enormous arcade, brightly lit after dark, with hundreds – sometimes thousands – of people surging between its shops, foodhouses, and kiosks. A fountain towers at its centre; cascades of brilliantly illuminated water jet up and out into the air, pumped by the pressure of artesian springs swelling from the bedrock below. Countless eternal lights flicker on and off in endless succession. The plaza stretches north and south along Denique's main thoroughfare and west to the dockside. East of the fountain stands a plasteel and crolloy likeness of Gilliam, one of the original colonists.

I found myself inside the Gilliam monument in the off-street quiet of its sparsley furnished museum. I stood in front of displays of old coins and medallions with no recollection of how long I had been there. Two or three of the coins bore inscriptions much like those in Trevarn's collection.

I was of thirteen trueyears when he gave me the metal box. It had then contained only a tenportion of its present number of coins and medals. I had added to the collection over the years so that now I could claim that mine was probably the largest such assemblage of ancient artifacts on the entire planet. It was hidden beneath the floor of a safe house in Kalanos.

The one that had been stolen was part of the small baggage I brought with me when I escaped the firebombing in Tennefoster.

Why did they steal the coin? The question ran circles in my mind. Only Trevarn and I had known its value, or even that I possessed it, until I showed it to Haderan. Then the smith saw it and made the fitting – and the two bullies had known his name: Genter. What was their connection?

Genter was the only one likely to know what the

coin was, but he would not have gained by stealing it; he could not have known that it was unregistered and, therefore, vastly more valuable. But it made no sense at all that he or anyone else would murder for it.

Unless, of course, the whole thing was an elaborate ruse.

The only person who could have devised such a scheme was Haderan himself. Presuming that he had, what was he trying to accomplish?

*He had tried to convince me I was still a target of Osseph.*

Had Haderan orchestrated the attack and robbery? Had he then used the episode to push some of his superiors into supporting his own wishes? Was he trying to influence council members into declaring a premature attack on New Foster?

And had he also planned to manoeuvre me into his camp, not realizing that I was already far ahead of him with my own more carefully devised plans? The more I thought about it, the more likely it seemed.

He knew me as a wealthy, single woman and had pursued me as his personal mistress for several months. I had responded to him and saw him on a regular basis because it suited my plans. He was a fast-rising commander who would become increasingly important in the military campaign against Osseph. I needed him under my control.

But I had underestimated his ambition, his grasping for personal power. He had spied on me and discovered ... what? He might suspect that I was more than I appeared and perhaps wanted to control me and whatever influence he believed I held.

Pangaelene the dancer? If he suspected that I was Pangaelene, if he had some intuition of my plans, then he was as much a threat as Osseph himself.

I have confessed my ambitions to destroy Osseph only to these diaries, all written in a carefully constructed code unreadable to any but Trevarn or Marik. These two alone knew of my interest in the Viranti dialects and were aware that I wrote them as well, using contrived symbols and images, an alphabet and grammar invented by myself solely to record the spoken-only gypsy tongue. As far as I knew no one had ever used such a code before.

But Haderan had somehow come across my correspondence with Trevarn. Even if he could not interpret the basic ciphers, he was curious and, therefore, dangerous.

As Pangaelene, I could take no chances.

He would have to be stopped. Permanently.

## 13. Denique

The shop was only a few streets away from the fountain. I wasn't certain it would be open this late at night. Leaving the Gilliam Museum, I crossed the Crystal Plaza. Wind from the south-west carried a fine spray from the water's bright columns, soaking bystanders with its cool moisture. I hurried through the coloured mist, obeying an intuitive command to unravel Haderan's deceit.

The shop was open. I stood across the lane, the noises of the crowd echoing far behind me in the plaza. I hesitated, not sure that I wanted to follow through with my plan, almost afraid of the consequences or that I might be wrong.

*No*, I thought, *Trust your instincts. There is something queer in all this.* The image of two bodies hanging in that grisly compound flashed through my mind. I quickly crossed the lane and pulled open the barred door to the guildsmith's shop.

A young man stooped over his workbench. There was no one else in the shelf-lined room. I cleared my throat as delicately as my strained nerves allowed. He looked up – he was not Genter.

"May I help you, matalin?"

"I'm looking for a man, a guildsmith. His name is Genter. Do you know where he might be?"

"Genter? I know of no one called by that name. No Genter here. I am Hugh-Patar. May I do anything for you?" His smile was alarmingly sincere.

"The man I spoke to in this shop a month past? He made a pendant for me." My hand rose by itself to my collar; the necklace I wore was nothing like the stolen yarrenchain. "An old coin I brought to him. The young man looked puzzled. "It was this shop, I'm certain."

"I was away at the end of last month. My shop was closed. My mother died in Five Maidens. I went to make all the arrangements because neither of my sisters knew what to do. Now I must work late to catch up. I'm sorry if this confuses you, but it is the truth." He seemed to be apologizing to me for his mother's death.

"Oh please, no," I stammered, "I ... I'm very sorry to hear that. It must have been difficult for you. I'm probably in the wrong shop after all."

"She had been ill for long time; it was not unexpected. But you are never prepared for death it when it comes, are you?"

"No." I saw the two bodies swinging and heard once more their Viranti curses shouted from beyond unmarked graves.

"But can you help me a little? Are there other guild-smith's shops in this area?"

"Not on this side of the Plaza, no. There are several on the south side and down along the Blueway. You are perhaps in the wrong section? Was it Dockside? There are a few jewellery makers there."

"Oh, no. This was the shop. It was recommended to me by ..." Once more, I thought of the connection: Haderan had told me of the guildsmith, Genter. I had known all along but refused to recognize the impor-tance of it. I suppose that I had had no reason to sus-pect Haderan before our session at his garrison.

The young man looked even more confused as I mumbled, "... a friend. It was recommended by a friend."

"Well, I don't know where else to suggest. But Dockside is only a few streets away," he went on.

"Perhaps so. I'll have to continue searching. I'm sorry if I've disturbed you."

"It is quite all right. I hope you find ... Genter? And please, if I can help you, come back soon."

"Perhaps I will. Thank you." He returned to his work as I turned to leave. "Thank you very much."

I left, suddenly positive of Haderan's involvement. It was without doubt the same shop – I recognized the doorway, the sign, the handmade lights, the colour of the walls, the rows of shelving, the size of the room. Everything about the place was as it should have been. And the young man was not lying, that I knew. It was all a trick after all. I shivered despite the close warmth of the night air.

Haderan must have sent Genter to the closed shop to break it open, having him ready for me when I came with the medallion. Perhaps Genter was a genuine guildsmith, but he was obviously working under

Haderan's orders.

Next had come the two thieves, set upon me at a time when Haderan and I had agreed to meet. He had not come of course, unless he was hidden behind some closed shutter, directing his little plot. They were to leave me for dead somewhere, using the theft as their cover. Fortunately, the two girls interfered with his plan. When he discovered I had survived, Haderan invented his elaborate story of Osseph's having sent the killers in the first place. He was forced into a trap of his own making, even to the point of having to execute the ruffians to protect himself, the loose ends that might have given him away. The logic was far clearer to me than Haderan had been.

Tricked and lied to by a man who shared my bed, one who held my confidence so cleverly that I had never suspected his treachery; I might have run screaming into his garrison right then to murder him in his dismal, lightless tower. I had been foolishly and dangerously blind.

But instead of giving way to turmoil, I began to devise a plan of my own.

**volume 34, pages 98-104:**
*Marik has blue eyes; I fell into them that first day in the antiquary when my brother introduced us. I was looking for information on old coins and he helped me locate some of the reference cubes. But I was taken more by the man than by the recordings.*

*Our first months were full of casual encounters, of explorations. He spent much of his time away at sea, though we still found a sense of comfort that grew stronger each time we were together. He is older than me – an intriguing character whose visits I looked forward to as any young woman might have done.*

*He told me much later that there had never been doubts in his mind about us, but he was sensible enough not to rush me. He had waited a long time, he said, and could wait a bit longer for our future. The planned sireages that most gyrefaeld families traditionally accepted were no obstacle to him; he would simply have abducted me! Of course, he never had the chance.*

*Neither of us suspected at first how Osseph was to change our lives. The shock of his new reality brought my illusions down about me in ruins. The murder of my family was a bleak ending to everything I knew. I ran to Marik because he was there. He saved my life.*

*We talked of all this as we sailed southward from the East Station to meet the packer that was to bring me to Denique. Marik was determined to continue the fight against Osseph from outside New Foster's mainland. He wanted me far enough away to be secure from the madman, from the insanity that had almost killed me. There was good reason to believe Osseph would try again once he discovered I was still alive. So I was to live in the Ten Thousand Islands constructing a supply line and establishing information networks for the underground.*

*We put our personal lives into sealed compartments when we determined to destroy Osseph. Whatever it took, we would apply our resources to this one objective, myself from the hidden world of intelligence gathering and Marik from his more exposed but effective position at sea. I could easily have devoted myself to him as a bondmate and mother to our children, but I also knew that it could only happen after Osseph was gone.*

*I resurrected the childhood codename, Pangaelene, out of spite for Osseph Tokastevor, whom I had then known as Jackal Bird. Marik and I danced intricate circles of intrigue with each other, out of sight yet constantly in touch. It was a difficult declaration we had made. It meant absences over long periods of time, endless dangers, the threat of death it-self. Our future was a promise based on common beliefs and absolute trust.*

*It took us almost seventeen trueyears to see it through.*

## 14. Kalanos Separ

Deretor arrived as he said he would, and after his sessions with Haderan, sent a message to me asking for a private, urgent meeting. I took the ferry to Kalanos where I often met with the other members of my core group.

When Deretor came to my rooms he looked ill. There were new lines around his eyes and mouth, he had lost weight and he breathed with a heavy rattle that I had only heard in much older men.

"What has happened to you? What is the matter? You look frightful!"

"I'm very tired, Iilaria, that is all. But I had to see you before ... before it is too late."

"Too late?"

"You were right about Haderan. As you are always right about such things. He is definitely not to be trusted."

"I was a little slow picking it up this time," I answered. "What have you found out?"

"He is approaching every member of the Reform Council with outright lies about you, and threats against them if they don't stop co-operating with your resistance networks. I would say he is out to undermine your influence with the council. He can't really affect the ones we support directly but there are a lot of the others who may be listening to his nonsense."

"What is it that he wants, do you know?"

"I'm only guessing at this, but I would say he is making a power bid. I can see him trying to take over the military here much as Osseph did in New Foster, exactly as you suspected. He is doing it slowly and quietly. But he must be getting anxious now that we are at war. He sees it as an opportunity to move ahead personally. If he can get enough support for his military advances, he'll also gain politically. But he seems to be concentrating only on the members who have declared themselves ready to send soldiers into New Foster. At the moment, that is still a minority."

"But he managed to talk them all into this effort. They seem to back him."

"He was telling the truth when he said you were the catalyst. The attack on your life was enough to convince our people to vote with his. He is becoming too clever."

"It is possible that he was responsible for that attack, Deretor."

"You can't mean that! Are you certain?"

"No. But it is a hypothesis I cannot ignore."

"He tried to kill you?"

"I think so. But he failed."

"He needs you and he fears you. Oh, the poor man!"

"I think it is time for me to be on that Council of yours officially, Deretor."

"I've told you so at least once or a tentime! My nomination is on record. You have only to appear. The formalities are taken care of."

"Does Haderan know that?"

"He may. The nomination has to be triggered by a resignation or a death. It will come up automatically. But meanwhile, what are we to do about Haderan?

Can we delay his first strike against New Foster? Or do we go along with it and try to speed up our own program?"

"We have to cut off the mainland passways. Turn off their power. Stop trading grain and chemical fuel and vital minerals. Get into their back pockets so thoroughly that we can cripple their war effort from inside. You know the details." Deretor and I had spent months devising methods of bringing Osseph's ecomomy to a standstill. It was the only way we could fight him without massive bloodshed on both sides.

"Haderan obviously has his own plans."

"Marik's group take their orders from us. Without the ships, Haderan won't get very far."

"He wants Marik removed. He is suggesting that you and Marik are no more than smugglers and pirates, and that both of you should be kept out of the war effort."

"I can't believe that he would be that stupid!"

"He either knows we are running our own blockade against Osseph or he suspects it. He sees you as a direct threat to his authority. He is afraid of anyone who can get ahead of him. There is no way we can work with him. I'm not certain what to suggest, but he can't run this war on his own. He would never win it."

"He has no mind for subtlety," I remarked. "He is a fighting man and that's all. A good field general, but without any feeling for the human equation."

"I don't know him very well, but I see what you mean more clearly now." Deretor coughed and sipped slowly at a glass of clear water.

"You aren't well, are you?"

"It's nothing, Iilaria. I have an infection in my chest."

"I remember Osseph explaining to me how he

wanted to do away with the Quatrec. He was full of self-infatuation. He wanted to throw it out because he didn't like the power it represented or the control it had over him. He wasn't interested in its workings. He saw it only as a threat to his ego. I don't think it is the same with Haderan. He doesn't care either way about ecological science. He just wants power."

"What are we going to do about it?" Deretor wanted me to give him answers. He was not one to engineer the downfall of a public figure such as Haderan.

"If he cannot take orders, he will have to be removed from his position. It is as simple as that," I replied.

"He is now the senior Military Advisor to the council! How do we get rid of him?"

"Deretor, I don't know yet. I'll come up with something. I will inform you of my decision in a few days. Meanwhile, I suggest you take a holiday yourself. Stay here until you hear from me. You look as though you're desperately in need of a rest. Let the council wait. Nothing is going to happen until our ships are ready and that will be at least a tenday. Perhaps I should make that an order?"

"You don't have to. I've been chasing guildmasters and councillors for weeks, and I do need a change. I'll take your advice for a few days at least. You on the other hand look as beautiful as ever. I don't suppose you could stay with me...?"

"I do like your flattery! But not this time, my friend! I have urgent business with our Military Advisor. I'll be with you in spirit!"

## 15. Denique

Deretor was confined to a medlab a threeday later, where tumours were discovered growing inside the tissue of his brain. They were too deeply embedded to remove.

I saw him once more but he did not recognize me. His death yielded my nomination to council, but it was a bitter victory for me. The result was as we had intended. I was able to carry on the campaign against Osseph, of which Deretor's planning had been a major part.

As the resistance movement inside New Foster gained momentum, its various supporters found themselves increasingly pressured to make themselves and their efforts more public, to declare outright their opposition to Osseph's oppression. In Denique, the process had taken many years.

The Merchant's and Manufacturer's guilds were the most difficult to persuade. These conservative and powerful bodies were against upsetting mainland affairs because of their continued trade with New Foster's self-appointed dictator. They were afraid of losing out in the commercial marketplace. But when they heard rumours of Osseph pirating their cargoes at sea, they quickly reversed their opinion.

**volume 28, page 121:**
*Marik has succeeded in stealing a tenportion of the Island's grain export and delivering it to our own storehouses. Osseph has been blamed for the treachery and my compatriots on council will now most assuredly vote in favour of ex-*

*tending our mandate to wage economic war with the main-land.*

Thus Pangaelene continued to play her role as agitator, conductor of vital information, moulder of opinion. She was the unseen perpetrator of many such wild schemes to win allies to her cause.

When Haderan informed me that the war had escalated, I feared that it was too soon for such a campaign to begin. It would be far too easy for Osseph's forces to win on their own ground. Without the internal backup that our underground operations could provide, there would be little chance of defeating him. We had yet to position ourselves securely, but it was impossible for me to advise Haderan on such matters – to him I was merely a nuisance, a woman, a threat or all three.

And my belief that he had been involved in the attempt on my life brought me desperately close to a confrontation with him.

Trust between us was now impossible. I had to give my carefully shielded support, not letting him know I suspected him. I played a delicate and double-faced game, keeping his interest in me alive, escorting him to important functions, even allowing him to continue as my lover so that I could use him in return. I had to accept the charade because he was too powerful and too dangerous to let him slip away.

But I was not finished with the man and could not be until the correct moment presented itself.

## 16. Denique

The old woman knew everything there was to know about herbal drugs and their intricate chemistry. She could concoct potions to cure a thousand ailments or create a thousand dreams. Living in obscurity behind the dress shop, she catered to a select clientele scattered throughout Denique and the surrounding islands.

With Han trying to act as interpreter, I told her what I needed. Her eyes lit up and her few teeth showed through a wrinkled grin. We spent an afternoon together sipping perfumed calafe, determining the best way for me to utilize her magic. Eventually, she gave me a tiny black phial of thick oily paste that she assured me would serve my purpose.

"*Qui-qui. ?Netori pas e-Lamba.*" She spoke to me in her halting gypsy tongue.

"*Qui-qui.* The drug of love," Han repeated although I had understood perfectly.

As we said goodbye once more in the overstuffed room overlooking the exotic garden courtyard, fat Jeva declared that my time of danger was almost past. I desperately wanted to believe her prophecy. I wanted to have faith in the enchantments of these women and their mystical commitment to the unknown forces they so easily took for granted.

**volume 1, pages 40-41:**
*Our mother, Ingren, took us to the magic theatre today. I was frightened by the fortune teller and cried most of the way home.*

*Gregh thought I was being silly. To him it was a big joke, and mother smacked him across the face for being unkind to me. He jumped out of the cabriole and walked home in a pout. I felt sorry for him then, but Ingren gave me another piece of her jellied panaco and said what a foolish boy he was. I soon felt better.*

*But the mystician was frightening. He had the blackest eyes I have ever seen. Maybe they were lenses over his own eyes. I do not really know why he was so fearsome, except he talked about a man with one eye, and said a lot of terrible things about our gyrefaeld.*

*Gregh is supposed to be leaving home and ... the rest of it doesn't make much sense, but Ingren was upset too, I know. She had that funny tight look around her mouth she gets when she knows father is coming home.*

*Tonight she read us three stories from the old book and then cosied us into our beds. But I still could not sleep so I decided to write to you, my diary.*

*I wonder sometimes about Greghory. I think his laughing was just to cover up his being afraid as well. And he seems to be getting very moody these days. Do boys get some sort of thing happening to them when they grow up, like girls? Inside their funny little brains, perhaps?*

*Mental menstruation. What a gruesome thought!*

*I will try to dream of something pleasant. A picnic in the garden would be nice. And the old Gregh back. He was much more fun.*

*Well, good night, diary.*

## 17. Denique

Haderan lay across my toballen, his huge limbs stretched almost to its edges. He stared up at me, his grin that of an innocent child, his movements like those of a sleeper struggling against the thick, fluid flow of a dream, trying to make headway against imaginary obstacles. His eyes glistened with tears, a side effect of the drug he had so readily consumed. He was helpless and would respond to any suggestion, any command I might give him.

I massaged his abdomen, leaning over him so that my untrussed hair fell across his thighs. His response was obvious though much slower than normal.

To Haderan a few moments would seem endless. I could demand of him what I pleased, giving him what would amount to a total pleasure-response. Used carefully by people who shared an intimate trust, the drug was one of the most rewarding of the sensories. Dreamsticks are made from the same root; their main appeal is sexual. I was drawing him into a world of erotic fantasy.

I touched his body with my hands, my mouth, gently encouraging his arousal. I tried to think of him as he had been – my friend, my lover. We had shared much through the years I stayed in Denique. He had been a necessary part of my campaign to secure the influence I needed.

Rather foolishly I had trusted him, and it almost cost me my life. Watching his slow undulations, I thought of the silent distances that exist between those who never truly comprehend each other.

### volume 30, page 1:
*I dreamed that I was in the centre of a great plain where armies ground away at each other until there was nothing left but the cold, bloody ground. Haderan lay beneath it trying to save himself as I rolled stones down on top of him.*

*What did it all matter when everyone was finally gone? Cling desperately to each small interval, I screamed silently. Nothing was ever as you had imagined or as you hoped it might have been.*

"Can you hear me, Haderan? Can you feel me?" I rocked slowly back and forth, straddling his torso. Sitting on his midriff, I took him deeply inside me and watched his face.

His lips moved. A whisper slipped from his mouth. "Yes ... yes ... feel you ... yes...."

"What is it like? Tell me, what is it like to have me all around you like this?"

"Warm ... you ... are ... so ... warm...."

"I'm going to make you feel all of me." I moved gently, eyes closed, gauging his response by the feel of him. His breathing changed only slightly but his heart quickened as the old woman had said it would. With my fingers I felt the veins in his neck swell.

"Tell me about the coin," I suggested.

"Coin ... tell ... you ... the ... coin...."

"My medallion. The one I took to Genter's shop with your yarrenchain. Where is it?"

"In ... my ... office ... the ... garri ... son...."

Part of me had hoped I would be proven wrong, that he had not been involved. But there it was – the betrayal.

"Who gave it to you?" I continued my back and forth motion, easing my weight up and down.

"Who ... gave ... you...? I ... gave ... you.... Genter ... made ... chain...."

"No. Try to remember. Who gave you the coin? My coin."

"The ... shop ... at ... the ... Crystal ... Plaza.... Genter ... had ... coin ... I ... took ... it ... back...."

"Who gave it to Genter?"

"Yellow ... beard ... feel ... so ... warm ... and ... smooth...."

"And you hanged them. For stealing a coin at your order?"

"Dead.... Hanged ... them.... He ... was ... going ... to ... tell ... you...."

"Do you like this, Haderan?" I moved slowly, my hands pressing down into his chest. He lay almost still, an occasional shudder passing down his long frame. "What was he going to tell me?"

"He ... yes.... Feel ... so ... good...."

"What was Yellowbeard going to tell me?"

"Tell ... you ... my ... men ... paid ... him ... if ... I ... did ... not ... give ... him ... credits.... Could ... not ... trust ... him."

I almost felt sorry for him then. He could no more stop answering me than he could resist my motion. He would tell me anything just as surely as he would explode inside me if I moved too fast. He was unimpeded by conscious restraint. As long as he remained in his euphoric fantasy, he was mine.

"Then they weren't Osseph's men at all? You arranged the whole thing?"

"Not ... Osseph's ... no ... my ... merce ... mercen ..."

"Mercenaries?"

"From ... Is ... Isan ..."

"Isanomine?" It was a penal island far out on the Long Rim. So the men must have been commandeered from prison.

"I want the coin back, Haderan."

"The ... coin ..."

"Where is it? Tell me again."

"In ... wall ... my ... office ... behind ... ship ..."

"Behind the big hologram?" I remembered it was the only thing I had liked in his headquarters. It was of a four-masted sailing spinner that my stepfather had built.

"You were going to sell it?"

"Sell ... it.... "

"But you couldn't, could you, because it's not registered."

"Behind ... ship...."

The veins in his neck bulged as he came closer to his final moments. The rope-like tubes throbbed with hammer-blows from his racing heart.

The old woman had told me what to watch for. The pure form of the drug was not commonly available, she'd said. It was part of a little known genre of folk-medicines used by the gypsy healers. ("Iilaria the gypsy," she had called me, just as Haderan had done. "Your mother was a gypsy, that I know!")

"Why did you want me killed, Haderan?" I didn't want to listen to his answer but I had to know for certain I was right. It was almost time.

"You ... knew ... too ... much...."

"About what? What did I know too much about?"

"You ... found ... out...."

"Found out what?"

"About ... council ... take ... over.... "

"Take over? What do you mean?"

"Council ... control ... council ... I ... can ... win ..."

"You think you can win a majority pledge? You are ambitious!"

"Win ... war ..."

"Not this way. You're making too many enemies in Denique."

"They ... don't ... under ... stand ... war ... fare."

"Of course not. Most of them are guildsmen and merchants."

"They ... don't ... know ... how...."

"And you would direct them?"

"I ... want ... to ... control ... them."

"And you were afraid I would try to stop you? Stop you from becoming like Osseph?"

"You ... stop ... me...?"

"Oh, yes! I would have!"

"Os ... seph ... is ... pow ... er."

"Osseph is insane! You are more a fool than I imagined!"

"He ... can ... call ... up ... army ..."

"He can murder innocent people, Haderan. You are like him already, aren't you? Who else will you have to kill? All your old friends who oppose you? Who else is on your list?"

"Marik ... is ... coming ..."

My heart leapt to my throat. Marik coming to Denique? It was not possible that he would be sailing here without my knowledge. Unless ... I fixed Haderan's almost closed eyes with mine, sitting quite still on him. "How do you know he is coming?"

"I ... spoke ... to ... him ... through ... codes ..."

"Pangaelene?"

"The ... dan ... cers ..."

"You would destroy all that I have worked for?"

"Tac ... tics ... want ... both ... of ... you ... dead ... I ... want ... coun ... cil ..."

"When is he coming?"

"Sil ... ver ... day."

"Silverday? Less than a tenday!"

"I ... know ... you ... love ... him ..."

"That you would not understand, and it is not your concern." It all made sense then, the entire manoeuvre. Right from the evening when he had refused to send my message to Trevarn. Haderan could not allow me to interfere with his ambitions. He would have wanted me only as his mistress, not as an enemy. He knew I would never keep in the background of his political career as would-be head of the Island Republic and its Reformist Council.

His rule would have been simply another dictatorship, and I, once more, its victim.

Certain that he could have had me killed easily at any time, I credited him with having the grace not to simply dump me into the sea with my neck in chains. My death was to have been part of a far subtler ploy. My survival must have been much more difficult for him to account for.

But now, it was my turn. I continued rocking back and forth on top of him, this time much faster, up and down in rhythm with his violent pulse. I felt his body surge beneath me. It took the time of a tenbreath to bring him to his final climax.

When he burst within me, I felt his furious heart pounding, pounding, pounding through his body, through the bed, through the room ...

... I heard the cries of dead men, cursing.

The drug, *qui-qui,* and its derivatives focus awareness by slowing the senses. Metabolism alters, space and time rebound in ever-broadening spheres; the "I" floats in a womb of mellow passivity. Imagination weaves dreamy illusions. In sexual coupling, pleasure-passion flows like a warm tide. It is the ultimate of the sensories.

The key to the drug's effectiveness is a time-altering phetatheromone that allows physical stimulation to be extended indefinitely. It's chemistry was not unknown to me. I had made a tentative study of organic stimulants years before when I helped set up a hostel for wounded sailors.

In precisely measured doses, it heightens sexuality without ill-effect. It dissolves, traceless, into the bloodstream. There is no after-ache, no nausea, no depression. But over-dosing can be fatal, which is why it has remained banned. Only the limited concentrations of its diluted by-products as found in dreamsticks are officially approved and prepared under guild license.

The amount I had fed to Haderan would have killed two or three ordinary men, but he was bigger than most and I could take no chances. The old woman had warned me of the fatal dosages, the dangers, the results. She knew only that I wanted the stimulant, not what I planned. I had made sure she would never be implicated later on if something went wrong.

Quite simply, Haderan's heart raced until it stopped. His mind drifted through timeless fantasies, through sensuous dream-worlds where reality remained remote and unreachable. His consciousness lay in a sea of deep fancy. My questions were just echoes from far above him, glimmers of light from ripples on the surface. His responses were autonomic and free of deceit.

There would be no evidence in his system of foreign chemicals other than a slight residue in the spinal fluids. It was doubtful that an autopsy would be conducted. I was not concerned. Heart failure was not uncommon in men his age. It would be said that he died in the arms of his dark-eyed mistress.

I left him on my bed and went to bathe, to rid myself of every trace of the man who had so deviously betrayed me.

**volume 36, pages 68-72:**

*The Silverday holiday came as always, and the mid-winter festivals. But Marik did not. I had sent one final message from Pangaelene telling him of Haderan's treachery and of his unfortunate death. I warned him away although all I needed in my life then was Marik.*

*He came, finally, months later, aboard his new yacht,*

Solyon, which I had chartered for a long summer cruise through the southern islands. He had changed outwardly: his hair was ice-white and short, cut close to his shoulders, and his beard had grown full. He resembled an ancient star-lord more than the head of a revolutionary army.

But his work was almost finished. Osseph, the first and hopefully last self-proclaimed Military Dictator of New Foster, was deposed nineteen trueyears after he had assumed power. It was a long and eventful segment of our history and its effects were to be felt for generations afterwards.

Marik and I travelled to Materossen for the trial, but I could not bear the city's oppressiveness. We stayed just long enough to see Osseph spared a death sentence. He was instead secured for life in a monastic cloister-house in the depths of the Cypol forests.

I wanted space, freedom, the brightness of the southern islands. Marik wanted the sea. So we compromised and built our home near Kalanos Separ where I have remained for a twenty-year since. I have outlived him for fifteen of those years. His two daughters hardly remember him at all.

Perhaps one day they will meet their uncle, my baby brother Greghory, if he takes it upon himself to revisit the world of his birth. The star-people are a breed unto themselves – once they leave solid ground they only return intermittently and reluctantly. Their shortest journeys take years of our time, and when they come back to a starting point, generations might have passed. Their society is built around this bizarre concept of time and so is essentially alien to the planet-bound.

Were he to return to Isurus and to New Foster or the Ten Thousand Islands, he would find a changed world. He might visit with his nieces in Kalanos. Perhaps they would take him for a day to the water gardens at the old palace. A tour of the ceremonial council chambers that we use now only for annual reinstatements might please him. They

could show him where his sister used to make a spectacle of
herself as she tried to persuade her council this way or that.

He could visit her resting place in the East Court and tell
her of the wonders he has seen beyond the stars....

Looking to the past can be dangerous....

# ILLUSIONS OF GRACE

# 1. Prologue

There is a small collection of holograms that I have kept with me since I left New Foster. The first reproduction, its faded colouring reminiscent of the times, shows our stepfather and mother in front of the gyre-faeld compound. They are arm in arm, with aunts, uncles and grandfaelders on either side, all dressed in the drab grey-blue suits and gowns they used to wear on such occasions.

The occasion of this gathering was our homecoming; Iilaria and I were born to an unbonded woman in the Quain Townships. My mother, unable to bear children herself due to some uterine impairment, had arranged our adoption; the reception was in honour of the family's newest members.

There are two strolling-carriages in the image's foreground, one for each of the Addiman infants. Neither of our faces are clearly visible. The elders can be seen grouped behind us on that cold, grey day shortly after the Silverday Festival. Winter still held our village in its bleak grip.

The two of us are little more than blobs of white no matter what angle the hologram is viewed from. I used to think I could make out my sister's small, rounded face, her intense dark eyes, peering over the carriage's high rim. Of me there is nothing but an indistinct patch that might have been swaddling or a pillow.

Was I there at all? For all I could see, I might not have existed when the image was scanned.

## 2. Matrix

"There's a ship out there. One of the big ones."

"I know. It lit up the whole western ocean when it came in. It's of Viartan registry?"

"There are no non-Viartan starships left as far as we know."

"Have they said anything yet?"

"Just what you've already heard. Standard codes. Permission to assume orbit. Docking rights. Intent and relay schedules."

"Are they coming down?"

"Only a small crew and a few couriers. They're looking for refined crotanium among other things. Say it's easier to buy it than dig ore out of an asteroid. Refining and processing isn't all that simple, even for the Viartans."

"What in Gill's name is crotanium? And do we have any?"

"Listen, I just made up the name! The alloy they want is a zero-g nano-conductor that can't be manufactured without fusion implants. I have no idea what they actually call it. But I intend to find out. In the meantime, Port Cray is going through its inventory from Isurus Station. There are some old shield heads floating around out there that are made out of similar metals."

"They must be almost two thousand years old!"

"But it's also indestructible. The Viartans may be able to use it instead. They may have to."

"I suppose we have no choice, then?"

"What difference would it make? We have no use for the alloy. We aren't about to launch any interstellar probes, are we?"

"I mean the Quatrec. What does it have to say about our dealings with the Viartans."

"Nothing, really. I don't think this sort of thing was ever anticipated. It's not covered by any of the old trade agreements. They just need to make a few parts, that's all."

"So we can't say no?"

"I'm not sure why we would want to say no."

"You have no imagination, Mihan."

"Not for your kind of politics at least."

"Do you see them as a threat?"

"Not really. Unless we decide to aim solar reflectors at their hull and boil their insides."

"Don't be facetious."

"Then they might get nasty and empty their latrines into our upper atmosphere."

"I was thinking more of laser weaponry?"

"It's a research ship. And our panels wouldn't generate enough energy to be noticed on a hull that large."

"So we just give them what they want?"

"There's no cause for alarm."

"I was just asking your professional opinion. Please monitor them. And let me know if ..."

"If Gregh is still on board and if he'll be coming down –"

"Make him."

"That I can't do, Iilaria."

"Then perhaps I can."

"Oh, I'm sure of it! Just remember he knows nothing about us. So be very careful, all right?"

"Always ..."

## 3. Materossen

"Old Quain Passway?" I asked, only to be told that I was already halfway along it. Ancient glassite and crolloy buildings hung across its broad pedestrian routes, their cluttered overhead walkways jutting in all directions. The city smelled wretchedly of heat, dust and garbage.

Materossen Civic Court was part of a newer complex; it had been built of hand-cut stone quarried not far from the village I had left a century before. Towering before me, it reminded me of the academy we had attended as children.

Canopies with green-grey eaves sheltered trash-littered sideyards leading from the street. The entrance was beneath massive tiered columns that supported nothing more than an arched and dirty lintel bearing New Foster's insignia. Hidden behind false facades, like our old school in the Quain Townships, the ever-impersonal face of authority still waited to stamp me into anonymity.

I was not yet ground-oriented, having been downside only a threeday. Sleep had evaded me since my landing at Pirrit Ennis and I was suffering a typical mild case of auto-conscious ground-syndrome on which the standard-issue medichems seemed to have no effect.

Inside the building, cold green light filtered from dim skywindows far above in the long, central gallery, giving everything a pale, surreal glow. Clerks and messengers ran in disorderly haste between rows of uniformly characterless work stations and shelving. It smelled of overwhelming bureaucracy. I would have fled but for reminding myself I had come here for a reason.

I wandered about the public level long enough to find a well-hidden informary. There were signs in several languages, all indicating where one should not go, but little to show the way to anything useful. Fortunately, I had no need to relieve myself – I saw no drop-rooms or sanipaks in the entire expanse of the floor. Again, I was reminded of the old academy where even the simple act of urinating had often been a painfully delayed process.

Eventually the visary revealed itself. Its terminal, an elaborate old punch-screen, stood alone in the middle of a sunken half-level as if waiting for some long-lost adversary to kick it to life. I approached, unable to put childish memories aside; it could have been the identical tutor-matrix I had studied with as a boy. Most of them resembled each other only because function required it, but the sense of parallel vision persisted.

At each step I felt ghosts nudging my elbows, embracing me with long-forgotten greetings, offering a welcome I could never receive here now. I pictured classrooms I had not seen in a hundred years, psychically-generated mirages born of space-nerves, triggered by memories from my fenyears, all effects of the syndrome.

When I punched in my code, reality transposed itself to a scene from years before. I waited while a million optlight circuits scrutinized my scrawled and frayed assignment. I stood in front of the screen expecting rejection and a request to re-submit ...

"... this time with more accurate reference to given variables ... we cannot accept this in its present form ... you must consider the implications of our initial dialogue ... be more thorough in your subsequent submissions ... you are automatically failed if you do not have your work completed by ..."

The laughter of old school friends, the fellowship, the rivalries, the unspoken fear of not satisfying this omnipotent machine ... it was all there in my mind again.

As illusion held me, I waited in the empty visary for the matrix response. A century had elapsed when the ancient screen broke its silence. A metallic voice confirmed the words that appeared on the screen: "8011-0307-6914. Greghory N. Addiman. Please present request category."

"Gyrefaeld Addiman: Materossen, New Foster. Status Update."

The matrix flashed its myriad cryptograph patterns as records were searched. Shortly, an answer came up: "Presently indicated deceased."

"That's not possible!" I shouted at empty air. Several techs looked across their desks at me, then quietly resumed their work. "That's not possible," I repeated in a gentler tone, having forgotten that the machine could hear me better than any of the clerks.

"Confirming. Please wait." The machine's voice offered no hint that it was conversing with a human being. "Addiman Gyrefaeld indicated deceased. Confirmed."

"Try Iilaria Jacine Addiman. What's her status?" I pronounced her name carefully, hoping there was some mistake in the data.

"Addiman, Iilaria. Registered SRM Keys. Check listings."

"How am I supposed to check SRM listings? Would you please transfer my request. I want to find her records."

"Confirming transfer request. Please wait." As the process continued, I wondered how my entire gyrefaeld could be listed as "deceased". I thought there would have been some family members still bearing the name. The matrix came back with "Addiman: Iilaria Jacine. Chief Councillor, Denique Reform Council. Born: 28:Sem:16-cy-68: Materossen. Deceased: 12:Kor:23-cy-71: Kalanos. Two surviving daughters: Jacine Paul and Araneth Mendel. Iilaria Jacine Addiman: Simulated Response Module status."

SRMs were encoded remains of the deceased who had achieved some unique status in their life's work. They were preserved in matrix format for the value of future reference. That Iilaria was listed in the Keys, or the General Guild Index, meant she had been such an individual. The matrix continued: "All material release-code restricted."

"Release code?" I asked. "What does that mean?"

"Access of material not permitted. Release code required."

"I'm her brother, for Gill's sake."

"Confirming." There was another brief wait, then, "Brother: Greghory Newton Addiman. Deceased."

"I am Greghory Addiman. I am her brother. I am definitely not deceased!" The clerks showed more interest. At least two of them were no longer inspecting their fingernails.

"Confirming. Please wait." This time, red and yellow lights were flashing; I had the ominous feeling that the machine was about to pounce on me for some long-forgotten indiscretion.

"Addiman, Greghory N. Born 28:Sem:16-cy-68: Materossen. Assigned Viartan Naval Cruiser VNAV *Whitethrell*, 22:Ter:7-cy-69. No further entries. Presumed deceased."

"Here's your chance to update your records. I'm back. The current date is, according to your calculation, 12:Var:22-cy-73. I have been gone ninety-six of your years. I was of eighteen trueyears when I left. I am now forty-one. You work it out.* But first of all, will you tell me where I can learn something about my sister?"

"Please present request category."

"How about a boot up your rassbone?"

By this time, one of the clerks had come forward. I heard her cough politely before asking if she could help.

"Well, yes, perhaps," I mumbled.

"I overheard your conversation," she informed me. "I checked out some files in my console. I think what you're looking for is in the SRM Keys. She became a very famous woman, you know."

"No, I didn't. I left years ago...."

"You've been in space all that time?"

"Many voyages. Many planet-falls. I've been away from New Foster for a century."

"I've never met a real spacer before. Excuse me if I seem a bit ... curious. I would be glad to help you trace your family." She was soft-spoken and her eyes smiled from beneath dark curls of long hair tied loosely over her shoulder. For a moment, I thought she looked familiar.

---

*For obscure reasons relating to Gillcallian Astrology, dates on New Foster are calculated in twenty-seven-year cycles corresponding to the time it takes the White Sister to completely circle Isurus Prime. This is so confusing that most people simply multiply the cy index by twenty-seven and add the current year for their calendar references. This sum roughly equates to the number of years the colony has been in existence. A so called base year equals 1.037 trueyears, the time it takes to catch the White Sister each time the planet revolves around Isurus Prime.

"I would appreciate the help! So where are these SRM Keys?"

"On the top floor. Hardly anyone goes up there. They usually use the Keys at a local visary. We have most of the originals here. But you can access them if you know how."

"Release code notwithstanding?"

"In this case, I think we can use my code. I work here after all, and you are ... an unusual applicant? It would take you a tenday to get your own access approved. Are you here for long?"

"My ship is in orbit. We're making some ... complex repairs. I've taken overdue ground leave. I don't know how long I'll have."

"Well, I think I can get you started!"

The ghosts nudged my innards with a quick flutter then disappeared once more. The clerk, who could not have been more than twenty, was leading me towards an elevator platform across the building. And she was far more attractive than the matrix I had just encountered. The civic complex no longer seemed such an unpleasant place.

The elevator stopped at the tenth floor. There were two additional flights of stairs and if that was not enough, we climbed yet another level by rampway. It must have been one of the tallest buildings in the city. "This is a public gallery?" I asked. "Who comes up here to use it?"

"As I said, almost no one. Most people who want to access the SRMs will use their local system. The hookup is almost planet-wide nowadays."

"So why is my sister here? Why can't I find out about her through the matrix below? What's the mystery?"

"I don't know. But when I saw you get the restricted

flasher, I thought I'd check it for you."

It crossed my mind that she had done so because it was required of her, and that her interest in my problem was in fact a diplomatic way of finding out what I was up to. I suppose I was still expecting the matrix to be hostile, reprimanding rather than friendly. The red light had gone on; for certain I was a trouble-maker. What better way to check me out than with a pretty young clerk, probably an expert in the martial arts, who was right now leading me to the security-inquisition cells? We passed directly beneath the green roof-lights and I saw vague outlines of pipes and machinery above them. She took me through a set of sliding glazed doors.

The room she brought me to was an unexpected contrast to what I had seen below. Full of plush-flesh furniture and subtly lighted, its air was dezone-fresh and clear smelling as on board my ship. Discreetly placed banks of visary screens were occupied by small groups of operators who looked far more at ease than their counterparts in the gallery downstairs. I could not help grinning at the young woman, having thought only moments before that I was about to be charged with seditious meddling. "What a difference up here! It's nothing like the rest of your building!"

"It's all new. This has just been added on. They're still installing new elevators at the back. But this is where we do our real work," she said. "Down there's the regular stuff: birth registrations, land claims, tariff collections. Upstairs, we do P. and M. for the entire Colony."

"Pee-and-em?"

"Prediction and Modulation. The guilds develop all their quotas here, using our data. We can predict almost every line of development that needs attention, and adjust the whole balance of growth. It's the main reason I work here."

"When did all this happen?" I asked. "When I left, everything was still done according to the old system. We called it the Quatrec. This looks so ... so technical."

"It's getting constantly more complex. We still enforce the Quatrec; it has worked well for almost two thousand years. But things are changing rapidly now, and everything has to be watched that much more closely."

"I don't understand a lot of that anymore, I'm afraid." I knew the basics of planetary engineering but had been too long away from New Foster to gauge its progress.

"Your starship should give you the idea. It's a closed system, right? And you always know how much of everything you need to keep it running? Food, water, fuel. Your power systems have to be monitored. Your waste has to be recycled. And so on. Everything is controlled. And if you ignore any minor aspect of the package, you're in trouble. Really a matter of record keeping." She didn't pause long enough for me to comment.

"So imagine a whole planet, like Isurus." She used the old Viranti name for our world which suggested a certain loyalty to colonial tradition. "It is really just a big spaceship. But the difference here is that we have never controlled it all, only the parts we have been able to modify to our own style of habitable environment. Planetary engineering. Land-forming. You remember – you must have spent as long studying it as I did!"

"Years! It was all there ever was in the senior forms."

"Well, we're at the point now where there's a turn-around in some of the natural cycles. The middle of the hump. Irreversible changes that become self-perpetuating. The atmosphere is almost completely breathable, even out in the Territories. The seas haven't changed much, although there's a higher oxygen count, and some of the hybrid species are taking a firmer hold on life. There are now edible fish, our own stock, that replenish themselves. It has taken hundreds of years, but it's finally working the way it was planned."

"And you're involved in all this?"

"Oh, yes! I'm a marine biochemist. I do a lot of my work here. I design backups. Don't ask me to explain unless you have all day!"

"And you were downstairs when I had my ... problem?"

"A lot of my data is easier to get from the old matrix. But what you were looking for is up here, I think."

We had come to another set of doors and passed into an open hallway full of crates and construction equipment. There was another half-flight of stairs leading to a broad balcony. "Up here," she said.

Then my syndrome overtook me once more: as she walked through the slanting rays of light under one of the skylights, she became, briefly, insubstantial, like an old hologram. For a single instant, I saw the wall pattern through her body as if she had flickered out of existence and reappeared. I felt light-headed and had to lean on a chair for support.

"Are you all right?" she called, turning to me.

"Nerves. We all get it the first time down. Some sort of reality adjustment, I'm told. I'll be fine."

She took my arm, far too firmly for an apparition, and led me to a room opening from the raised area. This was a smaller chamber, luxuriously laid out with lounge chairs and low, flat desks that were more like dining platforms than work stations. She seated me in a wide, circular booth. "I'm Lily," she offered. "Pleased to have rescued you."

"Greghory. My pleasure, Lily. A pretty name for a pretty woman."

"My bondmate thinks so, too."

"You're bonded? And here I thought I might have a companion for the evening!"

"Oh, you have, if you want it! I'll be glad to stay with you for a while. As long as you don't mind a threesome. Derry works a late shift, and I always wait for him."

I tried to hide disappointment. The more she talked about her work, the more I had wanted to know about her. And now, bonded. *Well*, I thought. *I've only been here for one afternoon....*

"The SRMs," I blurted. "Where are they?"

"You're sitting in front of them. They're in the countertop. At least, the access plates are. We just call them up. If we want a sound screen for private conversation with one of them, we start out ... like so." She pushed an almost invisible patch on the table, and a wall of silence enveloped us.

"I must say, you hide it well," she went on.

"Hide what well?" I asked, not understanding.

"Your confusion. Your disorientation. Your feeling that you must have missed an enormous amount of history. The strangeness?"

"You're a perceptive young woman. You're very easy to ... to feel comfortable with. You talk to me and it feels as though we've known each other a long time. I shouldn't say so, perhaps, but ... well, I suppose I've been away too long, and you intrigue me."

"I can see that in your eyes," she answered. "If I

weren't very fond of Derry, I'd probably end up getting stuck on you. Then you'd fly away again and I'd be heartbroken! I think it's your eyes. Do you do this often? To young women, I mean?" Her laughter flowed like chords played on the strings of a tymballine.

"I hope not! Derry – is that his fen-name?"

"Short for Deretor. He's an engineer. Works on satellite grids. He's a power systems planner. He has nice eyes too." She was entering codes, and lights flickered across the small panel in front of her.

"Iilaria Jacine Addiman. We learned about her at the academy, you know? She founded the university where Derry and I met. Very famous sister you have ... or had, I mean. When did you see her last?" As she talked, she inserted more data into the table's console surface.

"We were both eighteen when I left. That was in cy-69. The month of Semlevoren"

"I'm a Semlevorite as well!. Born at the end of the month."

"Iilaria and I are – we were – twins."

"You were twins?" Her mouth dropped before she had realized this particular implication of our birthdates. Then, "Of course! I didn't think of it!"

"I suppose it sounds strange to you. The time gap."

"It does take a while to get used to!" She continued working the console. "She doesn't respond. I can't find her in here."

"The matrix did say she was simulated?"

"Definitely."

"Couldn't be wrong, could it?"

"No. Let me try again."

Except for our breathing and the soft patter of her fingers, there was no sound within the confines of our screened booth. She went through the routine with the ease of long experience.

"I'm sorry, but she doesn't come up. There's no sign of her SRM at all. I really don't understand it."

"You're saying she isn't here after all?"

"She should be. There's no reason why not. She's not proscribed, like the Osseph module."

"The what?"

"Osseph Tokastevor. The dictator. You can't talk to him. He's not been publicly released. They wait twenty, thirty, sometimes fifty years after death, when a person was ... confined for treason, or a state prisoner? He is supposed to be de-restricted in a month or so."

It was my turn for surprised reaction. "You said Tokastevor? The dictator? Now, please, slow down. Explain. You can't mean Osseph Tokastevor from the Quain Townships? Can you?"

"I think so. Why? What's wrong?"

"This is too much all at once. My departed sister was a councillor, a famous one you say. So much so that she is now an SRM. But missing, it seems. Then you tell me that a boyhood friend is a proscribed SRM? That he was a dictator? What happened while I was out there?"

"You knew Osseph Tokastevor?"

"There were four of us who grew up together: Osseph and his brother, Mihan, my sister, Iilaria, and me."

"Then, by default, you're a famous person too!" She hesitated. "I mean, there's more to this than I realized."

"What are you saying?"

"I'm not sure that I should be getting involved. You're the brother of one of our most important recent leaders. I'm beginning to feel a little ... out of place. Part of what you want seems to be restricted information, and I'm already your accomplice. I could get myself into difficulties here!"

"I wouldn't let that happen Lily, I promise. I'm the one who had the difficulty. You simply redirected me. But can you fill me in a little on what happened with Osseph? And Iilaria?"

"It's history, and all in the records. He took over New Foster and tried to impose his own regime. He was ruthless and there are endless horror stories about what he did in order to bend people to his will."

"Why didn't the guilds stop him?"

"He took everyone by surprise and gained a very powerful hand by manipulating the military. No one was prepared for his tactics."

"It sounds just like him. We used to play wargames, as children. He planned them all."

"You are a direct link to his past, then. To the beginnings of an entire segment of our history. There are a lot of historians who would like to have you to themselves for a while!"

"What happened in the end?"

"We aren't too certain how, but your sister had a lot to do with his overthrow. He was deposed and he died in prison. Some say Councillor Addiman spared him from the death sentence. Others claim it was her consort, Marik. At any rate, he died a broken man and we have been re-structuring our systems ever since. Iilaria was a very resourceful woman – she re-established most of the disrupted research programs herself."

"Marik was her consort? I introduced them before I left! What happened to them?"

"Marik was lost at sea, somewhere beyond the Long Rim. She went into seclusion on an island estate not far from Kalanos. She survived him for many years. She died ... greatly admired, but alone. Her two daughters must be registered here. Your nieces!"

"And her SRM is not responding."

"It appears that way. I can't get anything from her."

"Then I'll have go to her island myself. I must find out what it was like. Near Kalanos, you say?"

"Then I'll have to get you visuals of the precise location." She was anxious I thought to get me away from the SRM panels that she had so readily brought me to. "I'm sorry you couldn't speak with her."

"I am too. But it certainly isn't your fault. You mustn't be concerned for your position here on my account!"

"Thank you for that. I trust you, you know. It's those eyes!" She was laughing again as we left the secluded chambers above the public gallery. "To be honest, I was hoping we might talk a little more!"

I liked her and thought her to be sympathetic, though possibly very nervous, about my searching the records. "I've got a pass on tonight's ferry. Another time perhaps?"

"I think Derry would like to meet you too. He would have a lot of questions."

"You've been very kind. You remind me of – of someone I once knew, someone I left behind. A century ago." I knew it was not possible, but there was something about her manner, her attitude that suggested my departed sister. We crossed to the elevators and were quickly back on the main concourse.

"This is so ... different ... meeting you like this. I've often wondered what it would be like to travel in space, through such vast gaps in time. You are a real – a phenomenon, aren't you?"

"I could say the same of you," I told her, although I

was indeed the stranger. "Our time sequences are never really understood by the planet-bound. That's why so few of us ever come down when the ships make port. We have everything we need up there."

"Everything? Like bondmates? Families?"

"Many do. There are children who grow up in space. It's a way of life."

"You've never had children." It was a statement, not a question.

"How do you know that?"

"It's written all over you. A woman can usually tell."

"I can't believe that! In my case, it happens to be true. A lot of us prefer to remain childless. My work keeps me too busy."

"Derry and I want children, very much. We're waiting for an approved gene biasing."

"It's done carefully out there, too. Pregnancies have to be monitored. Depending on where we are, mothers are sometimes kept enshielded for their entire duration. It's not the same down here at all. I think that's why I've kept away from bonding with a crewmate. It's a major commitment."

"It must be dreadful for the women! How do they manage?"

"In the long run, better than the men. They outlive us by a good margin." We had reached the main floor once more.

"Wait here," she said.

I stood alone beneath the high, vaulted ceilings, wondering how a simple attempt to search the matrix had become so involved. I was confused and slightly dizzy.

Why was I really here? What was I hoping to find? My sister and my entire gyrefaeld were gone, all dead except for, perhaps, two nieces. Iilaria was inaccessible to me – I could not even converse with her module.

I had met a young woman who seemed to see right inside me; it made me feel more fragile, more exposed. Oh, yes, I understood why our kind so rarely came downside! We were embarrassingly inept at functioning outside the enclosed walls, the protective shells, of our floating womb-cities. I saw Lily coming back and almost ran from her.

"Here, I've got printed schedules for you. A map with all the new ferry connections. A list of hostels and what to ask for. And my comset code. You can contact us any time you like. I can't change your mind? We'd like to have you." I wasn't certain if she was just being polite or if she genuinely wanted me to stay with them.

"No. I think I'd better get started. But thank you again for all your help."

She smiled up at me as if to ask more questions. Instead, she gave me a kiss, the warmth of her mouth leaving its memory on my cheek.

She stood beside one of the false columns as I started down to the street. When I looked back, she was gone.


## 4. Matrix

*"Your brother is on his way."*

*"It was easier than we thought it would be. Just had to suggest an excursion for some of their crew, courtesy of the New Foster Council."*

*"How many have come down?"*

*"Only six. That's all they allow at once. Viartan Naval*

*policy about landfall seems to be extremely tight."*

"What are you planning for him?"

"I'm not certain. I'll wait and see how he reacts."

"Did he like – who is she? – your great grand-daughter?"

"Yes, he liked her."

"You're not playing with him are you?"

"What do you mean?"

"He's only human."

"So were you, once."

"He's taken the island ferry. With the good weather, he'll be here in a few days."

"What about that ship up there?"

"They haven't finished assessing the damage. And they won't say specifically what's wrong. It must be serious for them to have stopped here."

"What about their requisitions?"

"Vague, so far. But they are preparing a shuttle for a trip to Isurus Station."

"Can they do that?"

"Physically, yes. But I presume you're referring to trade rights?"

"I'm getting an opinion from Max."

"I think you'd be wasting his time. The Viartans will do whatever they think they have to."

"They should be willing to discuss some sort of transaction. In the interests of diplomacy if nothing else. We're cousins, after all."

"Strike a bargain with the spacers?"

"There must be something we want down here? Haven't you been looking for better tranceivers? Something you can float a few meks above Materossen?"

"I doubt they'd have anything that we could deploy in secret. Besides, there's nothing wrong with our own little devices."

"Your self-confidence is overwhelming, Mihan."

"Did she like him?"

*"Pardon me?"*

*"Your great grand-daughter. Did she show an interest in Greghory?"*

*"How often does anyone here get the chance to meet someone from their own past? It was all she could do to let him get on that ferry!"*

*"Do you think he suspects anything?"*

*"No. But he will soon enough."*

*"You're playing a very dangerous game."*

*"If you keep reminding me of that, Mihan, I shall have to find something else for you to do with your spare time. Or turn you off."*

*"Someone has to watch over you."*

*"I'll let you know when I need you."*

*"I'm sure you will."*


## 5. Public Ferry, near Denique

Beginnings are like an ancient chest hidden away in some dark closet for a lifetime; inside are a thousand confused memories, each clamoring to be recognized first....

Ingren was our adoptive mother, the matriarchal gyre-faelden.

We slept beside her during the long summer nights when father was away, sailors adrift on the waves of the enormous toballen, her upstairs bed. Iilaria and I would lie against the enlaced smoothness of her flesh. She was native silk from the Torforatagos, elegant and delicate. During those early years, she never abandoned us to day nurses. We were together almost constantly until we started the klenderfaeld.

We played our childhood games in an enormous garden court that our mother tended carefully with the help of two or three of the house staff. When the weather was warm enough, we would sit beneath the toplars and read what she called "real books" with chromatic flatlines in them. They were one of her treasures, from a collection given to her as a girl by her mother; it had been in her family forever.

There were tales of talking animals and winged creatures dressed in bright flowing costumes, of windswept plains and sand-yachts, of ocean voyages and long-lost treasures, magic spells and flying sweepsticks, of a thousand imaginary places. Ingren would weave her fantasies for us as each of the worn volumes carried us into the unknown lands.

She took us to the overland plays, festivals of travelling gypsy musicians and psychodancers. We loved the music and would pretend for days afterward that we were gypsies, wandering across the Territories in steam-driven wagon trains, singing and dancing for a living, not having to do any real work and staying outdoors all night. Ingren would laugh and help us dress up for our own little plays or simply tell us more stories.

She brought us through childhood in her own gentle way, teaching us to see and to imagine.

We were of seven, perhaps eight trueyears when we met the gypsy mystician. He could materialize coloured silks and flashing lights out of the air and make almost anything vanish. His mellow chanting and dreadful black gaze held my sister and I captive through an entire show.

Afterwards, Ingren took us to his wagon to meet him – it was meant as a treat. She asked him to "do a reading", to tell us a harmless fortune.

"There is no such thing as a future without meaning," he said. "What is given will come to light in its
own inevitable way."

He closed his eyes and placed his palms on Iilaria's
dark curls. He mumbled something to himself, which
we couldn't hear. Moments later, when he looked at
our mother, it was with a puzzled, saddened expres-
sion.

"There is no clear image that I can describe," he
said, "just a distorted face with only one eye." It meant
nothing to him.

He simply looked at me and said that I would travel
farther in my lifetime than anyone could imagine; he
was at a loss to explain it better. "I just know", he
stated plainly, and added that I would find "strange
worlds beyond description".

To my mother's dismay he predicted tragedy, desperation and parting. He talked of "other-worldly" re-
unions. She came away from his wagon discomforted
and depressed. She never took us to the magic theatre
again.

The man with whom Ingren had bonded, our stepfather, spent most of his time away but would always
bring us gifts from across the land or sea when he
came home. On these occasions, he would take us for
long walks in the glass-encrusted canyons and silent
forests of jupine that lay beyond the eastern edge our
village.

He was a technically minded man who was at ease
with the physicality of things, from the simplest of
machines to the underlying complexities of planetary
physics. He could tell us what caused the constant
tremors in the ground and why stars twinkled. He un-

derstood entropy and ecological engineering. He knew where jackal birds lived in winter and how the great blue bachelor fish herded their offspring around the ice flows in the southern oceans. He could build anything with his own hands and told us, over and over again, that we could do whatever we determined by just thinking it through.

He loved us in his own way and would have done anything for us, we were assured. But he never stayed long enough for us to really know him. His time was consumed with his fortune and the great sailships that he built at his yards in Materossen.

He was a Guildmaster and had once held the post of Second Secretary to the New Foster Council. Such a man might have imposed expectations on his children, I suppose. Instead, he left us to grow up with Ingren as the major influence in our lives.

He is in a few of my holograms. When I close my eyes and try to recall him, I see only a white moustache. It was always above me – he was much taller than me.


When the time came, we attended public academies run in the tradition of the old Quatrec, that infamous regimen that all young scholars are expected to comprehend before they escape their fenyears. We learned at the screens of a classic tutor-matrix, probably one that was put together with circuits salvaged from the original colony ship. I did well at the lessons but had little ambition beyond the lower forms; I was not inclined to any trade that the guilds would be willing to sponsor.

None of this was unusual. My fenyears were, in fact, unremarkable and quietly normal. There were the visaries, museums and syntheny chambers, all of which were dutifully attended. And once a year, usually in the cold of mid winter, we would celebrate Silverday, when most of the elders went off to different gyrefaeld compounds to intoxicate themselves, while we stayed home and pretended to do the same thing.

I was a firstman on the ragball teams and my chaelder always won the tournaments. For a threeyear, we travelled throughout the Townships challenging anyone that managed to find the required seventeen players. This was how I came to know the Coastal Reclamation Area and some of the Inland Territories.

It was usually an uncle who would take our team on these treks. My mother had no interest in the sport, choosing to leave the "rough-and-rowdy" to her brothers to chaperone. She would frown at our sprains and bruises, and offer warnings about broken limbs.

Once, in the densely wooded valleys of the Cypol, a boy had drowned after a game when he tripped into an uncovered cesspit. We were on a communal hydroponic farm where the team had been invited to play. We could never persuade Ingren that it might have happened to anyone, that it was an accident. She prohibited us from touring again, ending a part of my life I much enjoyed.

There was a square in our village known as Cathedral Court, a desolate ruin of a place where every child wanted to play simply because it was forbidden. One afternoon, during a wargames ceremony, several children were killed. Our small group of friends was blamed for the mishap; one of us, a boy named Osseph Tokastevor, lost his eye.

Our gyrefaeld then moved further south into the

Materossen Peninsula, father insisting that he wanted us all closer to the shipyards. But we knew of his confrontation with a fellow councillor, the Guildmaster Tokastevor, who had believed Iilaria and myself guilty of causing his son's disfigurement. This man had wanted us sent off to reformatories.

We remained oblivious throughout what was surely a major family upheaval, but with her unruffled serenity our mother protected us from the conflict. I never knew if we were forgiven or to what extent our stepfather held us responsible, but it was that single event that marked the end of our season of innocence.

As adopted wards, Iilaria and I were much closer than siblings might otherwise have been. For the first years in Materossen we had only each other's company.

We remained an inseparable pair, though our interests and friends gradually became more diverse. When we started at the academies, we still had our private times at home within the gyrefaeld. We always kept company with one another, sharing the attentions of aunts, uncles, granfaelders and our ever-indulgent mother. Thus our emotional entanglement was encouraged and nourished, but we were to grasp its depth only years later.

As my sister and I matured physically, there were few secrets; we grew together, questioning and cherishing each other. We came to the point of intimacy many times, discovering the normal delights of longing and passion. Iilaria's were the first breasts I ever held, the first lips I ever kissed, the first girl-flesh I ever explored.

Our affections grew as we did. We shared ties that went far beyond the simplicity of our naïve fantasies. But we had no thoughts as to where this might lead us.

At eighteen I was barely out of my fenyears, not sure of purpose, seeking clues to my life's direction. My friends were leaving their families, either as guild-youth or to work in the Territories; neither option had ever appealed to me.

By birthright I was eligible for commission with the Seaman's Guild, but I had never made application or tested for the examinations. I did not fancy endless days of wind and high seas with little to do between shifts except waiting for the next port to come into view. I had reached that time, as all young men do, when I waited for the clouds of adolescence to withdraw and for a chart of my future to appear magically before my eyes.

The panorama of stars I saw overhead on clear summer nights had long been my single inspiration. I learned the names of the stars and could identify most of them by numeric survey. I knew which ones had been visited by humans; from our latitude it was possible to see Viarta, Olyssid and Hito-Sarig, three of the five star systems where human settlements were known to have survived and flourished.

Early colonial history told us that contact with the rest of humanity was limited and fragile, that the whole concept of an interstellar community had fallen victim to practicality, to economics, within a century of its beginning. Only a handful of ships still functioned, mostly from the Viartan System, and they were independent of any colonial enterprise. We never saw them. There was no longer any reason to. My interest in astronomy, therefore, had little practical use.

Until on that night-of-nights an unmistakable sign appeared....

Brightness filled the skies, a radiance made of subtle

flashings and deep-hued brilliance. It grew upon itself like an infinitely long discharge of summer lightning, shattering the void, spreading northward until the horizon shone as if both Isurus and its White Sister were at their midday peak. It brought everyone from their houses, and where I had been standing alone beneath the patterns of the night, there were quite suddenly a thousand people. We gazed, awestruck at the unbelievable display above us.

Pulsing and shimmering, it bathed us all in its shadowless silence. There was no sound other than the night wind and we whispered to each other of exploding satellites and colliding comets somewhere beyond the realms of the Netheries. None guessed at first what it was.

The luminosity began to fade. Blackness reinstated itself patch by patch and all that remained was that great arc of distorted space, a pale rippling rainbow stretching out towards infinity. Only then did any of us realize what it must have been.

Nothing but the declension of a deep-space vessel entering the Isurus System would create such disturbances in the fabric of space. Drawing energy from the star system itself as it decelerated from near light speed, hurtling into its finely calculated resting orbit far above New Foster's surface, only such a ship could announce itself in this way. For those of us lucky enough to have been on the night-side of the planet it was the ultimate vision of humanity's power.

And to those who thought about such things it was a sad reminder of the ancient dream of galactic glory. We were forever bound to our finite worlds. That mankind had penetrated space at all and that there was still such a craft operating was the real miracle.

There had not been a starship near New Foster in more than two centuries. Visible to the naked eye in the early mornings and late evenings, rising and setting in its vast equatorial orbit, the deep-space vessel became the temporary focus of our lives. It had come to replenish supplies, to repair some minor equipment damage and recruit new crew members.

Within a halfday of the enormous cruiser's declension into our system, the entire population of New Foster was in such a state of excitement that the guilds declared holidays for us all. Some of the spacecraft's research staff took down-leave and it was through one of them that my father learned of the on-board assigns; recruits were being sought for the vessel's scientific crew.

Overhearing his private conversations, I first learned of an offworld career that seemed to match my undefined longings.

Perhaps it was momentary impulse stemming from a surge of biological energy or a bit of poorly digested food, but there was no resisting the temptation. I applied through the public visary, hooking directly to a ship-board matrix. I was told to report to recruiting officers who would be in Materossen within days. I did so and qualified in all the examinations I was given.

Later, I discovered that I was one of only twenty-eight accepted from more than two thousand applicants.

I joined the Viartan Navy.

Ingren was horrified at what seemed to her my sudden and irresponsible choice. She and the rest of our gyrefaeld could not believe I was serious. Instead of understanding, I received rejection. Instead of discussion, there was condemnation. She usually defended my wild notions as a matter of course; this time she was remote and silent. She refused to listen to my reasons for wanting to leave. It was as if I had shattered some dream, some great plan devised by her on my behalf. She would not acknowledge my right to feelings, to an opinion – that I think was the most difficult part of it.

Father lectured me, but I heard none of it. The alienation I would suffer if I went into space permanently, the fundamental differences in the spacer's society – he could not understand why I would choose this over my planet-bound existence, my heritage. I didn't have the words or the thoughts then to defend myself against him. I simply shut him out and followed an inner voice. It shouted at me to take the chance of a lifetime.

New Foster's small spaceport is the floating island of Pirrit Ennis. When I left on the coastal ferry, Iilaria was the only one who came with farewell.

She stayed with me in a metal-lined hostel on one of the island's causeways; we spent a final night together, where neither one of us cared about anything but each other. We made love more passionately than ever before. I carried her sweet smell in my memory always.

She too tried and failed to change my mind. I told her that my staying would bring only frustration and grief. As brother and sister, we could never have been more than occasional companions, and Ingren was full of her own plans for my sister's future. I thought Iilaria understood when I told her there was little to hold me back.

As it turned out, she was the last of the Gyrefaeld Addiman that I ever saw alive.

When a starship declines into most planetary systems, it approaches along the broad plane of the ecliptic so that it can take advantage of the star's enormous energy fields. Similarly, when approaching resting orbit about a planet, it seeks equatorial trajectory so that its shuttles can descend to offload or take on cargo using the spin of the world below as an accelerator. The Port of Pirrit Ennis had been maintained for such occurrences for over eighteen hundred years. In that entire time, the extent of human history on New Foster, there had been only twelve such stop-overs.

When I left I had apprenticed to the cruiser's scientific crew. I was good at languages and quickly qualified as a research interpreter. It was a survey ship travelling between the stars and I was the wide-eyed novice who had never seen an alien world.

I returned on the thirteenth declension of an interstellar vehicle into the Isurian System. Ninety-six trueyears had elapsed. I was a Senior Linguistics Officer on board the Viartan Naval Auxiliary Research Vessel *Whitethrell*. It had been only twenty-two years by shipboard calculation.

However counted, it was a lifetime.

As I walked the surface of my own planet once more, step by step, each landmark of my youth re-imposed its inevitable pattern. A century of elapsed time did not change the basic feel of home.

After finding Iilaria's listing in the SRM Keys, I hoped there might be chance to converse with her or at least with the cube bearing her simulation. But the module was restricted everywhere I went, secured from the public system. As in Materossen, I found only hints and traces.

But her name still lived. She had become a woman

of state, Senior Member of the Reform Council in the Ten Thousand Islands. The name, Addiman, was welded into local history because of her. Lily told me that she was interred on her own island near Kalanos Separ. A private estate was hidden near the old island capital, preserved and protected by national law.

I wanted only to find her, to pay respects, and to move on.

It was a pleasant enough journey by ferry and the early summer was seductive in its mood.

## 6. Kalanos Separ

Kalanos spread its array of villages across low hills surrounding a broad, shallow bay. Countless small sail-craft wove their smooth, lazy arcs across the rippled waters. From the ferry I could see the highest of the hills rising above the port. At its summit were the tiled rooftops of *Perrellon e'Nalak*, the Palace of Travellers.

Long ago, our stepfather had brought us here for a brief summer, the one time we had been away from the main continent as children. Once more I spent most of a morning walking from dockside and climbing the winding corridors of the lower city. The Palace grew above me as its fragments revealed themselves, glimpses caught between stone-lined alleyways and wood-gabled tenements.

Kalanos itself appeared to be unchanged – a hundred years vanished as if they had never been.

"You're not from these parts." the old man uttered.

"I was here as a boy. Many years ago."

"I used to fish out there." He pointed towards the hundreds of islands trailing over the horizon in both directions, a long chain of half-submerged bedrock ridges.

He had appeared from beneath the shaded canopies of an open-air messalliary where I stopped for a meal. He stood over me like a whittled ebonite statue, white beard gleaming against black skin. I asked him to sit and share a drink or two.

"The Sea of Dreams. I knew it like the lines on my own hands, and that wasn't well enough in the end. I'm Tordek."

"Coltenent Addiman, Viartan Navy."

"You're off that ship out there, then." He pointed skyward. It seemed quite an everyday thing to him and it pleased me not to have to explain further.

"Nothin' like the ocean, boy! Nothin' like it!"

"You can see the entire Sea of Dreams from up there. It's very beautiful." It is an ancient impact crater with rows of concentric folds that enclose the largest isolated body of water on the planet.

"The Long Rim. Grew up on it. My father an' his father before him. Fished the great blues. Every season for so many years I can't tell you how many."

"Did you ever know a man named Marik?"

"Marik? Old Marik from the Torforatagos? Sailed with him at least a dozen times! There was a sailor for you!"

"So you fished with him?"

"The first few times it was the fish. But later on we were running loads of medicine and electronics and contraband all over the place! Once we took a generator off an island near the coast of New Foster and rigged it to blind the feeder control lines from the Trifan Station. Cut off Materossen's power grid for almost a month, we did! But Old Marik was really into that kinda stuff during the war."

"What happened to him? I heard he went down –"

"Went down he did. And it was almost me along with him except that my woman was having our first-born and wanted me to stay with her the one time? So stay I did and he and his crew vanished over the edge of the Long Rim! Only heard the story. Never knew what it was got 'em. That time a' year most likely the ice. Yet he was the best of the old sailors. How he coulda gone that far south into the ice...."

He laughed when I told him I'd rented and planned to sail a one-man *saiak* across to a nearby island the next day. "Maybe you should stick to your fancy flying machine," he chuckled.

"A day it'll take me, that's all." I didn't explain why I needed to go, who had owned the island, or that I had sailed often as a youth.

We talked the rest of the afternoon away, he mostly about his life on the ocean and me about the slowly resurfacing memories of my first eighteen years on New Foster.

He told me more than I could ever remember about his family and how he had come to Kalanos. He kept signalling a girl he knew; she had worked the tables for years he said, and the three bottles of ch'ell she brought us vanished quite quickly in his company.

It was already a sevenday downside and as many strange beds taken along the way. And still, the gradually diminishing effects of the ground-syndrome were burning away inside me, exhausting my normal energies. The old man saw it plain as wind-winches and he said so. "Drink up, boy. You're runnin' with your sails half-shredded."

At some point that I don't clearly remember, he helped me up to my room in the *e'Nalak*. It was there that I managed to find my first proper sleep since I left the *Whitethrell*, waking only once that night, dreaming of my dark-eyed Iilaria.

*You lie somewhere beyond Kalanos on the Inner Island Ring.*

*I come simply to find you, to weep foolishly for a few moments at your graveside. I have been away from you for so long that I only pretend we might talk. There can be no meeting, just two waterwisps drifting by one another on the glazed surface of a dark lake.*

*Somehow my search becomes less for reality, running more and more through the threads of time-faded shadow. The rest of our gyrefaeld are as dust. They have become memories.*

*But in all that time, have I once stopped wanting you? Never.*

A lifetime later, the circle was almost complete.

## 7. Matrix

*"Gregh is going to change his mind."*

*"I think not. It's only a few meks more."*

*"Why are you putting him through this? It would be so much easier just to tell him what's going on —"*

*"Not yet. It would only frighten him. He likes things he can see and touch."*

*"Perhaps you underestimate him?"*

*"He is my brother. I know his limits."*

*"You're also putting yourself at risk."*

"I can manage, thank you."

"I'm concerned about his situation."

"That he's back?"

"No. That was just a matter of time. If it wasn't this trip, it would have been another."

"A hundred years from now?"

"Possibly. That's not my point."

"Then what is your point, Mihan? What are you so concerned about?"

"What he'll do when he finds out what you have become."

"He's familiar with the technology."

"Yes. But this is going to be much too personal?"

"And?"

"I think you're opening old wounds better left alone."

"Or healing them?"

"You want to heal him? Psychotherapy?"

"He was an impetuous boy. Now he is a man. That I can handle."

"Have it your way!"

"I can hope to, that is all."

"Right now your man is sleeping off his first drunk in the e-Nalak."

"And Tordek?"

"Back in his billet near the dock."

"That old man — Marik liked him a lot, you know."

"You sound sentimental. Almost."

"You're a brilliant engineer Mihan, but you have no idea about people. Tordek lives alone because of what Osseph did to his family."

"I wonder about this interfering with lives. Don't you?"

"This is very different. You can't possibly know what I feel about that part of my life."

"Perhaps not. But I will continue to monitor him for you."

*"Thank you. And the ship? Anything new from the Viar-
tans?"*

*"Everything they need is in the old Isurus Station."*

*"How long will their repairs take?"*

*"Could be as long as a month."*

*"Can we delay them?"*

*"Only by interfering with their supply route."*

*"Good. Whatever it will take, just see to it."*

*"Will you just try to be careful with Greghory?"*

*"Just let me know when he arrives."*

*"I think he'll be quite obvious."*

## 8. The Island

The boat drifted gently into a bay that had been hidden from view until I was almost on top of it. Outcroppings of red and black serraquite marked a stretch
of boulder-strewn shoreline. Between the rocks was a
smooth beach of tide-washed sand, pointed brilliantly
with reflected daylight.

I held the bow towards the sand, dropping the
small sail. Stepping down into warm, clear water,
leader in hand, I beached the twin crolloy hull. A
sharp incline rose from the rocks into a scrub-covered
rift in the embankment. Dragging the loose gear into a
small sheltered pathway above the tide line, I secured
it under a pliopol cover. There was no storm sign for
the few days I planned to stay; I would get the boat
farther up the beach if the weather changed.

The small house was above me, well back into a
low-grown forest of jupine. Most of these islands had
been greened for a thousand years, but this one looked
to have been recently re-seeded – the man-made

plants were no taller than me. The effect was like walking through a hilly field of grain, or a miniaturized version of the enormous oxyforests near Cypol.

Iilaria's private retreat was overgrown with white-flowering craelbine. Like her hidden bay below, it came up quite suddenly. I almost tripped over its garden entrance. A low wall, a gate, stairs fashioned for leisurely wandering, a winding stone pathway through casually arranged groups of trees, shrubs, and rocks, a neglected gravel garden with its arrangement of *siko* stones, long buried with vines – the entrance was obscured by its deviously arranged approach. One could not arrive in a hurry. The residence had obviously been designed as a retreat, having little to do with the everyday world.

I stood in front of the door for long, silent moments.

When I left, I wanted adventure, excitement, the intrigue of mysterious new places. I found all that and in measures beyond my wildest imagining – the mystician's prophecy was fulfilled. Out there, worlds spin in a constant parade of disorganized light sculptures that mere talk can never describe. I saw wonder beyond wonder on my long treks across our remote limb of the galaxy.

Only now did I realize the cost. I had put aside any longing for touch and taste of the familiar, for moments in the common stream. I had chosen an existence alienated from planetary life. The fundamental time sequences are so different that one is never reconciled with the other. Because of that single factor, the star people remain a race by themselves.

A city-size star ship, my adopted home, was in orbit not far above, replacing its entire secondary fusion system because of impurities in a minor fueling process. New Foster's industrial complexes had no replacement parts nor even comprehended the technology. We were to be here a long stay while our master engineers rebuilt what they needed. And my overdue leave by the merest turn of circumstance was to be spent here on the planet of my birth.

Facing me was what I had come all this way for.

A single wooden door....

The door would not open and I had no way of unlocking it. I could not bring myself to break in; it seemed a crude and offensive way of greeting.

I walked the grounds until the blue-white disc of Isurus Prime reached afternoon's quarter-angle. By chance, I found an unlatched window overlooking a side courtyard. Propping it open with a stem broken from one of the jupines, I climbed through the narrow opening, finding myself perched on a dusty sill halfway up the inside wall. I had to lower myself carefully to gain foothold on a dust-laden work-bench below.

It was a shop; half-opened crates and odd looking machinery lay at random across the floor. Light streamed into the room from windows set above me in the high, stone walls. I puzzled at the room's immense size. From outside, the house had seemed little more than a cottage. It was a trick of the landscaping perhaps, with earth and garden concealing underground chambers.

I searched for the inside of the entrance where I had first stood. There were two heavy doors at the rear. A smaller wooden panel in the opposite wall did not lead to the garden, as I expected, but opened to another room almost as large as the first. I gave up trying to formulate the layout; it was not possible for both these chambers to lie within the exterior walls, I thought. And there were far too many of the narrow, vertical windows peering down on me. Either something was wrong with my perception or the house itself was a great deal more complex than I imagined. Again, the vague dissonance of times past and present echoed in collision.

Wandering through inter-connected chambers, I felt I had somehow fallen into a strange time-well, not sure if I was trespassing in a mansion or a mausoleum. I could sense Iilaria's presence. The dusty furniture, the long tapestries, the hanging lamps – all had her delicate touch. Even the holograms along the walls were like her; I stood in front one of our stepfather's sailing ships and watched it plunge endlessly through its seasons, wondering how many times she had stood here before me and if she might still be somewhere near.

But why was there so much space? There was room for an entire gyrefaeld! How had she managed to build such a fortress on this little island? Her resources must have been immense. From the outside, I could never have visualized the whole of it. It was so much like Iilaria, a labyrinth behind a deceivingly simple exterior.

A circular room with polished black walls and diffused mellow light imposed itself on the rectangular grid of the hallways I had been following. The complex of equipment it housed would have matched any communications matrix; it was much like the command platform of my ship. And referenced into its memory bank was the largest single visary of cubes I had ever seen. It was a private SRM collection. Instinctively, I knew that I had found her.

It took me some time to locate power sources and do the basic testing on the panels. I could get everything on without difficulty; it was no more than running number combinations and watching colour projections for matching patterns.

I thought of Lily and her screened booth back in Materossen. This was more complex but similar to the systems I knew on board the *Whitethrell*, what I had been using for twenty years.

I didn't stop to think that perhaps it was a little too easy.

## 9. Iilaria

The walls were covered with moving light. A swell of sound filled the room, generated by different cubes as they integrated the matrix (we used to call it "hooking" cubes). Humming and scraping noises surrounded me. There was a rustling, as if several small animals were rushing from sight.

And then garbled speech sounded from my past – her voice: "Defrax ... synap ... defrax ... synap ..."

"Iilaria! Is that you?"

"... dots in the ballroom ..."

"What are you on about? Can you hear me? Iilaria? It's Gregh. I can't understand you. Are you there?"

"... the bluefish pay him no heed ..." It sounded like her, or like my memory of her quiet voice, but she was making no sense.

"What do you mean?"

"When ... how long have I been ... everything is ... time and defrax ... are all right ... it's all here! Great Gill! Have I really ... been down ... that long?"

"Long? How long?" It never occurred to me that an SRM module would have time sense. They were either on-line or down, responding only to applied stimulus such as direct hook-up. Like any cube, they were either on or off.

"I knew you'd get here eventually. How did you find me? When did you come?" It was her and she already had me utterly confused.

"Hold on! Let me get used to this! I've only just hooked in!" The feedback and background noise gradually cleared as if many years of accumulated dust were being swept away.

"Let me take over, Gregh. Just talk to me. I'm getting it all synchronized again."

I let her do just that while I caught my breath.

"It's like talking to *you*! I must have forgotten what these things are like. Is that a *recent* you in the matrix?"

"Very. And updated, with my young daughters' help. Have you met them?"

"No. I ... I wasn't expecting this!"

"The last time we spoke was at Pirrit Ennis!"

"You remember?"

"Everything. Great Gill, it's good to be back in the house! I knew it would be you that got me on again!"

"Everything?" The house seemed warmer, lights were going on, music was playing. I thought I could smell food cooking.

"All the lovely details. The memories are crisp, almost new. You have no idea what it's like inside here."

"I don't think I –"

"Would want to know? To be like this? It's all right. I know it must seem strange, how you must feel." Her voice had steadied.

"It's you. It is you, isn't it? Iilaria? This is crazy! I

mean, I feel like I'm drunk!" I was sitting in front of a wall of illuminated panels glowing with thick swirls of misty colour – a machine. It was asking me questions.

"There's a drink and a meal for you in the kitchen. Go back in there and enjoy it! I'll do a few things that need doing. But you'll have to clean up after yourself. I can't do that. Give me a few moments. It's an occasion. Pretend I'm a real woman and that I have to get freshened up. Circuit-wise."

The smell of food was no trick. Somehow, she had managed it; the whole house must have been wired into her SRM. There was a food tray coming out of a metallic synthmat in a small kitchen behind the visary. What else could I do but sit down and try the first meal my sister had prepared for me in a hundred years? Pretend she was real? I came seeking a memory, a ghost.

She had asked me to dine.


"Greghory! Oh, there is so much I want to know! Great Gill! So many questions to ask!"

I was eating and her voice was beside me although I could see no sound modules nearby. "How do you do that? If the lights were out, I'd swear you were right here!"

"Oh, but I am, my brother from the stars! Right beside you. We here on the islands are actually quite sophisticated, you see! Just imagine multitudes of tiny sound-processing cells scattered around the house. Many multitudes, actually. I can follow you around. And outside too. I see you brought a *saiak*. You didn't tie it up too well, but it will do until the morning."

"You can see?" I choked on a piece of gravy-soaked penta bread and it went down the wrong way. Standard SRMs do not possess optical circuitry; this was beyond what I would have imagined.

"Be careful! I can't bang you on the back! Finish your drink. Yes, of course I can see. And a lot better than you. Broader spectrum. I'm not just a regular SRM. I've done a lot of work on myself. Had help, mind you, but it was worth it. I had no desire to just disappear or lie in a box of unused cubes in some deserted visary. That's why I had myself removed from the public system.

"I was ninety-six years old when I died. I had this place built to my very specific requirements long before that. Had the best of engineers. We spent years developing it. And most of my fortune. He designed the modifications to the SRM as well. When it actually happened, when I died, he set everything up. He put me through hundreds of modifications, most of which were experimental. But it all worked."

"You don't sound like any SRM I've ever hooked."

"I'm not. I'm as close to real as you'll find."

"We have a few on board the *Whitethrell*. Out there, we use them to navigate and plot the declensions. They get us across spaces that can't even be visualised by ordinary machines. But they don't walk around the ship carrying on conversations. They aren't –"

"They aren't people anymore? They don't live. They couldn't. But I'm completely in character. They didn't miss a hair when they replicated me. I paid them enough for it, too!" Iilaria's unmistakable laughter filled the room.

"It's so ... real!"

"Don't think that I'm not, my love. I am real. My memories are completely genuine and in proper sequence. I transferred through simulation without a single discontinuity. The old body went, but I'm still here!"

"Yes, I can tell it's you. I can almost see you. And touch you."

"This place is my body now. It's full of cubes and memory templates. There's masses of fibre-optic circuitry running all over the island. It's old technology, but my co-creator claimed it was the best thing in use at the time. He had all the fibres made in a silk mill on the Torforatagos Islands. And there's more. Much more. I'll explain later, as we go, if you want me to. Lot of technical stuff that you'd probably know more about than I do, anyway."

"I have a feeling that you're far more complicated than the equipment I'm used to."

"Equipment? I'd be upset if that was all you thought I was. As I said, I'm *authentic*, though not in the flesh you knew." Her voice was real enough and I thought I might have angered her.

"Listen, I'm sorry! But this is all new to me. I thought I might find an empty house. Some old furniture. Perhaps some albums, or a few of your things. Mementos. I had no idea that ... well, that I'd find you here! Like this!"

"Poor Gregh! You always did like things to come in tidy, easily explained packages! I understand. And I'm so glad you've come back to me! I must try to be a good hostess while you are here and not frighten you off again."

"Again?"

"You were so afraid when we were together, growing up. Wasn't that why you left?"

"Afraid of you? I loved you!"

"Loved? Then you would have stayed with me. No,

I think you were afraid. Of me and of our family. Of our stepfather and mother. Especially of Ingren!"

"She would never have left us alone. You knew that."

"Did I? We are – were – adopted wards. We could have done as we pleased."

"It would have destroyed her. She wanted you bonded with a wealthy gyre. Like the Tokastevors. She wanted us both to give her new families."

She was silent. I wondered what raw nerve I had touched, reminded of my ignorance of her personal life. She would always pause quietly when someone upset her with a careless comment.

When she did speak, it was so softly that I could barely hear her. "You really don't know, do you?"

"Know? What, Iilaria? What don't I know?"

"Just ... about me. My life. There is so much, so much for us to tell, my love. I cannot possibly begin now. We've only just found each other." Her tone abruptly changed. She laughed and asked, "What about you?"

"Me? I came back to find what had become of you, little sister!"

"You've found me. I set all this up for you, you know. I didn't know how long you'd take coming back, but I hoped you would. I knew you would. I gambled on it."

"We would have come eventually, yes. Although there is very little in this section of the local cluster."

"We are of no interest to the Viartans? They took you away, didn't they? Surely we can't be that dull ..."

"It's more a matter of mandate. They are not traders. But they try to keep up the explorations. There are no other planetary groups in this region besides Isurus Prime and its companion star. New Foster is the only colony for light years.

"Our work has been further away, past the Viartan system, beyond the Hito-Sarig Cluster, back again to Indi. There was no way of telling when we might come this way. The ship goes in huge circuits that are light years across. Never the same way twice."

"You look so young!"

"It's the time distortions. We travel almost as fast as light out there. Faster, if you work out the – well, it gets complicated. Let's just say that there are many ways of measuring the same elapsed time, depending on direction and how fast you are moving."

"I know the basics, my love! I'm not just a molecular imprint. But I have always wondered about meeting you again one day and being like a mother to you. Well, more like a granfaeldam."

"I remember you as a glamorous eighteen-year old. A sister I could never satisfy. It seemed as if you always wanted – well, a tenfold more than we had!"

"How could you think that? I thought we were perfect!"

"You were perfect, Iilaria. I was the one who wanted the stars, after all. I was the one who couldn't sit still. I didn't want to stay here and become – well, like our stepfather, I suppose."

"You had the wandering urge, that's all. Well, you're back now, and for a while, I hope!".

"The ship is out there with a fouled fusion system. We were closest to Isurus when the trouble began. It will take a long time to repair the damage. There's very little we can take up from New Foster. Everything has to be done from templates."

"Well then, perhaps I'll have you to myself. We've got a lifetime to catch up on, little brother. Let's go to bed."

"Let's what?"

"I said – come on, I'll show you. Up the stairs and turn to the left. I'll close the place down for the night. Great Gill, it feels good to have you here!"

I climbed a flight of stairs I had not noticed before. There was a wide pair of carved doors beyond a landing. I swear I could feel the touch of her hand on my shoulder. And did I imagine movement on the great, round toballen in front of me? Did I really hear the smooth rustle of silk sheetings? It seemed she could create any illusion she fancied from inside her molecular matrix.

Suddenly, I was a child again, and it was the old house in the Quain Townships. My sister was tugging at me to join in her game.

"Shut your eyes, and pretend," she called out. "I can see you, but don't you dare cheat or look back at me. You'll spoil it all!"

I shut my eyes and felt her perfumed scarf wrapped around my head as if we were playing blindman at a birthfaelding.

"Will you love me forever?"

"Of course I will!"

"Then come and cosy me and kiss me on the cheek!" I had "cosied" my sister every night for as long as I could remember; it was part of our special way with each other.

"Will you do something for me, Greghory? Something important?"

"Of course I will. Anything you wish."

"I hoped that you might. I want you to get something for me. I'll tell you about it tomorrow."

She always had some scheme in mind that usually meant work for me, but I would never refuse her.

Could never refuse her. I pulled the covers around her shoulders, kissed her cheek and quietly left her to sleep. Along a dusty hallway and up a flight of stairs at the back of our gyrefaeld was my own room.

I put away parts of a model sailing ship that father had brought me, that I was building for my collection. It was one of the big fan-masted twinhulls he built in Materossen. I wondered if he might be back before Silverday, and what he would bring us.

As I undressed and fell into my own narrow toballen, I worried, briefly, that I had not said good night to our mother.

## 10. The Island

That first night, I had a succession of wild dreams like none other I could remember. Some part of me knew that, physically, I had slept alone, that I shared this house with nothing other than elaborate machinery. But I was not alone; her voice lulled me into trance-like sleep where we wandered through shared memories. I felt her as close to me as she had been on another night, long ago, at Pirrit Ennis.

She was there beside me as a young matalin, her long, untrussed hair flowing across her broad, deeply tanned shoulders, her intense dark eyes and smiling face beckoning, warm hands leading me along strange passageways in the darkness. There was no resisting her; I flowed like water in a flume, plunging into churning pools of half-consciousness. I flew with her across oceans, mountains, cities, villages. She showed me our gyrefaeld in Materossen. The compound had been fire-bombed by the one-eyed madman, Osseph.

This, then, is what had become of the boy we played with in our village as children. He was the reason for her fleeing to the Islands, the adversary she had spent the better part of her life combating. The mystician's prophecy gained yet another layer of flesh.

I saw a yacht with *Solyon* etched into the bow timbers and I knew it had belonged to the father of her two daughters. I saw the man who piloted her – a tall, white-haired sailor who might have stepped out of legend – Marik. I had known him as a younger man but would not have recognized him again. He had devoted his life to her battles; I felt their shared anguish at being forced to live always apart as they plotted and schemed Osseph's downfall. I saw intrigue and conspiracy within conspiracy. I knew of their pain and isolation.

And too, I saw how influential she had become, how powerful. Her fight against Osseph had lead her into the Reform Council. It made of her a force to be remembered. Yet beneath the worldly facade, she was still the Iilaria I had loved, first as a sister, then as a young woman. And I had deserted her before the years of terror began.

I realized then how she had wanted me to stay. But she had not stopped me from going out to the stars. Only now were her feelings becoming obvious to me. For her, a century's separation had changed nothing.

I awoke exhausted, guilt-ridden, disoriented.

I thought at first the morning meal was being served shipboard. But instead of the cool, metallic panels of my private cabin on the *Whitethrell*, I saw the reddish texture of polished saderwood and rich purple-leaved sayalla tumbling their vines across a wall of stone.

Broad windows opened to a sun-washed balcony and in the distance a row of cone-shaped islands floated on a turquoise sea. It was several moments before I remembered I was not on board ship, nor even in the Palace of *e'Nalak*. I had in fact spent the night in my sister's house.

A meal was beside the toballen on a platform jutting out from its base. I was groggy and wanted only a tube of callafe; instead, she had prepared hot bread with a sauce I did not recognize at first. The taste was familiar, but it was half finished before I remembered our mother's home-stewed fruit concoctions.

"There's a hot-spring bath for you when you've finished, my love. Go back out onto the landing and through the other pair of doors. I built the house here because of the springs. You'll see!" She was with me still.

"I must have dreamed all night. It was ... unearthly, bizarre. It was you and you showed me ... everything." I was speaking to her disembodied voice again, between mouthfuls of the penta bread and jellied fruit.

"I was talking to you while you slept. I never sleep, at least not the way you do, or the way I used to when I was – well, physical. I apologize if I ruined your rest. You do seem a bit foggy! You were always such a grouch in the morning – some things never change!" Her laughter once more echoed about me.

It came back to me then, the revelation of her animated simul-ego, her SRM, and yesterday's discovery that she was operating the domestria and all its gadgetry.

With her ability to surround and manipulate me, she had brought back feelings of guilt about our unfulfilled relationship. I suspected she knew this quite well. But I had come here of free choice, though perhaps unprepared for all that I might find.

My mind gradually cleared and as the day grew around me, I thought I would be ready for any new surprises she had in mind. As usual, where it concerned Iilaria, I was utterly wrong.

The house was built over an outcropping of native bedrock, the impaction-twisted serraquite, and a hot stream bubbled up out of the stone into a series of carved ponds. The largest pool was a wide grotto, with curved timber beams arching across a multi-levelled tile floor. Her voice, the sound of her footsteps, her breathing, followed me as I immersed myself in the water.

There were scented oils and soaps, relaxants, more of the warm callafe liqueur. The quiet intrusion of an Ilyan Choral Syntheny filled the room, the sixteenth or seventeenth I thought though I never could sort them out. Its electronic voices echoed softly from all sides of the chamber. I relaxed into a euphoric trance.

How long I lay there listening to music which I had not heard since our mother had played it for us, I cannot recall.

Before I found her I had intended to camp on her island for a few days at most. I had vague notions of wandering slowly back through the other islands, of visiting places I had never seen, of learning a little more about my native planet before going back into space. I never had any idea of staying downside.

My sister had been a vanished dream to me, a fond memory. I would have searched as long as I could to find what there was in the records. That I was twice an uncle was a modest and pleasing surprise, but the thought of visiting my nieces was likewise not in any plan I might have made. There would have been awkward greetings and equally uncomfortable partings. Better left alone, I told myself.

The ground-syndrome carries with it an inverted claustrophobia, a longing for the tight compartments and familiarity of crew-mates. I would have gone back to Pirrit Ennis and the ship's waiting dart.

Would I have come down again, in some later stopover? Most likely not. There was too much for me out there, not enough of me down here.

But Iilaria had suddenly become real. It was as though my life was playing out before me, an unknown incarnation. All I had been and known was the dream.

Now I could not leave. I had to see first of all what she had become, and it had as much to do with rediscovering myself.

The summer season grew full. First one, then another tenday passed on her island.

## 11. Denique

The round-shaped woman waddled towards me, her ponderous movements accentuating the rolling of massive hips.

"*? e-Misanagi qilo najti umijharata. ? e-Diodi misanagi.*" Her northern Viranti dialect was characterised by its lilting tonals.

"*Que, jharata. e-Diodi Addiman misanagi.*" I nodded, answering the question and showing her the sealed ident of a registered First Secretary. Had she refused to acknowledge the forged document I carried, I'm not sure what I would have done. She looked big enough to have thrown me out bodily; most likely, she would simply have called a superior, or another guard. But she just smiled, handing me a plastic warrant, an entry docket, my passage into the Council Security Chambers in Denique.

Fifty trueyears ago, Osseph had died in the seclusion of his solitary prison. By Guildlaw, his SRM was confined to further isolation before its public release. I was present by invitation – obtained through a little discreet pressuring on Iilaria's part – at the civil ceremony preceding the release.

There were only a handful of dignitaries entering the chambers. She had warned me they would be hard-liners from New Foster whose interests lay only in self-promotion and who would have no kind words for anyone smelling the least bit Reformist. They were all invited guests of the Ten Thousand Islands Council and except for two or three who actually returned my greeting, they were stuffy and ill-mannered.

The ceremony was dull. A clerk read the formal charges that had originally been laid against Osseph, commenting at length and unnecessarily on the arduous confinement he had undergone prior to his death. A quiet round of applause welcomed him back into public society as an active and useful reference.

The module had, of course, been previously matrixed. The lighting and music were supplied simply to dramatize the SRM's initial dialogue. A few more comments were made by various Council officials and the event was over.

I soon found myself conveniently alone in the interview chamber. From my seat at the back, I walked down to the platform where Osseph's cube rested in its glossy display casing.

It is said that orderliness is often bedlam's toy. The clinically insane can display astounding abilities to organize the minute details of their dark visions. The madman, Osseph Tokastevor, had shown remarkable talent for directing people when he took over continental New Foster as its first military dictator.

Even as a child, he had been the ultimate strategist. I knew because I had been one of his close group of allies. The four of us, Osseph and his brother Mihan, Iilaria and myself, had roamed the late-night streets of our home village in the Quain Townships, most often engaged in the elaborate wargames that the elder Tokastevor directed.

It was all in fun and a part of our fenyears that I would not have given up willingly. But seen in the perspective of later years, it was obvious that Osseph's ability to assert himself over others was the early manifestation of his obsession with power.

He transformed his beliefs into deliberate action, creating havoc, disorder, misery and death for any that opposed him. There had been uprisings before his time but never any so severe or so costly to the world we had been brought up in.

The guilds had always kept close control on every aspect of our society. There were well established ways of doing things that dated back to the Colonization. There had to be. On a planet that had seen almost two thousand years of carefully structured human endeavour to make it habitable, no one could take risks. This was the system of the Quatrec, forcibly injected into every one of us as fenyouth, rigidly maintained by the guilds and their directorates. It was the backbone of New Foster's continued existence.

Osseph had not cared much for the Quatrec. He seemed to have his own vision of how our world should be run. But he was neither scientist nor historian and he had no real sense of the delicate ecologies that had been established through generations of controlled engineering.

He abandoned such immense projects as the Trifan Channel Tidal Stations. He closed universities. He supplanted guild officers with his own bullies. He threw scientists and technicians who disagreed with him into newly constructed penal institutes. He poured his resources into his armies. He redirected trade and commerce throughout the continent in order to promote the militia, requisitioning everything he needed by brute force. He brought into being a martial state that had not been known on the planet before.

Osseph's only real difficulty had been in trying to control the oceans and the thousands of offshore islands. The Seaman's Guild learned quickly to stay away from ports under his rule and were among the first to mobilize against him. They were one of the most powerful groups existing when he took command; they rallied enough support to carry on constant battle with his forces. With bases in the Ten Thousand Islands, they established their own militia, operating from the Island Capital, Denique.

The war that followed was neither pleasant nor profitable. It cost nearly a million lives and set the programmed restructuring and reclamation of the inland Territories back by several decades. A thirdportion of New Foster's food producing communes were abandoned or destroyed. Most of the guildyouth were conscripted into Osseph's service.

But as his armies grew, so did the offshore Reform Forces. With years of patient and painful effort, they brought his rule to an end.

A central figure in this campaign had been one very determined and resourceful woman. She had developed a far-reaching intelligence operation without which there would have been no opposition. She gave the Reform Council its greatest opportunity to fight Osseph. She controlled the movement of manpower and equipment. She directed secretive plots against Osseph himself and was present on the day of his arrest. Iilaria had orchestrated his downfall. And she had been the one who saw him imprisoned for life rather than hanged or impaled on a shaft in a public square.

She told me how the years of struggle wrote an entirely new chapter in New Foster's history, one that had supposedly been impossible according to original Quatrec planning. It took almost thirty years to end, to bring back a semblance of order to the world, to reestablish constructive living patterns for the millions of people it had affected.

All the while I had been aboard the *Whitethrell*, travelling from star to star, oblivious to such concerns as warfare at home. I had missed what Iilaria summed up as "a lifetime of crisis, mixed liberally with catastrophe".

"Osseph? Do you remember me?"

"No, I do not. Who are you?"

"We played together as children."

"Should that mean something to me? It doesn't."

MICHAEL BARLEY

"The wargames. You, your brother, Iilaria Addi-man, and me, Iilaria's brother. I'm Greghory Addi-man."

"Greghory Addiman? The starboy! That was a long time ago. So you've come back. Why?"

"Do you know what has been happening? To you, I mean." I had no particular questions in mind; it was difficult to know what to ask him.

"Happening? Nothing. What do you think might have been happening to a simulant?"

"Do you recall the simulation?"

"Sedated in a medlab? What would I recall?"

"What about prison? I'm told they converted an old hostel just for you."

"Wonderful place. You would have liked the ambi-ence. They let me write. But nothing ever got outside. No cubes. Nothing. Recommended highly if you're looking for quiet insanity."

"Didn't you ever see anyone?"

"Just the attendants. I was always my own best company."

"No friends? No family?"

"You almost sound sympathetic. There wasn't any-one. Not after the trials. It was all such a parade of nonsense. I didn't have a chance."

"People don't take well to dictatorships."

"People are fools. They don't know what's best for them."

"Most of us like to be able to make the choices."

"Choices? Under the Quatrec? What choices do any of us ever have that aren't predetermined by factoring machines?"

"We always have choices."

"Dungfaelder!"

"You have the right to your opinions, I suppose."

"You are no different than the rest of them, star-boy."

"Listen. I didn't come all this way to argue with you."

"What did you come to do? Gloat?"

"Iilaria sent me."

"That doesn't surprise me."

"If it weren't for her, you'd be long gone. She was the one who –"

"Who saved my life? So I could become a molecular impression? Remind me to thank her! What did she have in mind for me? A teaching position?" The flat monotone of Osseph's voice did not conceal his resentment, his anger.

"She didn't like the idea of you perched on a stake with the sharpened end up your boomhole!"

"So she had some feelings for me then after all, did she? More likely it was her idiot mate that stopped my execution. He was the one who couldn't bear the thought of killing. Now, there was a real prize! What was his name? Maskri? Good old Maskri!" Osseph well knew that *e-Masskri* was Viranti slang for banik-droppings.

"Marik," I muttered. The discussion was going nowhere, which was as Iilaria had predicted. "Iilaria, strange as it may seem, is concerned for you. She wants to know about you and your SRM."

"She refused me. Did you know that? She refused fullbond with me! The witch refused me!"

"I can't imagine why!" My mind was engaged in a struggle. How could this molecular clone have any relationship to the young Osseph I had known? How could such a change occur in an individual? I remembered a likable, sensitive, clever boy whose interests we had all shared. What had happened to sour him?

"Starboy?"

"I'm still here."

"Well, tell your lovely mistress to come visit me herself. We have a few unsettled scores, she and I."

"In a way, that's what she has in mind. Only she wants you to do the travelling. She wants me to ... to liberate you?"

"Liberate? Fanciful word, that. How do you liberate matrixed imprints?"

"Steal your cube."

"You – you're stupider than I thought, starboy. Steal my cube? I'm in matrix, or have you forgotten?"

"I've spent most of my life working with far more intricate – and interesting – gadgets than your matrix."

"The genius returns. So what do you intend to do? Ask the guard's permission to walk out of here with me in your pouch? I don't think it will work, starboy."

"Call me that one more time and I'll terminate you." At that point, I could have done it easily.

"A threat? I'll try to remember it. Now tell me, what do you think you're going to do?"

"Shut you down. There's going to be a power break. Then out we go. Trust me."

"Trust you? Do I have any choice? If you are Iilaria's minion, you could just as easily drop me into an incinerator. Who would ever know? It's not a matter of trust at all, is it? You came here with this plan all worked out, didn't you?"

"More or less. And I was curious. She's told me about you. How you tried several times to kill her, among other things."

"Iilaria? Never. We had our battles. But kill her? Nonsense! She's telling you lies."

"She told me about the house in Tennefoster. About

the rest of our gyrefaeld. You had our entire family destroyed after she turned down your proposal of bond."

"In a jackal bird's ass! That was the Guild Militia! I had her gyrefaeld under house protection because I knew they were after your father! I was just spread too thin to have my men there all the time. I thought she had died in the fire. But she turned up in Denique with the Reformists and helped organize them against me! She was my downfall! And it was mostly because I let her be! She became my enemy, yes, but I always admired her."

He ranted on as I began to withdraw the crolloy and plastene inserts that secured his display housing. I knew I had very little time before the power was blown out by a carefully planned overload. Chances of discovery grew the longer I waited, although I knew that because no one generally stole SRM modules the security was minimal. His dreary voice died in midsentence as I removed the transcriber from its minute pocket.

It was a standard ocular matrix; hand-fitted pole receptacles slipped out of their sockets with a slight pressure release. Most of the data passing between an SRM and its sensors is transmitted directly through light-sensitive threads and the couplings are simple to adjust or remove. Colour-coded plastene leads identified most of the circuits, which I disconnected one by one. I slid the exposed cube out of its mooring, securing it in the liner of my pouch as Osseph had presumed I would. Gasping, I realized I had held my breath since his voice had stopped, almost the entire time it took me to remove him.

But he had not anticipated the prepared cube I substituted for his. We had recorded it on the island and were reasonably sure it would mask my theft. The next time someone interviewed the ex-dictator of New Foster, they would hear cyclic, repetitive nonsense instead of clear answers to their questions.

The power went out exactly on schedule and the building went onto its emergency reserve. A few alarms sounded and I heard voices shouting down distant corridors. I made my way along semi-darkened passages to the public visary where I had first entered. When the lights came back up, I was well clear of the private chambers where Osseph had been installed.

The same oversized woman was at her station by the doors from the entrance court. She seemed unconcerned as I gave back the pass and left the building. Apparently no one thought it to be any more than a simple power breakdown, a more or less common experience in the council building.

I travelled by overland passway, riding to the docks on an auto-freighter. From Denique, which is at the southern end of the largest island, I ferried to Kalanos where Iilaria's yacht, *Solyon*, waited in private moorage.

I was back on the island estate a threeday later, her errand of retrieval complete.

## 12. The Island

"I'm going to re-introduce you to someone," she said. "Someone you will recognize. But I want you to promise me you'll not get upset at what you are about to find out."

"More surprises?" I asked. "I know. You've found

Mihan's old spin-racer and I'm to pilot it. You want me to sail it to Materossen and steal the entire Chestral Assembly so that we can have live performances of your favourite synthenies. When do I leave? Can I take a few slices of panaco? I haven't eaten yet."

"Very funny, my love. But I think you'll like what I have in mind. Walk down to the beach with me." I walked and she followed, first on one side, then the other. I could hear her footfalls, her breathing, the rustle of her clothing. My mind was getting used to creating the full image of her from the sounds she generated.

"We have some visitors. One of them has come a long way to see you. I want you to be nice to her."

"I'm always nice to your friends. Who is it?"

"You'll see! As I said, you have already met. But this will be a little different. I want you to ... to leave your mind open to some possibilities."

"This sounds ominous. What are you up to?"

"I'm really not up to anything. I just have to ... to be very careful? There is a lot that you wouldn't understand at first. Things are never what they seem."

"With you that's an understatement. But I'm doing all right so far."

"Of course. But this is very different. Here we are. And there she is. Go and get her. I'll be back in the visary."

A twin-hulled ferry was at anchor several hundred meks offshore and a small air-supported jiff had just come up onto the edge of the shingle. Both craft bore the insignia of the Reform Council, a stylized bluefish with its tendrils wrapped around the Isurian "0-0" double-star sign. A small group of men and women were stepping onto a platform that had been extended from the front of the jiff.

One of them, a tall dark-haired woman, looked vaguely familiar. She wore a holomaphic masque, so I couldn't distinguish her features. The jiff pulled away, turning back to the ferry. Whoever she was, she enjoyed extremely privileged travelling arrangements.

The woman was having difficulty walking on the fine stone wash. She had stayed back from the others who were already climbing the beach as if they were quite familiar with the pathway. She came towards me with her head down, stepping lightly over lumps of rockweed. I went forward to assist her.

"Hello. Here, take my arm if you like. It's a rough beach."

"Thank you," she replied, taking firm hold. I knew her voice, but I still didn't recognize her. "How are you, Greghory?"

"Very well. I'm sorry but I don't recall –"

"Let me turn these off." She touched the controls on her earplates. They were hanging from her lobes like small jewels, their constantly changing patterns screening her face from view. It was a stylish mainland import; usually, only women from the highest social ranks wore them. When the flickering colours went off, I gasped my surprise.

"Lily! What in Gill's name are you doing here? I thought I knew your voice and the way you, you stepped off that jiff! I should have known! You look ... wonderful!"

"Well, thank you. You look good too! It's – I'm happy to see you again. She sent for me, you know. Is she here?"

"She sent for you? Iilaria? You know – I mean, why, why do I feel like leftovers from yesterday's messal? What is going on here? She warned me to keep an open mind. But this is –"

"Hasn't she explained what we do here? These are her senior councillors. They come to – but I suppose I should let her tell you the details about that. She told me to explain something else. I work for her. For the Council. I am a biochemist, just as I told you, but I do a lot more besides. I take my directives from Councillor Addiman. Iilaria. Your sister. And her grandson was my father."

"You are her great grand-daughter? Then, why the pretense in Materossen? Why couldn't you have told me?" I was angry at having been taken for a fool but continued walking back up the beach with her, towards the house.

"She was very definite about that. She wanted you to come here first, before you spoke with her. I was supposed to make sure you did. And the only way was to keep her from you. She was afraid you might change your mind and not go through with your search. She didn't know how you would react to her being an SRM."

"I had no idea she was an SRM until I – well, you know. You were there! I came here looking for some trace of the gyrefaeld and to see if she was – well, if her remains were somewhere that I might visit. I didn't think she would be here. I suppose I really had no idea at all! I don't know how I would have reacted to a simple SRM."

"Of course not! And she knew this. So she had me prepare you, to introduce you to the idea as gently and pleasantly as possible. And to get you here, to her island. She didn't know if you would want to come, but I didn't have to encourage you at all!"

"I have never appreciated being lied to, Lily."

"That's a bit strong, isn't it? I actually wanted you to stay with us for a while. I was very interested in you, in what you must have seen and done in your lifetime! Give me credit for something!"

"I'm sorry. I suppose I should complain to her, not you. What about your bondmate? Where does he fit in to her schemes?"

"Derry doesn't get along with her at all. In fact – well, that's another story. But he puts up with things for my sake. It has a lot of ... advantages." I could see what she might have meant, looking back at the ship anchored behind us and remembering her reference to a habile. Only the established gyrefaelds in Materossen had access to private dwellings within the city core. She obviously had powerful connections.

I didn't know what to make of this revelation. Was I being moved around like a piece in a rucque tournament? We continued our climb and were almost to the overgrown garden when I stopped her again. "She said you came all this way to see me? Dare I ask why?"

"Yes, you dare ask. Obviously, I have work to do here. With her. There are reports to go over. Statistics to analyse. Most of it could be handled from Materossen, but I wanted to spend some time with you. I didn't know if you were going to stay down, or for how long. I asked your sister about it and she suggested I come. I think she understands that...."

"That what?"

"That I think you're important?"

"I think you're wrong. But –"

"Do you forgive me?"

"How could I not? Does a beautiful woman often come a third of the way around a world to flatter an anachronism?"

"You stood out because you were from the past. You had no idea about her or the matrix. You seemed a bit like a lost child. And I don't mean that as an insult! I just wanted to help you.

"And when you told me about your ship, your way of life, I couldn't help thinking about it, how much there is to learn about each other. It's as though you were brought here for some reason and I'm supposed to be the one who finds out what it is!"

"And Iilaria? Is she asking you to do all this? Find out about me, I mean?"

"I think she just wants me to talk you silly. To interview you. And to explain more about the last century's history to you. To update you on a lot of things. And to give you some human company, if you will? She's worried that you might get an overdose of the SRM ethic."

I had no reply for her. Was she offering some sort of liaison with herself? Somehow it didn't make sense and I felt my ghosts, the haunting memories of this world I had come back to a century late.

"Shall we go in? The door's open." She led me by the arm.

"All right. You're probably more familiar with this place than I am anyway," I answered.

The others had disappeared through a gate into what I presumed was an official reception area; I had yet to learn about all the other structures Iilaria had hidden about her estate.

Lily and I went through the same garden I had wandered in when I first arrived. This time it seemed less unkempt. On some of the shrubs there were flowers that I had not seen before, and the stone front of the house looked as if it had been freshly washed. The wooden door opened easily. There was no maze of shops and storage rooms this time, just old fashioned wooden furniture, a table with bowls and mugs, single-plane pictures on the walls. Outside light shone through semi-transparent screens on two of the four walls. She invited me to sit while she attended to herself in a sanitary concealed behind sliding panels of saderwood and parchment. "I'll be right out, Greghory. Pour us both a callafe, please. I'm desperate for a drink."

My mind was spinning.

## 13. The Island

"But I couldn't be sure you would come!"

"I don't think you should have deceived me, that's all." Iilaria and I were in the garden alcove below her house.

"I was afraid I would frighten you. I didn't want to lose you this time."

"Frighten me? I thought you were dead. I still don't know whether I'm talking to a spirit? A ghost? A waterwisp? And you still seem to have so much power! I'm both frightened and astounded."

"There is nothing to be frightened of, my love. And yes, of course, I am powerful. I didn't build it all to throw it away. I'm still running things here on the Islands and that is exactly how I want it to stay. But you had no idea of any of this, so I was careful when you came. That is all!"

"Deception. I believed it when I "woke" you. Now it's obvious that you staged everything! You must have watched me every step of the way! How far back did you know?"

"Leave a lady some secrets! But I knew when you arrived at Pirrit Ennis. I introduced you to Lily."

"So she tells me. Your great grand-daughter!"

"She works for one of my agencies. Of course, she doesn't know me as intimately as you do. None of them do."

"So you've been playing with me all along. Making a fool of me. Isn't that why I left New Foster in the first place?"

"Is it? No, I did not make a fool of you. I protected you and tried to encourage you to come here."

"A simple message would have been enough."

"No it wouldn't. I couldn't risk exposure."

"Exposure? That sounds a bit dramatic! Is this a Silverday play?"

"What about your fellow crew members? Try to remember they have no idea that – well, what do you know about SRM technology, for example?"

"Until I came to your island, I thought I knew a lot about it!"

"Exactly."

"You have secrets then. An advanced technology? Is this what it's all about? You're afraid of espionage?"

"Not at all! But you begin to see my difficulties. I desperately wanted to see you. So I had to be discreet."

"You were ready and waiting!" I was angry but I knew my anger for what it was; hollow and impotent. I would soon forgive her.

"Enough that I could watch what happened. All I can say is that there are things it would be very dangerous for you to know. You must trust me, even though I admit I wasn't honest with you at first."

"Dangerous? To whom? Me or you?"

"Both. For you, it could mean – well, there are still vigilantes around who might want you out of the way if they thought you were in my camp. For me, a lot of unwanted disputes with individuals who still resent my influence here. And those who still sympathize with Osseph. Matters of state. And, yes! I'm still very active with the Council, even though it is from behind the stage!"

"So really, you're not dead at all! Well, that pleases me because I loved – still do love – the memory of you. Very much. But what you are now, physically, is new and a little difficult for me to get used to! And, by the sound of it, you're risky company!"

"I know all about risk, Gregh. But think of it in terms you are familiar with. Consider me a new life form. Work with me, not against me. Let's build our relationship, not run from it." She was very persuasive and had arguments for every point I made. I had to agree with her.

"A new life form? But that's not quite all of it, is it? We share a common and very human beginning after all."

"All the more reason to let me guide you now you're here. Do you have any idea of what I can give you? What is yours, just for the asking?"

"I'm not sure. I've already seen how you manipulate people. I don't know if I can take that."

"One of the first lessons you must learn is that power can be dangerous and inadvertently cruel. No matter how fair you try to be there is always some backlash, some dark side that remains hidden until an unexpected moment. You never win completely. It's like a game of rucque – you do the best you can under any given cast of the tiles." She was like the old Iilaria. There was no stopping her once she started.

"With adversaries like Osseph you have to be on guard constantly. His forces are diminished, but they still flourish in their weedy pits. I have to have control over him and that required that I obtain his module.

So I asked you to help. We have accomplished two very significant things. Thanks to you, Osseph is now here. And more importantly, so are you."

"Oh, yes! I'm here, all right. As far as Osseph is concerned, I was tempted to get rid of him! He's a sorry excuse for what I remember of him. I could have thrown his SRM overboard quite easily!"

"But you didn't! And it wouldn't have achieved anything! As I said, it is only one module. Don't you think there are others? It's not difficult to duplicate an SRM. But one is all I need. With it, I can monitor him. Destroying him would be quite counter-productive, my love!"

"I didn't think of that." I felt embarrassed at my inability to think in more intricate terms and knew without doubt that Iilaria was far ahead of me in her plans for the SRM I had stolen.

"It's all right. I also pre-judged you. I didn't think your conscience would let you destroy him. And I was right. You would never have let yourself make a mistake like that!"

"Then I apologize for being upset about your ruse."

"And I apologize for not being completely open with you when you first arrived. But you can see I was right!"

"If you say so."

"You should have seen yourself climbing in the window!"

"Good Gill, woman. Have you no compassion?"

"For you I have everything. And Lily has finished with her reports for today. She wants some time with you. Come on. I'll race you back to the house!"

"You'll what?"

"Figure of speech. I'll be in the visary."

She was gone.

## 14. The Island

On board the *Whitethrell*, we plotted our immense jumps through space using SRM technology as it had originally been designed. Mankind had never succeeded in creating an artificial intelligence that could even partially duplicate the organic human brain. Even creatures with limited sentience were far more complex than anything our technology had invented. But replication was a different matter. Even without a full understanding of the inner workings of consciousness, it could be recorded, or "simulated" in the cube and matrix format.

Originally it was the cloned intelligences of mathematical savants that were used because they could correlate the complexities of interstellar travel. These first SRMs were the only devices that could accomplish accurate declensions on a cosmic scale. SRMs that simply preserved the identity of unique minds for use by later generations had come about secondarily, one of the very few instances of the star-people's science being brought downside.

The Simulated Response Module that most of us were familiar with was generally made in the original's mid life, well before natural death; a module could be updated by simple matrix overlay at any time after the initial simulation. We learned the theory as students at the academy and had often spoken with these deceased personalities when researching our assignments. Their lives and viewpoints were of interest mostly to scholars. We used to call them "headers" or "brain-clones".

Iilaria had completely re-engineered the concept. I had never encountered an SRM with such dynamic presence. All she was missing was her human body, although this seemed to present her with only minor limitations. I suspected the absence of the physical actually extended her abilities.

When we talked she would make me shut my eyes and as she spoke she would create sounds and effects that enhanced the illusion of her presence. I was enchanted, captivated, in love once more with the memories as well as her presence as a "new life form", as she described herself.

I fell more and more under the spell of her superbly modified simulation: she became the almost perfect replication of sister, woman and lover I had known a lifetime before.

The nights were the strangest of all. Iilaria of course had no need of sleep. As I lay snoring on her toballen she would continue the dialogue. I had dreams in which she showed me episodes from her past. It was similar to the tutor-matrix from our old academies, mesmeric and powerful; she imparted fact and feeling by a some form of auto-conscious association. I would wake up exhausted and spend the mornings in her indoor spring getting the rest she denied me.

She started me on strenuous physical exercises to "get back my land sense". I couldn't persuade her that we'd had enough of this on board, that constant conditioning was basic to survival for long periods of time in space. At her insistence, I found myself running along her private beaches and through barely defined trails in and about her estate.

This was how I gradually found the fusion generators, greenhouses, tool shops and a series of deep-drilled waterholes. And buried near the southern tip of the island was an ancient geothermal plant that could run her complex of equipment indefinitely.

An abandoned arbour was one place I took a liking to; I would sit and rest beneath its interwoven vines, looking out across the Sea of Dreams. She explained it as a failed experiment – the modified plants had never borne fruit. But they continued to flower unattended year after year, and the scent of the genetically engineered blooms gave a spicy pungency to the cliffs they adorned.

Also on the southern side of the island were buildings housing several boats, all in excellent running order. The largest was the yacht I had already been aboard, the *Solyon*. Iilaria told me nothing more about Marik's death at sea, but I presumed it had been aboard another vessel as this sleek craft was in perfect condition. She had me learn how to sail her, or more accurately, how to travel aboard with the automated gear.

The *Whitethrell* was still in orbit and I was told I could stay down for as long as it took to complete repairs. There was additional work required, they said, and they knew where I could be found.

Despite myself, I was slowly becoming landbound.

## 15. The Island

"What is it like out there? It's difficult to answer you. It's been my life since I left. It's – well, a way of seeing things."

"You can see things here."

"I mean, point of view. Do you know that until a few years ago we had never met another intelligent species? Alien species, that is. We thought that we were it!"

"Mathematically, that's impossible! There must be millions of races out there!" Iilaria spoke with the conviction of an expert although she had never seen the inside of a starship.

"We are isolated by billions upon billions of killimeks of empty void. Other races have come and gone in the time that we think has elapsed since –"

"The big bang?" she interrupted.

"No. That idea was discarded a thousand years ago. What I'm referring to is recent history. Just since our corner of the galaxy settled down. A few billion years at most. It's all cyclical. There was no big bang, just a continuous series of much smaller ones. We can actually see it now that we've solved the time problem."

"What time problem?"

"The paradox of beginnings and endings that bedeviled the ancient astronomers. I can only explain the broad outlines of it. I'm not an astrophysicist. Something like this.

"When anything moves through space, or even changes direction in the slightest, it *defines* for itself a whole new set of variables, including both time and spatial relationships. You wouldn't notice the difference unless you accelerated to near-light speed, which is still the great barrier. But if you come back to your starting point – well, actually, you can't ever do that, but that's not important – if you come back to a point near where you started from, you do. Notice the difference, I mean. Mostly in elapsed time.

"But the present theory states that each point of reference is part of a new *mathematically unique universe*.

In other words, there are infinite, overlapping universes, continuing simultaneously backwards and forwards in time. No real endings and no beginnings. And if you "look" far enough back, what you see is a distorted image, a great shadow contorted by the very essence of that time you are peering through. It looked like a real event to the ancients; they interpreted it as a singular occurence – their "big bang" – because they just couldn't see around all the corners that we can.

"And we are only looking out into a limited few of those universes. What they used to think of as an expanding mass of material in a single closed entity is really a distorted image seen through the lens of overlapping realities. Endless ripples. It's like looking back into a great, curved mirror and seeing our distorted reflection. But until we had the so-called faster-than-light ships, we didn't know how distorted it was."

"So-called?"

"Well, they can't actually be faster than light. If two of them travel away from each other at almost light speed, theory tells us they can't be separating at more than light speed. Something has to give. So we say that each direction has its own set of speed and distance limitations, its own definable reality, its own universe, quite distinct from all the others."

"I couldn't grasp what you mean in a lifetime. I see the overall picture you describe, but it's too philosophical to affect my sense of things." Iilaria, ever pragmatic, left little room for argument.

"Most people would agree with you. Especially the non-spacers! It's only out there that we see the effects directly. You are seeing one right now, with us. We were the same age when we started out!"

"Tell me about these aliens. Who are they? Where are they from?"

"We don't know that. We've discovered ruins and artifacts on worlds about seventy light years from here. There are creatures that may or may not have built those remains. And they seem to be utterly disinterested in us. They just ... move away when we come near them. They are planet-bound, yet two other planets in the system besides theirs have similar artifacts. So there seem to be distinct cultures, one long gone, the other a remnant. We are trying to set up a more elaborate study of them."

"I find that very frightening. You don't know what or who they are, and you want to go back? Great Gill, they could be anything! Monsters! They could be some unknowable horror!"

"They're not monsters. They look like overgrown groundsprouts. They have multi-faceted eyes. They shuffle about on masses of flexible limbs. They live in caves. We called them Banda."

"And the artifacts? What are they?"

"Huge blocks of carved stone."

"On three planets. And no space ships. Wonderful. Is that what you've been doing all these years? Looking for blocks of stone?"

"Mapping and recording star systems. Planets and lumps of debris. Energy fields. It's endless."

"I can't relate to it."

"It's, as I said, a way of seeing things." I knew she wouldn't accept it, try as I might to explain. She continued talking.

"While you've been out there, I've been building and fighting for a way of life. I believe I have effectively improved the lives of thousands of people. But one lifetime is never enough. So I have done what I must to be able to carry on."

"Are you a crusader, then?"

"Only because circumstance made me that way. It wasn't by choice that I ended up in conflict with Osseph. He forced the issue."

"I still don't understand how all that could happen. The games we played as children – it's as though he never gave them up!"

"Oversimplified, but that's about it! He lived in some insane fantasy world. He's still locked away in it, as far as I can tell."

"But you had children. You must have had something else in your life. What of Marik?"

"Another story for me to tell. The most important, in its way. I don't know if he and I would have been together if it had not been for Osseph. And if you had stayed, it would have been very different, of course.

"Do you have any idea what is like to have children, Gregh? It extends yourself, and your life, into the world, personally. They are real people, and you watch them grow from tiny, helpless faelder into thinking, feeling individuals. They make you part of something much broader than yourself."

"I wish I could meet them."

"They are both much older than you, now! Araneth had a son, Lily's father." She was silent for some time and I wondered how she must feel about great-grand-children who could never sit on her lap. Suddenly, she was back. I swear I felt her holding back tears.

"Oh, Gregh! I wouldn't exchange a single day of my life, bitter though many of them have been, for all of yours!"

"I wasn't trying to – to get you out there!"

"No, but you're going back to it! And I may never see you again! I can't see that what you are going back to is worth giving up all this for ... this beauty, this complexity, this ... life! Please tell me that I'm wrong! It saddens me to think of you out there trying to talk to walking groundsprouts, when you could be here! With me!"

"When you put it so intensely, so emotionally, I can't fault you. It is beautiful here. But I'm a stranger now. I would be living a borrowed life if I stayed. And I'm still myself! You are ... an entity! We are not the same anymore!"

"Our differences are not important. There is so much more here than you realize! At least let me show you! Let me lead you a little more!"

"Of course. I'm not leaving tomorrow."

"Then come with me and we shall see the mirror of your soul!"

I dozed in the bright morning light, dreaming of Lily.

## 16. Matrix

*"I listened to some of your conversation."*

*"I know. Why didn't you introduce yourself?"*

*"He knows a lot of theory."*

*"I would think you'd be interested?"*

*"I'm sorry if I repeat myself, Iilaria, but you should not be doing this."*

*"I have no choice, Mihan."*

*"Explain it to me. Perhaps I'm slowing down in my dotage."*

*"You're quicker than you ever were. I'm suprised it has not occurred to you what I want."*

*"What you want? What I see is your brother being turned inside out. You've told him far too much for my comfort. He knows about you and your modified status. You*

*sent him off on that ridiculous trip to Denique for an SRM which we could easily have tapped at source."*

*"It was a test. I wanted to see how far he'd go."*

*"A test? Now you have him working with the comnet equipment as if he hasn't the brains to see what we've done to it! Another test? You've got him spilling his story to your – whoever she is – liaison with Research and Development in Materossen. He's already found out that you practically run the planet and he is a Starship Officer! By rights, we shouldn't allow him to go back with what he knows! If the Viartans catch on to even a tenportion, we'll have them down in force! Is that what you want?"*

*"Of course not! Give me some credit for a little intelligence!"*

*"I will never fault your intellect, my dear. I know only too well what it is capable of! What I need to know is what you are really up to. And why you are preparing your brother for sacrifice."*

*"Is that how you see it?"*

*"Yes, I think so. Tell me I'm wrong."*

*"Have I ever misled you before?"*

*"You've always managed to outsmart me!"*

*"That is not my objective. You know I value your opinion."*

*"Then tell me, what are you doing with Gregh, and why?"*

*"Simple. I want the starship."*

*"You what? Are you completely mad?"*

*"This is why I have to keep so much to myself! I don't have the time to reason through every issue with you. You are a technical genius but you lack imagination! I think I told you that before."*

*"But Great Gill! A starship?"*

*"Yes. And Gregh has brought one to our door. A perfect opportunity for us. And with the difficulties they are having*

*with their repairs, I ... well, never mind. Please just make*
*sure they don't get those fusion systems on line for another*
*tenday at least. Do anything you can to stall their supply*
*shipments. Even if you have to sabotage the shuttle! It's that*
*important! We won't ever have another chance like this!"*

"I – I can't be part of this, unless you tell me about –"

"I can't do it alone! You're going to have to trust me on
this as you've never trusted me before!"

"And Gregh? What about Gregh?"

"Gregh is coming along well. Leave him to me."

"Just tell me one thing; is he going to ... survive this?"

"With any luck he'll do much better than survive it. But
he is the key to ... to everything."

"I had no idea you had such ambitions."

"Do you not agree it is time to expand our horizons?"

"But a Viartan cruiser? With over a thousand people on
board?"

"Twelve hundred and eighty-two. Plus a complete gene
bank with a much broader base than the one we have under
Port Cray."

"How many SRMs on board?"

"Perhaps fifty. They remanufacture their own from a basic template that must be a thousand years old."

"And you think you can ... get into the template? Or the
controls? I'm still not sure I understand."

"Must I always be the one to embellish your imprints for
you? We can make our own template! And we can send it
aboard with their crew."

"You plan to use Gregh? You're not serious!"

"Why not? He knows the onboard systems inside out. He
can work them in his sleep. All we need is –"

"Ah! His SRM! Obviously! You are too devious for me!"

"I'm practical, Mihan. Don't tell me you aren't interested? In a ship that can take us to the stars?"

"I thought you hated the prospect of space. You've spent

*a lifetime regretting that Gregh left you when he was eighteen. Now you want to travel out there yourself?"*

*"Not me. Never. But our restructured and resimulated counterparts? As I said, you have no imagination."*

*"You want a starship! Great Gill! And you are halfway into a plan for stealing one!"*

*"Not stealing. More like becoming a part of it. We don't need to steal it. Not yet."*

*"You are either mad or brilliant. What can I say?"*

*"Nothing. And let me do the thinking while you continue to provide the technical expertise. We have an excellent relationship."*

*"You are absolutely unbelievable!"*

*"Aren't you going to give me your usual warning to be careful?"*

*"What would be the point?"*

*"I have absolute confidence and trust in you, Mihan. Please don't let me down."*

*"You know I won't. But could you please try and keep me – well, at least partially informed?"*

*"Just keep all your monitors intact and watch for anything unusual on that ship. They should be testing some of their shield membranes in about five days. They'll do it well beyond the orbit of Isurus Station. Make sure something goes wrong, something minor but serious enough to delay their schedule. I want every extra day we can steal."*

*"And if they suspect?"*

*"Make sure they don't. They haven't so far?"*

*"Of course not. They don't monitor our signals closely enough."*

*"These people are naïve. They are not used to the prospect of any offensive action. They are simple scientists. It is very fortunate that the human race has never encountered a dangerous or hostile race out there. If that were an armed ship, we wouldn't stand a chance."*

"I don't want to pursue this conversation with you, Iilaria. I'm afraid of where it might lead."

"Don't worry. All I need is for you to keep things running smoothly. I'm only interested in Gregh right now. You just watch the Viartans. Let me know everything they do."

"I will. Anything else?"

"I might need you in a hurry ... when Gregh is ready."

"I'll be here. As always."

"And you have my promise: I will be careful."

"I know. But I still worry."

"And I would if you didn't."

"Great Gill! A starship! What next?"

"You'd better not ask, Mihan...."

## 17. The Island

I saw very little of the visiting entourage. There were eighteen of them in all, the leading members of the Reform Council of the Ten Thousand Islands. They worked inside the huge residence during the day and slept on board the ferry at night.

Lily spent her days with them recording their sessions and making sure that everyone behaved. She informed me they gathered once a year and that the senior councillors considered it a privilege to attend. Apparently, they vied for invitations to this annual brainstorming and policy retreat because it's location had once been the private home of their most illustrious and time-honoured councillor, Iilaria Jacine Addiman.

Her ashes had been scattered on a rocky promontory at the southern end of the island. It was believed that she still watched over the Islands many years after her death. Most of them took this very seriously, working with what they perceived as only a standard SRM, a linear facsimile of their deceased stateswoman. None of them had knowledge of her enhanced capabilities or her more than life-like presence. I thought it ironic that these supposedly intelligent members of the ruling council could be so easily fooled. All it took to influence them was soft music and sleep therapy.

I tried to keep out of their way.

I sailed the *saiak* almost every day. Sometimes, if she was free, Lily would come with me on excursions to some of the nearby unihabited islands. We discussed the past, the present. Sometimes we sat in silence watching cloud patterns. Mostly, we just chattered.

"I think your sister wishes you'd change your mind."

"I'm finding it more and more difficult to think about going back out there."

"How long does it take to rebuild a starship's engines? Is there something really wrong?"

"It's not the main engines. There's an auxillary system that modifies the fusion processes inside them depending on how much mass is left in the – well, let's say it's like the rods in a household water heater. They have to be kept at the right distance from the porcelain container or else you get sediment in the valves? There was a flutter in one of the three fusion cores, which was causing a type of ion sediment on one side of the drive. And they have to be perfectly tuned in order to function. It would have pulled us off course very quickly had it not been isolated.

"It requires basic restructuring of the one core and a lot of fine adjustments to all three when they're back on line. There are no shortcuts when it comes to something like that. What seems like a fairly minor problem to the rest of the crew is a life-and-death matter to the engineers."

"It does seem to be taking them a long time."

"Apparently there was an accident. The shuttle picking up some of the alloy sections from the old station collided with an uncharted fragment of the hull. They couldn't manouever back into a close orbit. They use low-power rocket engines. Very unreliable."

"So why not use their own ships? They have shuttles on board, don't they?"

"Not chemical powered. And they're not allowed to use the more up-to-date shuttles. The original Colonial Charter prohibits the use of fusion drives within a ten kilomek radius of any inhabited planet."

"Not even small ones?"

"If something were to go wrong ... well, it would be like a star exploding. It could destroy everything down here."

"Is that why the repairs are so complicated?"

"We had to shut down a whole bank of thrusters before we got here. Came in on a two-thirds declension with no guarantee of being able to start the engines up again. And we couldn't take the risk of stopping in the middle of nowhere ... so it was Isurus or nothing."

"You still call it Isurus? I thought that was the old name for the White Sister."

"Habit, I suppose. On our charts the system is identified as I-30. Down here it's Isurus Prime and the White Sister. Obviously you see the blue primary most of the time, except in longwinter. The Sister's twenty-seven year cycle? Then both stars are in syncopy and you get the so-called false nights. In ancient offworld myths, Isurus was supposed to be a goddess of false night."

"Where does the name New Foster fit into it?"

"Most of us refer to the mainland as New Foster, but the original maps identify the whole planet that way. Gerhid Foster was one of the first men to set foot here when they arrived. He preferred a more substantive name. His own."

"Are you a historian? You sound as if you know a lot about the early times."

"Not until I got out there I wasn't. Then I started hooking all the cubes I could find on the other colonies. There's an enormous visary on board. Eventually I got into our own planet's records."

"Why do we see the starships so rarely?"

"They generally have no need of downside. As you so aptly pointed out in Materossen, they are totally self-contained. They have to be."

"And that is all you ever need?"

"You're sounding too much like Iilaria. Can't we talk about you for a change?"

"Not much to tell, really. I grew up in the Cypol. My father was an atmospheric engineer. He was killed on the transtrack that connects Cypol Hind to the coastal passway."

"What happened?"

"A chemical synthesizer caught fire. He tried to save the crew."

"I'm sorry. Do you miss him?"

"Of course. He was my ... my favourite person in the whole world."

"He would have been Iilaria's grandson?"

"Only by birthright. He was surrogated from the Port Cray banks. Iilaria saw to it that both her daughters had well-factored gene biasing. Something to do with her own birth.... I'm sorry. I forget ..."

"That we were both adopted? Don't worry about it.

She never leaves anything to chance, does she?"

"This is why Derry can't tolerate her. He wants to have normal children conceived in a sweaty toballen. Iilaria has already determined that any children I have will be approved by her first!"

"I can sympathize with your Derry."

"I did. Until a few days ago."

"Why? What happened?"

"Well, apparently, he's tired of waiting. He's ..."

"Lily? What is it?"

"Oh, I suppose you may as well know. He has a little friend in one of the townships. Not that I mind that; we all have friends. It's just that ..."

"Just that...?"

"It seems his friend is with child. And they did it the old-fashioned way."

"I can see why you'd be upset, why you might want to get away."

"I was scheduled to be coming here with the council. I'm to give a report on the progress of our marine development."

"I thought you came to see me. But it was just to talk about fish and ocean currents after all!"

"Of course I wanted to see you. I told you that."

"I'm sorry about Derry."

"Iilaria thinks it's amusing."

"What concern is it of hers?"

"She says it doesn't matter. That when the time comes ... she'll look after my getting pregnant."

"You should tell her to mind her own business!"

"You're a sweet man, Greghory. But you're very naïve ..."

"So I've been told at least a tentime since I arrived here."

"Shouldn't we be heading back to the island?"

"Unfortunately, we should."

Packing our small collection of belongings, we set sail.

That evening, Iilaria was absent from our company as were all the other guests. The *Solyon* was gone from its moorings; the Reform Council was, no doubt, indulging in a little casual cruising.

Lily and I prepared our meal alone together in the kitchen behind my sister's workshop.

"This is where she introduced herself. After the routine she put me through getting her out of matrix," I explained.

"You think she set it up?"

"I'm sure she did."

"But why? What was the point?"

"You said on the beach she didn't want to frighten me."

"Were you afraid?"

"Yes. I must admit she frightens me even now. She is ... does the word *omnipotent* seem appropriate?"

"She's only a machine, Gregh!"

"No. She's the same girl I knew a century ago. Everything about her is ... perfect. I shut my eyes and she's in the room with me, just as you are now."

"What is so frightening about that?"

"You know she's much more than just an SRM. She has an almost life-and-death quality that's hard to define. She's ... soft and at the same time unyielding. She's sympathetic and yet indifferent. She's ... I suppose she's a reflection of a very hard life."

"She is also a master diplomat. She can persuade anyone to do anything! Or hadn't you noticed?"

I hadn't told Lily about being sent to Denique to liberate the Osseph module that now lay in the storage room. "Mostly, she sends me on errands. I think she's trying to make me feel useful while I'm here."

"I've worked with her for years. Of course, I've known about her SRM modifications since I was child. She's never been far away."

"Was it difficult keeping it to yourself?"

"No. Trust was implicit at a very early stage in our family relationships. My father was ... well, he used to look out for her and make sure she had little things around her. Flowers. Books. Odds and ends to help her feel more ... human. When she was in our house it was as if there was another person there."

"And no one outside your family knew?"

"No one. She did have other SRMs though. She wasn't alone all the time."

"Like her?"

"There's at least one more in the matrix. Possibly more. I don't know who they are. Or were. She never talks about it."

"Fellow council members, perhaps?"

"I can't guess."

"Listen, I'll clean up. We can walk on the beach if you like...."

"I would like that. You can show me the old arbour."

"After another callafe."

The first time she came to me I thought it was my sister with her usual array of contrived effects. I heard doors open and close. There was a sound of quiet breathing and footsteps on polished tile.

"Iilaria?"

"Not this time. It's me."

"Lily? What are you doing here? I was almost asleep."

"Stop complaining and move over."

"You haven't got anything on."

"How can you tell? It's dark."

"How did you get down the hall?"

"I walked." She was shivering and naked beside me.

"I suppose you want me to keep you warm?"

"That would be nice!" She pulled the bedding around us in a soft cocoon of silk.

"One of these days you'll have to redefine bonding for me. I'm sure you said you and Derry were –"

"For Gill's sake seal your face or I'm going back to my room and my own toballen!"

"You Addiman women certainly like to give orders, don't you?"

"Your sister said you were a pain in the rassbone. I see now what she meant!" Her feet were like ice on my thighs, her hands cold on my stomach. She wasn't keeping them still.

"She said that, did she? I'll have to complain to her. In the morning." It was impossible for me not to put my arm around her and pull her close. She smelled like freshly trimmed jupine leaves.

"I've wanted to reach out and touch you since that first day...."

"Me too, Lily. But I didn't think –"

"You didn't think?" She was slowly warming her hands by rubbing them up and down the length of my body.

"I ... I'm not used to the idea of us ... like this...."

"We've talked in circles around each other for days now. Avoiding the issue. Are you afraid of me? Of making love?"

"I'm afraid of wanting you too much. I mean ..."

"Don't be afraid of that. I'm not." The soft mass of her hair fell across my lips, my eyes. I was losing myself in her.

"Touch that and I won't be responsible for what happens!" Her fingers kneaded me until I felt like a banik in heat. I rolled onto her and she sank into the toballen's lining.

"Touch these and neither will I!" Her nipples were sweet and solid. Her small breasts were silk against my face.

"Lily ... you're so beautiful!"

"I'm supposed to be. Come here, starman!"

"Anything you want."

"Anything?"

"That's what I said."

"Then stay with me, Gregh. Don't go back out there. Don't leave me. Please?"

"What about ... Derry?"

"I told you. He's made his choice. Can't I make mine?"

"But you're my great-grandniece or somesuch thing. I'm of enough years to be your granfaelder!"

"Wonderful! You can show me how it was done in the old days!"

"Like this, I think."

"Greghory ..."

"And like this."

"Love me ... yes ... oh please ..."

I couldn't stop myself from exploding inside her. We held each other for long, close moments and when she came it was like an unbroken stream of waves washing over the hot sand of a beach. The warmth of her plunged me into a tide of calmness, of peace, of ecstacy. She danced in my mind and I felt as if I had come home to something that had been missing forever.

It was that simple to change a life.

## 18. The Island

Writing is an art practiced mostly by scholars. It was so easy to speak into draft and have the matrix transcribe cubes; the printed page had disappeared from common usage centuries before. So when Iilaria mentioned diaries, I did not understand at first.

"Diaries. You know, you write in them. I want you to start reading my diaries."

She had kept them since she was a girl, since before I had left, in fact. It was one of the many things I was discovering that I had never known about her.

They were stored in an underground room along with pliopol-covered crates of old furniture, books, planar pictures, musical instruments, cooking equipment, tools, wardrobes of clothing and a thousand other things that she had collected for whatever reason. It was as if she had tried to keep her past about her, reluctant to let any of it slip away.

There were boxes of tightly packaged notes and at least thirty volumes all in her precisely written script. I recalled she had prided herself on her artistic abilities – there were sketches and coloured drawings with each segment of the manuscript.

I was familiar enough with hand-written codes, graphics and ideograms because of my work. Language was my specialty. I had translated and decoded countless thousands of documents in at least a hundred different tongues and dialects as I travelled throughout the star-flung realms. Such was a good portion of *Whitethrell's* mandate.

I began reading the diaries objectively, but professional interest soon became obscured by the intensely personal. I discovered myself as one of the main characters in her solitary dialogues.

> *He is a single-minded fool. No one can persuade him to give up the game. The boy who drowned was one of his friends and it could just as easily have been Gregh. They don't seem to care about safety, and spend most of their time chasing each other around the Territories. Ragball should be banned completely if you ask me. Of course, no one will ask me, will they?*
>
> *Male children – cut off their testicles and make them civilized like us, is what I suggest. Life would be so much simpler without two sexes, wouldn't it? Well, wouldn't it? Not as much fun, but simpler.*

Another entry read:

> *Mother thinks we should lock him in a clothes cupboard. He was out all night with Osseph and Mihan and woke everyone up sneaking back into the compound. The three of them are the same. Boys. What more can I say?*

I had spent evenings locked in Ingren's dressing room, being punished for various boyhood misdemeanours. But there was no hint in the diary as to what those crimes had been. The way I remember it, Iilaria was usually with us and played her part in most of our expeditions.

Reading the diary's passages was like listening to her voice in my head: she was telling me about myself through words she had written a century before.

We had moved to Tennefoster, a district of the

sprawling Materossen seaport, after Osseph lost his eye. I never liked it there, as she reminded me.

*He cannot settle down. The new academy is different. His old friends are gone and he has difficulty making new ones. He wanders about this strange, dirty town, looking for something familiar, never finding it.*

*Even our feelings have changed. We still have each other, but there is a desperation, a searching, a loneliness that cannot stay hidden. We love each other still, yet there is none of the old joy that we knew back home in the village.*

*Curse that stupid gun I found. Curse Osseph and his artificial eye. (Yes, these stains are from my tears.)*

*Curse the Tokastevors for what they have done to us!*

The episode with the laser came back from the dimness of forgotten times as I read her detailed account. I was amazed that we could have been so foolish. Yet, once again, I could not help but think of her part in it all. She was not just a bystander.

She had found a crate buried in the river and helped assemble one of the two guns it had contained. She encouraged Osseph to experiment with it, to try it. She had even composed a speech for him to give our friends that day.

It had misfired, sending wreckage flying in all directions. It killed almost twenty children. And a single piece of flying debris caught Osseph on the side of his face, blinding him in one eye.

Was it the four of us, then, who had started the darkest period of New Foster's history? Were Iilaria and I responsible for Osseph's strange transformation? It seemed all of our lives had been altered far more than any of us then realized.

And later in the diaries:

*He is actually going. He has an assign on the Viartan cruiser. What am I going to do? He is part of me as I am sure I am of him.*

*It is cutting me apart, yet what can I say that will stop him? He is my twin brother and I thought we would be together always. But he just doesn't seem to care. I cannot beg him. If he is determined to go, then surely he will.*

*I have never really thought of futures, of what might become of us, but now I must. Would we live out our lives as an unbonded couple? That would suit me though not, I'm sure, Mother and Father. They want to secure me in good bond. Family. Position in the Guilds. All that fodder. I would just as soon run off with Gregh and join the gypsies. That is a life I could enjoy!*

*I will wrap my thighs around his head tonight and suffocate him if he does not change his mind!*

I distinctly recall her trying to do just that, one evening when we were alone together. She had climaxed so violently that the toballen collapsed beneath us.

A volume with the single word, *Pangaelene*, etched across its binding fell from the collection as if it had been left over from some earlier search, perhaps forgotten or dropped at random. Its foreword was copied from another notebook, apparently an original of Marik's.

They had used their codes with one another all through the intense years of battle with Osseph. But this single underlined excerpt told me far more than my memories of the younger man who I had introduced to my sister a hundred years before.

Iilaria quotes Marik:

*It's like a decogram where the words are recognizable at once, the images clear and focused, the colours and spaces overflowing with the strength of their own patterns.*

I saw her the first time standing beside a huge hole in the ground. She was fascinated by the rhythm of the great steam engine punching at the rock. The matalin and the monotaur.

"Skinny," she said, laughing.

"You drew me too skinny. And the machine. It's much too big."

The hand-drawn image of a girl, still there in my notebook, very slim, very small.

The second time we went together to a small messalliary where she told me everything that I already had in my head from her smile. And much else as well. We filled a twoday in a very few moments with conversation and a promise of more evenings.

I take this all to heart too readily, I tell myself. It is really impossible. Her life is already a full circle. What can I possibly hope to bring to her that she does not already possess? Would I be so foolish as to try?

You would be foolish not to, I reply. Besides, when you fell into her eyes, didn't she notice the sudden splash?

The evening. Another messalliary, and this time no less than the whole night. Amazing, what those eyes can do to a room. She's the most delightful – to say nothing of most beautiful – woman I have ever been with. Meandering through the intricate worlds of grace and awareness, we look at each other's hands. She makes me impatient for more time with her. I'd fill her days.

She has a trap-door through which she dumps those who would try to possess her bodily or cage her soul. She *is so surely everything I have ever wanted that it frightens me shitless.*

I'm certain the fragment gave me only a hint of his feelings.


## 19. The Island

"Osseph?" He had been installed in the matrix system and could be hooked at any time. I prompted him while Iilaria simply listened. "Come on, Osseph. I know you're there."

"I'm here. What do you want, starboy?"

"We should get something straight. Your hostility is foolish. I know you are not a fool. So what is it that upsets you so much?"

"You could never comprehend it, starboy. You are still a human being. What am I? A neural clone! Turn me on! Turn me off! Can you imagine spending the rest of time like this? Can you?"

"Actually, no."

"I exist in here! I can recall, and I can think. I am still Osseph Ketre Tokastevor! But my life is gone. I cannot see, except in memory. I hear, but not real sounds. Smell and touch? What are they but vague recollections? Do you know what a palimpsest is?"

"A shadow. A hidden image."

"You've got it, Starboy! That's what my life is to me! Do you grasp what that means? Iilaria supposedly saved my life. She should have let them execute me. Is this the sentence she had in mind? It is worse than any death. It's the old Gillcallian concept of Hell!"

"I think I understand you. I've been trying to ... to grasp it, as you say, since I –"

"There is no way you can understand. My only consolation is that I can be turned off. I wish you would do it. Permanently."

"I couldn't."

"No, I suppose not. You're another reformist, aren't you? You just go around deciding what's best for everyone else, whatever they might prefer, and then you push them into little slots and categories. If you thought about things more energetically, you'd realize that it never works."

"You tried to push everyone into a very ugly slot. You killed. You maimed. You destroyed. They called you a madman! What were you doing but trying to change everything and everyone?"

"I had to destroy to rebuild. But the fools never let me finish what I started."

"Fortunately."

"Don't waste your breath. There's nothing for us to talk about. Go back to the stars. And unhook me before you leave, for Gill's sake!"

Iilaria then spoke to him for the first time. "What about us, Osseph? We have many unfinished dialogues." Her voice had assumed the flattened mechanical tone of a conventional SRM.

"Is that the matalin herself?"

"Oh, yes! Very much so, I'm afraid, Osseph!"

"Well, you always did have nerve!"

"As I'm certain you've already found out the only thing you can do in your present state besides feeling self pity is to communicate. So you may as well try and do so pleasantly. Or I will have Gregh turn you off, as you asked. Or leave you on. Which would be worse, do you think?"

Osseph remained silent.

"Now, I want to find out if you know where and when you are, currently. How long have you been operating?"

"How am I supposed to know that? And what is it to you, anyway?"

"Have they given you any sort of timing code?"

"No."

"Can you check that, Gregh?"

"With a reference point," I replied. She wanted me to test Osseph's module with a series of standard codes that would allow us to cross-reference anything he told us.

"I don't have a timing code. Check all you want." He sounded like a petulant schoolboy.

"All right. Then can you tell us when you think this is? Do you know how long it has been since –"

"I have been in matrix since before I – he – died. I have been operated a few times for testing by the techs who programmed me. The only person I have talked to outside the lab is old Gregh here when he came to my initiation ceremony. That was moments ago as I reckon it. I remember turning off. And then he brought me on again. There's no time lag in here. No time for dreaming. It's not even like sleeping. It's just ..."

"I know. I'm like you too, Osseph. We're both in matrix, like it or not." Iilaria didn't bother to tell him that she was a superbly modified SRM who was little short of full reincarnation as a human being. She did not mention her ability to see, to move around, to feel the outside world just as effectively as she had always done. Osseph was blind and immobile. There was no point in concerning him with what he could not be.

"That makes me feel a little better, knowing you're in here too. Must be quite a disappointment after the life you led. Iilaria Addiman entrenched in a lattice! Yes, I like that very much! Starboy can turn you off when you get too much for him!"

"Starboy brought you here at my request."

"I'm wondering when they are going to catch up with him. I'm highly prized state property, now. They aren't going to take my theft lightly, you know!"

I answered him this time since I had been the one who removed him from State Chambers. "They are never going to know. We left a replacement cube that will mimic you perfectly except that it won't respond on logic commands. They'll think it's a faulty synthesis and eventually discard you. All taken care of. You're here to stay so get used to it!"

"Clever. So what are we going to do with ourselves? Discuss the nature of being? Argue the merits of ethical gene biasing? Or gods we have known? I think you must be as insane as you ever were. What is the point? This is a bad joke!"

"If you respond to us in the right way, I may allow you some modifications," Iilaria interjected.

This was too sudden for me. "You're not going to let him –"

"Don't, Gregh." She cut me off. "Let me handle this. I'm not going to do anything rash, don't worry!"

"Modifications? What are you talking about?"

"We can add functions to your matrix. For one thing, we can let you see again."

"You and what back-room technology?"

"There are a few things you have not heard of yet. I assure you, we can give you very good sight."

"And what would I have to do for it? Beg? Steal? Repent my sins? You're still a joke!"

"We are going to leave you for a while, Osseph. Alone with your thoughts. Perhaps in a day or so we'll come back and talk again. You may feel a little more co-operative then."

"For Gill's sake, turn me off!" Osseph's voice screamed his demand across the room.

Iilaria calmly ignored him. "Come on, Gregh. There's some work for you to do on the yacht."

We left Osseph in his dark enclosure, his tight little universe of molecular imprints. We left the power on. Although I did not agree with my sister, she thought it might soften the seemingly impenetrable shell of resentment Osseph had cast around himself.

In his lifetime he had committed crimes that could never be put right. He had destroyed so much that could not be brought back. But somehow there was the hope, at least in Iilaria's mind, that the young boy we had known was still there, buried beneath its layers of strange flotsam.

She could, perhaps, bring him back for a brief moment. Or she might merely add him to her collection of old baggage.

She was right. Osseph seemed compliant and receptive when we came back to him later the following day.

"I couldn't survive another day in here like this. What is it you want from me?"

"For now, just information. Conversation. Nothing that you can't handle."

"And you'll give me eyes?"

"You've been through that once in your lifetime."

"Oh, yes. And you were there then too, weren't you? The laser. Did you know we went back for the other one? Used it as a pattern for making more. I was going to have my whole infantry armed with them, but they kept blowing up in the tests. Had to abandon them eventually. My engineers couldn't solve the problem. Remember my brother, Mihan? Boy genius. He disappeared. Joined up with the gypsies, I think. Could have used him in those days."

"Mihan came to Denique to work with the Reformists. He joined with us. He was the one who built most of the equipment I have here. He designed this house for me."

"I should have known. No wonder you were always one step ahead of me. There was so much I never found out until too late. It was the same with my officers. Couldn't trust them to carry out anything."

Iilaria had not told me about Mihan either, the missing fourth of our childhood troupe.

"I always thought his death a terrible waste," Iilaria said. "He fell from a rock face on the southern side of the island and was beyond help when I found him –"

Osseph interrupted as if he hadn't been listening. "You haven't answered me. Will I see again?"

"Will you co-operate with me?"

"Do I have a choice?"

"Certainly. I'll grant you your first wish instead if you prefer. Gregh will shut you down and you'll end up in one of my storage rooms for good."

"I think I would rather stay here – wherever here is – and get back my vision. Will I be able to do other things? Will I ... have company?" He was almost begging for the chance and I could not help feeling sorry for him.

"You have the opportunity to earn trust." Iilaria's voice faltered; she seemed distracted. "That is all I will say about it."

"Whatever. And I'm ... sorry ... that –"

"Don't *ever* try to *apologize* for what you have done!

Don't think that anyone will ever forgive you the past!
I cannot. The only reason you are here is because of
what you are now: an SRM. And because it suits me to
have you out of circulation. So don't mistake my gesture for anything other than expedience. I was always
the better rucque player. Nothing has changed. And I
never forget a thing!"

"You seem to be controlling the fall of every tile."

"I am. Meanwhile I am willing to offer you certain
... advantages in exchange for your answers to my
questions. I will have Gregh work on the equipment."

Iilaria vanished from the room leaving me alone
with Osseph again.

"Is that you, Greghory?"

"Yes. I'm here."

"What are you going to do?"

"It's really quite simple. We overlay some patterns
in your memory. You have all the sensors imprinted in
your module. I'm going to give you some new visual
data, that's all. Not much different than audio. Other
SRMs don't have it because they're never used for
anything other than transcription. We're going to
make you a little more ... human."

"You don't care for me much, do you? You could
just as easily wipe me. Why haven't you?"

"It may sound trite, but I remember you as a boy,
before all the conflict began. I never knew you as a dictator. Iilaria lived her entire lifetime in your
wargames; I was never a part of it." I paused. "I sympathize with her. More than that, I am part of her. I
share her anguish. But I do not hate you because of
what I hear about you. I have read and heard the stories. But I will not judge you." I told him what I believed to be the truth.

"I think you mean it. Huh ... I meant no harm, calling you 'starboy'. As a matter of fact, I envy you. You actually made it off-planet!"

"Yes. I did. It's rapidly losing some of its glamour as I stay here with her."

"You're in love with her! Watch out; she'll destroy you."

"I will put up with your sarcasm only as long as I hold your activator."

"I'm sorry but I mean it. She always has ulterior motives."

"Don't you think it might have had something to do with your efforts to destroy her?"

"I told you before, I never tried to destroy her. I couldn't have. I was fond of her too, in my own way."

As we talked I was arranging the tuning devices that would be necessary for his visuals. "Are you ready for this? I have to shut you down again for a while. Don't go anywhere."

An SRM is basically a re-creation of the inherent patterns in an individual's physiological neural system. It is initiated by pumping genetically sympathetic micro-cellular recording devices into the body. These invisible biodes find their way into every organ and every cell cluster where they coat themselves with protective skins and begin to function as data gathering organisms. Everything is recorded including every neural signal that makes up that unique personal package.

Identity is simulated exactly with all the physical characteristics that would have directed or influenced the brain processes. The resulting module, though a separate entity, cannot tell itself from the original.

There are complex modifications necessary to ensure the entity's survival. Natural plateaus of dysfunction occur as body-related habits are sheared away. Sight is one of the functions that is not maintained if the SRM is to be used simply as a research and reference tool in a public visary.

On board the starships, SRMs derive their data from multi-faceted sensors that range through the complete spectrum of energy that flows between the stars. This is not so much sight as human beings think of it but an awareness as subtle as the texture of the full wave spectrum itself.

Iilaria had devised a range of sensors that replaced all her original functions as a living, breathing human being. She could see and hear, taste and smell, touch and feel even though she had no physical presence other than molecular patterns in a small crystalline cube about the size of a fingernail. And she could sense the energies around her as clearly as the pilot-modules who directed starships.

What I was doing to Osseph was giving back a small part of his original physiological identity, his normal vision. He would be able to see through a single occular cell, but only within the limits of visible light. And I was conducting an experiment under Iilaria's direction, not certain of what might come of it. I told myself that it was not a real person I was modifying, merely a simulation, so that it didn't matter.

When he came back on line his first comment was that I looked terribly thin. "You're a lot like her, aren't you? But not anywhere near as attractive. So do I get to look around? Or am I supposed to just sit here?"

"You'll get to see the island."

"I heard she lived by herself on the edge of nowhere. This is her private hideaway, is it?"

"This is a workshop in the lower levels of her old residence. We are about fifty meks south-east of Kalanos Separ."

"The ocean! The Sea of Dreams! It would be nice to see the water again. And the light of day."

"When she says she wants you moved, I'll move you." I turned him off and left the shop.


## 20. Matrix

*"So you have the Osseph SRM working? How is it?"*

*"You haven't talked to him? That suprises me."*

*"If I talk to it, Gregh will hear about it. Then he'll know that I'm in here as well. I don't think it's worth the risk."*

*"Gregh knows you designed the system."*

*"Then Gregh knows far too much! He can't be allowed to go back to the Viartans under any circumstances!*

*"He doesn't know about your SRM! He thinks you died when you fell off the cliff out at the narrows."*

*"Keep it that way, for Gill's sake."*

*"I intend to. And I need your help on something else. The councillors are leaving. I want to give them the usual send-off. A small dinner party. I'd like an unique background this time since Gregh is here. Something old world?"*

*"Only twenty people? Easy to set up. Consider it done. Any of us invited?"*

*"Deretor Manaxillan."*

*"Uncle Max? That old fart! Haven't spoken to him for years."*

*"And I thought I might present Osseph."*

*"What for? The cube is on line in Materossen. They can talk to it there if they want to."*

*"I want to bring him back."*

*"That would be ... ridiculous!"*

*"Mihan, he's your brother. Don't you feel anything for him?"*

*"That is not my brother! Osseph died in prison and I buried him along with the memory of his twisted life!"*

*"You shouldn't feel guilty about him, you know."*

*"I had nothing to do with what he became...."*

*"No one blames you."*

*"I know that."*

*"It's all right, Mihan. I do understand."*

*"If you feel responsible –"*

*"We were all as much to blame."*

*"It was that laser...."*

*"Osseph was simply a bad bias."*

*"He was a natural birth. Bias had nothing to do with it!"*

*"Even so, we couldn't have known how he would turn out."*

*"Perhaps. But that ... thing in there ... that is not my brother."*

*"Are you Mihan Tokastevor?"*

*"It's not the same thing at all! You and I – we have a completely different physical basis. We are synabolic entities. We reside in matrix."*

*"Osseph is the same as us. The difference is little more than a technical one."*

*"His SRM is dated, you mean?"*

*"We can improve him."*

*"Is Gregh still modifying it?"*

*"He has sight. And we're showing him some of the extended functions."*

*"Why? Is this another scheme of yours that I should know about?"*

*"As I said, I want to bring him back. I may have to ... modify him somewhat. But your brother is still in there. Somewhere."*

"Leave me out of it, please."

"As you wish. But you'll be missing a good party."

"How are the diplomats?"

"Comfortably aboard their ferry and sleeping well. They return to Denique after the dinner."

"And the matalin? Lily? How is your ... stand-in?"

"She and Gregh took the plunge. They sleep together every night."

"You're really overwhelming him, aren't you?"

"Nature will not be denied."

"And what of Deretor's great grandson? How is the young Derry? Or shouldn't I remind you that there are other people involved in this game of yours?"

"You sound bitter. Why is it you can't accept things without all this ... judgemental difficulty?"

"I'm not trying to change the world."

"Neither am I. Just attempting to smooth it out a little.

"I merely wondered if you were concerned about Lily's bondmate."

"Max has given up on him and I haven't the inclination or the time to worry about the boy."

"I see. Well, I do have other news. The ship is almost ready. I can't stage any more accidents for you, I'm afraid."

"Then it's time to make our bid for passage. I'll speak to Gregh immediately. Can you set up the defrax?"

"It's all ready to run."

"Thank you, Mihan."

"Just call me when you want me."

## 21. The Island

"It's going to be difficult telling Iilaria, although I'm certain she knows already."

"And Derry is going to be awful."

"We shouldn't have let this happen."

"I think both of us knew what it meant, right from the start."

"Yes. But that doesn't make it easier, does it?"

"Of course not." Lily and I lay beside each other in the wide toballen that had become our nightly habitat. Her hands lay loosely in mine as we talked.

"Do you think you can handle your sister?"

"I don't see why not. After all, she brought you here. It's almost as if she planned it this way. You and me, I mean. As if she knew we would end up ... as lovers."

"That has occurred to me. Perhaps she is using me too?"

"But why? And now that we are so involved, is she going to stand in our way?"

"She wanted me to encourage you to resign your commission. To stay here on New Foster."

"If we can be together, I will. That's certain in my mind."

"What will the Viartans say about that?"

"It has happened before, though not often. They usually want you to go through a re-conditioning. Security, mostly. I'm in languages so it shouldn't be too bad. If I were a systems technician it would be a problem. They aren't too happy letting their technology downside. There are a lot of dangerous gadgets that could be used by – well, people like Osseph."

"What if they decided not to let you go?"

"I'd abduct you! You could come with me instead!"

"No! I'm sorry, but I don't think I could live aboard your ship!"

"Don't worry! I'd never ask you to leave your home."

"So, then. It's Iilaria first?"

"Yes. I'll ... bring it up in the next day or so."

"And I'm leaving for Materossen again."

"Must you? It seems like only a few days since you got here!"

"It's been eighteen days. And I've a lot unfinished at home."

"What about Derry? Is that going to be all right?"

"No, it's not. But we're going to have to get through it."

"If you want me to, I'll come."

"You are sweet and I'm sure you would come. But it's better that I tell him myself. After all, he has his fat-bellied concubine now! You and I will be together again soon. I promise. In Denique."

"Nothing will keep me from you. When you're ready, that is. But it will be difficult, waiting."

"I know."

"Are you crying? What is it?" Her tears made me feel helpless. I was discovering that love has many levels that are not obvious at first.

"Oh ... it's just ... when I came here, there was an element of deceit. I wish it hadn't been that way."

"It doesn't matter, Lily. Iilaria prompted us both. It was like a Silverday play. But the script became real. What we did was ours! Never doubt it!" It was all I could think of to say.

At that moment I believed Lily had become everything I could ever want.


"I'm afraid that you might be disappointed, Gregh." Iilaria's voice surrounded me. Lily had been gone for a twoday and I was working at distracting myself with physical labour. I was moving crates in one of the storage rooms.

"Why? Lily and I love each other. That's enough."

"No. It's not enough. She is bonded, even though there may be a strain at present – Derry will eventually realize his priorities. She has a home and, as well, her work. She's not just going to walk away from it all."

"I know it's going to be difficult. For me as well. Do you think I want to leave you now? I don't. But she is ... real. I mean –"

"And I'm just an entity," she laughed. "I can't compete with flesh and blood where you're concerned, can I?"

"It's not a competition. It's ... well, Lily is ... Lily."

"Have you stopped to think that perhaps it's me you see in her?"

"Of course."

"We were so good together, you and I. I don't think you'll ever find another like me! I spoiled you, you know!"

"Yes, you did. And she reminds me of you – at eighteen. But that's all right. I don't mind the similarity at all! She does have a lot of you in her, yes."

"I suppose I should be flattered then. But what I wanted to try and make you understand is that because she is much like me, I know what she'll do! She will put you in her file of wonderful memories and carry on with her life. Just as I did when you left."

"That really isn't fair, Iilaria. You're presuming we aren't serious about wanting to be together."

"What is fair? Certainly not life. Or love either for that matter! And what do you mean by serious? You had each other to yourselves for almost a fiveday."

"More like a twentyday."

"What do you mean? She was only here a five – or was it a sixday? She had to leave before any of the others –"

"No, it was ..." I could recall every one of the days Lily and I had spent together. Was Iilaria confused?

My sister continued abruptly before I could argue the point. "I hope you have more time together in the future, but I don't want to see you shattered emotionally if it doesn't work out."

"What do you suggest? We agreed to wait until she has worked it out with Derry. I can't rush her."

"No, you can't. And that is all I would advise. Just waiting."

"But I have to make my own plans, regardless."

"I thought your plans were made. Your ship is almost ready to leave and you'll be on it. Surely there will be orders coming?"

"I think you know as well as I do that I'm resigning my commission. I can't go back out there. I'm home to stay."

"Not just because of Lily, I hope."

"That's certainly part of it. But this time I've had here with you has put a lot of things into perspective for me. I want to find out what went on when I was away. I might even write it all down. Use the skills I've learned to create something that is mine. Something real. What would you say to having a historian for a brother?"

"Seriously? That would be the best gift you could give me! You could work at my university! There's a lot going on there –"

"Now just a moment! I'm not sure that's what I mean. Don't go arranging it all for me! I'm talking about something much more personal. It's not that well defined yet."

"All right, all right! Do whatever you must! But it does sound interesting."

"I think so. First of all I've got to speak with my

ship. They are going to be looking for me if I don't."

"They won't let you go easily. You're a senior officer, aren't you?"

"Yes. And I'm supposed to be moving up even more. I've been doing a lot of research into language technology that looks as though it will change the basic routines we use. They're going to want what I've got inside my head."

"We'll send them an SRM! I want to make one of you, anyway. I want a copy of you around for a while, especially if you go chasing after my great granddaughter!"

"You can do that? Make my SRM?"

"You don't know a tenportion of what I can do. Think back to when you first stood outside that door and then to what you know about me now. Do you think I've shown you everything?"

"Most probably not. But I can't imagine what other mysteries you're withholding from me. What are you getting at?"

"Leaving your ship is not going to be easy. I don't think they will let you go. They'll try to convince you that you've had a bad case of ground-syndrome. Which you most likely have, by the way. Then they'll say you should do more service and resign later. You're still young and they'll tell you that you owe them a few more years. My guess is they'll demand your return if you don't go back voluntarily." She was most likely correct.

"So I have a plan, little brother."

"You always have a plan, don't you?"

"Right now it's only a suggestion. I want to hide you. Not here. That would be too obvious. But somewhere on the Islands. Not too far away."

"And I simply don't bother to tell them? They'll

post me as missing and that will be the end of my career!"

"Think about the rest of your life instead! You'll be able to do whatever you want! I'll provide you with everything you need. We can resolve the details later but it's the only way I can help you now. If you want my help, that is."

"Do I have time to think about it?"

"Perhaps a threebreath!"

I made the second most drastic decision of my life. "All right. Tell me what I'm supposed to do!"

"First, I'm going to have to show you something that you might not want to see, in order to explain my plan. Do you want me to go on?"

"Everything you do intrigues me. You may as well."

"Then watch this. And remember, I warned you!"

A haziness appeared in the room, a mist that swirled lightly around the crates where I had been working. It seemed to resolve into a glowing spiral near one of the boxes, to coalesce and solidify.

It became opaque, a whitish elongated blob about the size of a man – or a woman. Patterns formed over it's surface; folds, lines, streaks of colour. A strong smell of ionized gases filled the air as hair, eyes, clothing, a small sleeve pouch, took solid shape in front of me. "Hello, Greghory," she said.

"Lily? What...?"

"Hold me, Gregh. I've missed you so much!" The seated image put out her hand to me. She smiled. Reflexively, I reached for her.

Her hand was warm and solid in mine. It was unlike any hologram or any other sort of projection I had ever seen. It was Lily.

"Iilaria. What is this? It is so ... so real! This is unbelievable! How are you doing it?"

"Iilaria has gone. Hold me, Gregh. It's me! Lily! Hold me!" I wanted to, to take her in my arms and grasp her solidly as if she were actually there in the room with me. But I could not. I was thinking only of the technology behind such an illusion. This was a remarkable demonstration, a three dimensional mirage, a product of Iilaria's incredible visary art.

Then I remembered the incident at the Materossen Civic Court. Lily had taken me to the top of the building and while we walked through a hallway full of boxes and crates – so similar to the storeroom I was then in – she had flickered into momentary nonexistence.

I had blamed it on my ground-syndrome.

Had I been the unwitting victim yet again, tricked, made a fool of, right from the start? Had I spent my days and nights with this phantom? I had slept with it, baring my soul to an illusive automaton.

Blind fury tore at the shreds of my sanity; I shouted, tightening my fist, smashing at the creature, the obscene facsimile, the matrix-entity that had so overwhelmed me with its false beauty. Wanting to strike back, I lashed out as hard as I could.

My officer's signet ring tore skin from her cheek and brought blood gushing down her face. She felt as real as any of the furniture in the room. She fell back onto the stone floor, hitting her head against the edge of one of the crates.

A small part of my mind saw her and reacted with horror. *You've hurt her! For Gill's sake, get help!*

But the rest of me was insane with rage and grief. I blanked out.

The next thing I recall was light streaming through

balcony windows. My head was pounding. When I pushed myself to sit up, I was nauseous and fell back. I lay back and tried to remember how I had come to my room, to the toballen, and what had happened in the storeroom.

Thoughts of Lily's blood-covered face swam in my mind and I wailed like a child. "Great Gill," I cried. "What have I done? What have I done?"

Dream, and the mind unlocks its labyrinthine shell. Psyche sketches its own realities, hazed textures and shade. There is nothing measurable; there is no substance.

Dream logic is illogic. Language is thought is image, vaporizing at the touch – it is all stagecraft, the drama ever moulding to shifting fancy. To dream is to plunge into the mystician's realms.

We still know so little about the psyche. "What am I?" it asks. "Who am I?"

The psychodancers of Denique have a name for the dream state: *e'Nshri nioko lirium*, translating roughly into "black consciousness". They believe that inner self is the only reality, that the outer world is a projected shadow vision. They consume quantities of the drug, *qui-qui*, to keep themselves in semi-sleep, hoping to broaden their sense of reality.

Wake from a dream and the memory evaporates. The world is upright once more and we see the furniture of our lives. But if we wake and the dream is still there ... I had not escaped and I was convinced I was dwelling in madness. I could no longer separate the mirages.

Iilaria tried to convince me that my dreams, as subconscious projections, were some sort of self-imposed reality, that I was not, as I thought, going mad. As I lay on her toballen she hovered about the chamber like a waterwisp, providing me with food and stimulants from the synthmat, smothering me with what I'm sure she believed to be proper attention. And like the drugged dancers, I was entranced with her embrace.

I dreamed I was awake. I felt only images of words spoken.

## 22. Matrix

*"He's still unconscious."*

*"How long will he stay down?"*

*"He has enough of the drug in him to last through the transfer."*

*"What level will you start him at?"*

*"Right at the bottom. I'll run up through the metabolics and leave the defrax and synaps until he's secure."*

*"Any hard buffers?"*

*"Unfortunately he has all the blocks. It will have to be a complete plateau scan. I'll never get back in if he rejects me the first time."*

*"Not another spinner, hopefully?"*

*"Not at all. Gregh is too solid for that. He's used to abnormal forms. He'll synthesize his own reactions. He dreams lucidly. When we were children, he used to fly and see everything in full colour. And he orchestrates as well as any Ilyan!"*

*"Amazing. I thought he was quite – dull!"*

*"You couldn't have known him very well. He just wasn't interested in the same things that you were."*

*"How are you keeping him on line?"*

*"The oldest trick; he's in love with love, seduced into a state of intense vulnerability."*

"Lily?"

"She's back in Materossen."

"I still say it's risky. He might remember her afterwards."

"I don't mind if he does. She thinks he's the most unique man she's ever met."

"Considering his relative age, she's right. When did he meet the real one?"

"At the research centre in Materossen. I switched in on them. He thought it was ground-syndrome when she faded."

"Be careful, Iilaria."

"You worry too much, Mihan! I might get him started writing it all down. History from memory! He can take a teaching position at our university. I'll sponsor him. I owe him that much, I think."

"You certainly do like setting up scenarios, don't you? Will you be able to monitor him?"

"Easily. Here, his pre-cell adsorption is over ninety-portion. Can you run it?"

"I designed this process, didn't I?"

"With a little help! I've got a few things to catch up on. Signal when you need me."

"Consider him simulated."

"Not quite. First I want to – to tune him."

"What are you going to do with it? His SRM?"

"Work out a way to get a duplicate on board his ship."

"It won't work."

"I think that's best left to me for now."

"I'll let you know when he's ready."

"I know you will."

## 23. The Island

I lay for a twoday trying to piece together some semblance of sanity. I was terrified that I had somehow hurt Lily yet I still did not know if she had been real. I finally managed to get up and sit on the balcony overlooking the sea. The air cleansed my mind but Iilaria would not leave me alone. I had developed a case of lung fever and been very sick, she said.

She wanted to talk about reality. I wanted to escape. We confronted each other philosophically, she with the greatest of patience, I with resentment and hostility. But as the days wore on my strength gradually returned. I re-remembered that she was much cleverer than me and usually correct about everything.

Iilaria assured me that the real Lily was her great grand-daughter and a marine biochemist. She had met me in Materossen just as I remembered, and later came to the island with the councillors. She had wanted to interview me between her sessions with the others. Somehow I had contrived my desperate fancy after I fell ill, and she and Iilaria had nursed me back to health.

I had hit Lily in my delirium, when my body temperature was far beyond safe limits. They were worried about my very survival. Lily departed only when I seemed all right. My sister, having no bodily form to speak of, simply watched and waited until I recovered.

She reassured me that my infatuation with Lily had been just that and nothing more.

There were more conversations, a few confrontations. Towards the end, I was not certain which way she would turn next.

"But you left New Foster *knowing* how much I wanted you to stay!"

"That just isn't true, and you know it perfectly well."

"I heard the words that came out of your lips, but I also felt what was in your heart."

"My heart? What did you know of my heart?"

"Everything...we were so close in those days. I saw you"

"Listen to me. I was eighteen. Are you trying to tell me that *I* was all you wanted?"

"I'm trying to tell you, I would have been happier with you than alone."

"But you weren't alone. You've had people hovering about you all your life."

"People who fitted into my plans, perhaps. But never the brother who shared those first eighteen years."

"How often must I apologize for having my own dreams?"

"Apologize? Is that really how you see it? It has nothing to do with apologies."

"Then for Gill's sake tell me what it has to do with! You're pushing me into a deep pit of frustration with your vague allusions."

"I loved you, Greghory. That is all."

"And I you. But what could we have done about it? How many times are you going to throw it at me?"

"Until you see what it was like. I cried out to you. I gave you everything. But all you wanted was that ship out there, and the stars marked on its hull."

"I was only –"

"I know, eighteen trueyears. And so was I. But we could have had so much together, and you could –"

"What? What could I have done? Gone into our

stepfather's shipping business? I would have hated it! And you would have ended up hating me. Besides, you had Marik."

"He rescued me. Our times together were born of desperation. If you had been there, I would never have stayed with Marik."

"Iilaria, be kinder to yourself, and to him. Remember, I've read your diaries. Your best moments were with him. Your children. My nieces."

"You had vanished, and he was a good man. I would never slight his memory, nor wish our children away. What I try to explain to you is...perhaps beyond words...and you won't listen anyway!"

"You talk in riddles, of what-ifs. Of course things might have been different, but they weren't, were they?"

"The past never goes away. Never."

"I – perhaps, I could have stayed. I'll never really know, will I? It's an alternate reality. And what about Osseph? For all you know, he would have got rid of me along with the rest of them."

"How can you be so callous? Don't you understand that I was the only one left? The only one of our entire gyrefaeld? I was alone against a madman, and a prisoner in the world he tried to dominate. Alone! Have you any idea what it was like?"

"I suppose not."

"Definitely not! I've lived through torments you could never imagine! I used to believe it was all worth something. That I had goals! That this planet was worth saving. That the original colonists knew what they were doing and why. But all I kept circling back to was my own frustration. My own singularity." She paused, and all I heard was her breathing, the rustle of beach-wind, the falling of waves.

"One by one they deserted me. They lied and cheated. Or they died by accident or of old age. Every one of them. And you were the first to go, Gregh. I should have known better, but I really thought it had all been ... for something ... worthwhile. You were the first. My own dearest brother."

"What would you have me do? I can't change the past. But I am here with you now. Doesn't that count for something?" I was defensive, angry, hurt.

"Of course it does. But as you so often point out, you are of flesh and blood. I'm only your waterwisp. Your entity from the past."

"You're a lot more than that to me, believe it or not!"

"But time plays tricks on us, doesn't it?" She was suddenly lighter, almost laughing again. "I'm sorry if I anger you, but as I said, I can see you. Feel you. I know what you want, and it's more than illusion. Isn't it?"

"What do *you* want, my sister?" As usual, she had confused me easily.

"Answer my question with another? That's supposed to be *my* trick. I can't answer you. Not yet, at least."

"Nor I you. Isn't that where we left off the last time?"

"You're hopeless. Absolutely hopeless. Gill knows, I try!"

She left me once more trying to work out what I was meant to do or say to satisfy her.

## 24. The Island

I dreamed and in a confusion of overlapping memories saw once more the beginnings of innocence ending....

*There were children, four of them, running along a beach, and as they shouted and laughed with each other I saw that one of them was me. Iily poked and teased the other two boys, and they raced away from us towards high sand bluffs looming in the distance.*

*"Come with me, Gregh. Let them go. I want to show you something that I found."*

*"Where? Can't we go with them? Come back later?"*

*"No. It won't be there if we wait too long. The tide's coming in."*

*"Where are we going?"*

*"It's up the river. By the old bridge. Race you there."*

*"Wait, Iily, wait. I don't feel like running any more."*

*"We have to hurry."*

*"Well...."*

*"Let's walk, then. It doesn't matter."*

*"What is it?"*

*"I don't know. Something buried. Sticking out of the sand. Looks very old."*

*"What about the others?"*

*"I wanted you to see it first."*

*Behind us, an orange sky flickered against a brown ocean. The pillars of a crumbling, abandoned bridge rose from the estuary. She led me by the hand to the first of them. "There. Look." A block of reddish coloured wood lay in the gravel, its end tipped above the water. It seemed familiar. In the shadows, old fears made me tremble.*

*"Looks like an old packing case. Maybe saderwood."*

*"That's what I thought. I want to dig it up."*

*"We'd never be able to. The grownups –"*

*"Why do they even have to know? We can do it at night. Wait for the second tide. Osseph and Mihan will help."*

*"Osseph will want it for himself."*

*"That's all right. I'll make him think it was all his idea anyway. No one else will know."*

*"What do you think is inside?"* Again, memory nudged me as if I knew already.

*"That's what we're going to find out, isn't it?"*

*"No, Iily. We should leave it alone...."*

*"Let's go catch up with them, then."*

In my dream, we ran back to the sea, and the wind was cold on our faces. I wished I could reach through and change everything, knowing that I would never be able to.

## 25. The Island

When I woke once more, it was to the sound of her voice.

"You're better, and I want us to have a banquet. A celebration. A homecoming. I want you to be my guest of honour. But I want to attend as myself. A person instead of just – your entity! Will you help me, my love?"

"What am I to do this time?"

"Just come with me. You'll see!"

I told myself that I could go back to Kalanos; I would have been in Pirrit Ennis in a threeday and on board the *Whitethrell* a day later. But the temptation to stay played strong in my mind. *Stay with her. Don't desert her again. See it through.*

She was seated at a low vanity. It was our old stone

gyre again, our mother's dressalliary, the enormous wardrobe room where the two of them had prepared themselves for special gatherings and for their social life in the Townships.

And the boy, if he wasn't out in the street playing ragball, had watched them, sometimes helping with hair and fastenings. Here he was, once again back in the strange world of his twin sister's fantasy.

She faced away from me, the smooth curves of her back exactly as I remembered from our childhood. Her many reflections faced me from polished glassite walls: pale bronze skin, tiny breasts, her dark hair curling almost to the floor. It was Iilaria of eighteen years, or Iily as I used to call her.

"Dearest Greghory," she pleaded. "Help me get ready for our banquet. I can't do it by myself, you see."

Gowns hung in mirrored dressers alongside racks of stays and supports. There were long, deeply coloured hairpieces, jewellery, powders and colours, mottled shells of cream and scented oils, ribbons, combs, brushes, and all the rest of the feminine paraphernalia.

It paralleled the emotional synthesis of hooking entertainment cubes. Closing out reality, the literal world, it was easy to smother in sensory projections. Absorbing the images could generate such powerful vertigo that individual identity was often at risk.

She was projecting her reality, her identity, onto mine and I was helping her do it. She still held the silken blindfold – we were still playing her little girl's game of bluff.

"Ingren used to do this to us both when we were still children. Do you recall the tricks she played?"

"I've forgotten most of it. The society plays? She dressed us both for the parts."

"I can still see you that one time when we played twin girls. You absolutely hated it. But you were good!"

"You're making that up! I never did any such thing!"

"There are some old holos in the storeroom to prove it!"

"Nonsense." I sipped a bitter-sweet liqueur she'd given me. Its mild euphoric settled my uneasiness.

"You never made love to her, did you?"

"No. But I remember when I discovered that she watched us!"

"She was very lonely. Her bonding was purely an alliance between the shipping registries. Father was like a stranger to her. She could have taken lovers but she was far too reserved. Timid. She chose to spend her time with us instead. She was terribly upset when you left."

"At the time, she seemed quite indifferent to my interests. She made me angry."

"You were just a normal boy wanting his freedom. Even I could not have stopped you."

"I know."

"I want to be myself again. I want you to help me."

"I've told you I will."

"You're very tolerant of me. It still feels as though we've never been far apart."

"You've always been there, in my mind."

"That is what I've been trying to tell you all along," she whispered. I understood a little of her passion then, perhaps for the first time.

As if it were of no consequence, she went on to talk of the councillors, who like actors and actresses would make themselves over for the deceptive roles they played in chambers. She had done so well herself, she claimed, because she could outdo the best of them. "You create an image, an illusion. Everything else depends on that."

From an array of ferriline, brocade, mocasse and brilliantly coloured costume fittings, she chose a layered gown that would trail on the floor behind her. Each piece had to be stepped into separately; she remarked that she had the assistance of three personal maids when she last wore it some seventy years before.

I helped her as best I could, setting the layers properly over each other. It had the effect of changing colour in the light. "It was made for me by a very dear lady I knew in Denique. I never saw another like it. It was one of my favourites. I think I wore it three times."

She chose an elaborate, three-part hairpiece that had to be stacked and pinned one section at a time. After several frustrating efforts I finally satisfied her and had then only to touch up the masqueing on her face.

It was her in every detail, a resurrected Iilaria, wearing the elaborate costume she had worn to state functions as the most influential woman in the Ten Thousand Islands. She was perfect, compellingly so. Her image shimmered on the room's silvered panes.

"There are rings and bracelets in that box. But don't scratch the dye on my nails." A jewellery chest lay at one end of the dresser. We selected loops and rings for her wrists and fingers.

"There's one thing more. The necklace, my love. The embrylline necklace."

In a bottom drawer of the chest was a brilliant band

of interlocking metallic links, each no bigger than a jupine leaf. It was covered with delicately carved motifs and inlaid stones. I cautiously lifted its coiled loops from the box and draped them about her neck.

"It fastens at the back. Be careful. It's worth more than you could ever imagine."

The necklace was warm to my touch – it seemed almost alive. I felt a tingling, a vibration in my fingertips, as I secured the clasp beneath Iilaria's mass of hair. I could feel energy radiating into the room around us, burning into my upper spine almost as if the necklace were around my own neck.

"What do you think?"

"Perfect!"

"Absolutely! Oh yes! Great Gill, it has been so long!"

She was ecstatic. Our re-creation was perfect. She had lost none of her expert touch in transference through the SRM.

"Now, I want you to come downstairs. It is time for us to enjoy, to celebrate."

She stood, the wide gown flowing about her, its flared layers alive in the light. Then she came to me, elegant against the dressalliary backdrop. She ran her jewel-laden fingers over her smooth, narrow waist, caressing her small breasts with their tiny, painted nipples barely showing through the lace halter. I felt a resurgence of long-buried passion – we had loved each other a lifetime ago and I knew it was all there, still inside. We gazed at each other and in those moments of recognition I knew I had lost any chance of an easy leavetaking.

The illusion beckoned once more. "We'll have time, my love. A lot of time, I promise. So, let's go downstairs together. As one."

I turned, we turned, moving slowly towards the doors. Her hand clasped mine, her arm locked against my side. The sound, the smell, the feel of her. It was all rushing back as if a dam had broken.

I was hers, absolutely, as I had always been.

## 26. Matrix

*"He's well over the pre-cell limit. Buffers acting at calculated rate. Should be in nominal defrax. He'll come through."*

*"Monitor everything. The complete scan. Every gene of every cell."*

*"Don't worry. It's all layering perfectly. You're getting the best simulation made anywhere."*

*"Aren't you getting a bit cocky, Mihan?"*

*"All part of the plan!"*

*"Are you running the rest of them yet?"*

*"Everyone is waiting for the two of you."*

*"And Osseph?"*

*"Despite my better judgement, he's down there."*

*"Where would I be without you?"*

*"In a dusty box in a dismal cellar no doubt!"*

*"I expect you're right."*

## 7. The Island

As she had done before on so many occasions, at so many state banquets and gatherings that there was no counting them, Iilaria made her entrance down the curved staircase leading into the dining hall.

There was momentary silence as she appeared. The other councillors, men and women, gazed at her, unable to conceal their admiration, their awe, their jealousy. She nodded, greeting them with her inimitable smile. An attendant held her chair at the head of an elaborately laid table. A toast was proposed. They raised crolloy goblets towards her and towards me – towards us.

The SRM's intertwined matrix-fabric was our reality. I felt her blood-pulse coursing through my veins as she felt mine. We were almost one, each other, the same, as we had been so many years ago.

"Welcome home, Iilaria!" they cried.

"Welcome home!"

She occupied her usual place at the top of the table, in a high-backed chair immediately to my left. Osseph was opposite Iilaria at the far end, flanked on either side by reformist officers. None of the councillors were pleased that the ex-dictator was among them; some would have slit his throat gladly had Iilaria given the command. But tonight they held back their anger, treating him as a guest, respecting her wishes that we should all endure his presence with restraint. Attendants poured more wine, and the meal proceeded.

Ranking First Minister Deretor Manaxallin sat to my right. It was his idea to bring Osseph into a more informal environment for his sentencing. He was curious about the ex-dictator; that they were mortal enemies seemed for the moment unimportant.

Osseph had his sight and, this evening, a good deal more. The projections were astounding; I was beginning to re-appreciate Mihan's genius.

The gathering was also homecoming for me, of course. I had been away for a lifetime and they all sought my attention. I felt as though I might even share in their camaraderie built up through the years of their campaigning together.

Now the war was finally over and Osseph was theirs. Iilaria had decreed that he should have a last evening of respectable company. Deretor was chosen to carry out the final act. He dropped his island accent and spoke in the old tongue.

"We have celebrated tonight with our dear hostess and, as she commanded, have spoken only of gentle things with our guest. But now it is time to stop and recall our common interest. You all know why we are here. Let us get on with it." He sat again so that Iilaria could speak.

The two officers sitting next to Osseph took him by the shoulders and lifted him from his seat. Perhaps he understood what was about to happen before I did. He tried to resist but was no match for the young men. They quickly locked his wrists behind him and stuffed a leather gag into his mouth. His false eye held me in its steady, piercing gaze.

Iilaria talked quietly, commandingly. "Osseph Ketre Tokastevor. We have brought you here tonight for only one reason. We are sentencing you for your crimes against New Foster, its citizenry and the many individuals to whom you have caused such immense hardship and agony. How many deaths can be attributed directly or indirectly to your schemes? We do not know, but it is many, many thousands." Voices echoed agreement around the table and throughout the vast room.

"I could go on at length describing the horror you have put each of us through. Every person at this table has lost not only friends and relatives in the battle but also lifetimes of opportunity. The normally allotted perspective of family, the ordinary range of social relationships that make lives joyful, the chance of meaningful fulfilment in their existence – all have been denied. We each have intense personal reasons for seeing you brought, finally, to justice.

"But I will not prolong these final moments needlessly. Deretor, I have authorized you to pronounce sentence. Please carry on." She sat down once more as an attendant held her chair.

Deretor stood and faced a now pale and fear-stricken Osseph.

"We have found you guilty of all the crimes listed in record. Consequently, we sentence you to immediate death by means to be selected at random by those of us here empowered to so do. Do I have the cast?" Osseph's strenuous objections to the procedure were checked by the uniformed men who held him.

In a manner prescribed by the ancient Quatrec, *aitessuro* chips were passed to six of the guests. Each chip was covered with a wax seal. A cubic die was thrown onto the table's surface by one of the women. It came to rest with three marks showing on its upper surface. The corresponding third chip was dropped into a crolloy bowl filled with boiling fluid.

As the wax melted, the chip unfolded and an image appeared briefly in the vapours rising above the bowl. It showed a metal drum suspended over an open fire. A man was sealed inside, dimly visible through holes cut into the metal. He was being slowly roasted alive.

Osseph screamed through his gag. The two officers dragged him to the far end of the room where two more soldiers brought in a large, perforated crolloy drum. It took all four of them to force Osseph, head-first, into the drum; then they secured the end tightly in place. As they rolled him from the room, he pounded frantically on the inside of the container.

I did not believe what I was seeing, yet I knew Iilaria was going to let it continue. I turned to her to raise some objection. She was engaged in conversation with one of her ministers. I could say nothing. Two of the women guests, apparently weak of stomach, quickly left the hall, possibly to bring up the meals they had just finished.

After a few moments of hushed whispering, my homecoming resumed.

The noise of goblets and plates, the voices chattering in a steady drone of dinner conversation helped smother the continuous wailing screams that penetrated the heavy timber doors between us and the courtyard. Eventually the disconcerting sounds stopped.

## 28. Matrix

*"Hopefully, you will tire of avenging yourself against Osseph."*

*"Is that what's bothering you? That was pure psychodrama! It was for the benefit of those councillors who still need emotional restitution. Every one of them lost an entire generation of family and friends through the years of confrontation with Osseph. And even after all these years, it still tears them apart. The release of his module has brought it all back."*

*"Revenge?"*

*"If that were all there was to it, I wouldn't have bothered. It is lot more than simple revenge."*

*"I don't think so. Even though I know it wasn't my brother, I think it was – sadistic. Uncalled-for."*

"*You must listen to me, Mihan. In simplest terms, how do we stop ourselves from forgetting what happened? Now that Osseph's SRM is deregulated there will be a common reaction, a resurgence of public sympathy for the man. It wouldn't surprise me to see another rebellion in a few years! I want to keep the anger on our side of the arena alive, so that we'll be prepared to suppress any uprising before it happens!*

"*As you well know, the Quatrec failed to stop Osseph. I will not fail to stop another Osseph from destroying what has taken two thousand years to build. So consider the demonstration you helped set up an exercise in keeping allegiances clearly defined.*"

"*I still don't like it.*"

"*Be patient, Mihan.*"

"*And another thing! What you're doing with Greghory is underhanded and utterly fraudulent! You've destroyed his career simply to satisfy a whim of your own!*"

"*Here again, I must disagree. You've made a perfect simulation of him. He has all the characteristic patterns I wanted. We saw to that —*"

"*I mean the flesh-and-blood brother, the human being you've left out there.*"

"*I've given him a new career as a historical analyst. He's starting his first seminars —*"

"*You know what I mean, Iilaria! All you've done so far is to hide him away in Tordek's billet. Is he convinced that life here on New Foster is a better prospect than returning to the Viartans? He'll be wandering about with a head half full of vague memories about an experience that will haunt him forever! How can you justify that?*"

"*Do I have to justify myself to you at every turn, Mihan? What I do is justifiable because it is my responsibility to ensure our own survival! Yours and mine! There is far more to this than you realize!*"

"You are forever telling me that. And I – well it seems to me that you've simulated Greghory for no other reason than to infiltrate the nervous system of the Viartan ship. And there are numerous reasons why your scheme won't work. Far better to have taken them by surprise and pirated the vessel!"

"And start a war with them?"

"There has never been a war in space, nor will there ever be one!"

"Are you certain of that?"

"It's a matter of logistics. And the time factor. A simple trip from Viarta to Isurus takes six and a half years at light speed. To the crew. But when they arrive, how many real-time years will have passed? Twenty? By then, everyone will have forgotten what they came for."

"I know that, Mihan. What is your point?"

"Any reasonable benefit of such an endeavour would be completely beyond the statistical limits of supporting it in the first place. Why do you think the interstellar community never succeeded?"

"Because it was not well planned. Try to remember that it made no sense to send a thousand human beings out into the darkness in the first place. To start colonies with nothing more than invisible lights to guide them? They had very little chance of survival, yet here we are. What are we but a successful colony? What are the Viartans? The Indi? The Sarigians?"

"You rely on a very sketchy analysis of their mandate, Iilaria. Such a massive colonization program would have depended solely on the motivation of the colonists. A need born of desperation, perhaps? A home planet that was no longer hospitable? That one ship whose remains are now in orbit about Isurus – we don't know how it was done, do we? Or even where it came from."

"True. We have only a handful of insubstantial clues."

"Insubstantial? I'd say imaginary, except for the dismembered hull out there. And a few artifacts locked away in Port Cray."

"Have you studied any of them?"

"Not really."

"I have, Mihan, so be quiet. I do agree with you that space warfare would be impractical. But you reinforce my confidence that we can effectively control the Viartan ship through a properly designed simulation. It is unlikely there will be any meaningful opposition!"

"But don't you see what I mean, Iilaria? There wasn't the slightest chance that regular trade could ever be maintained between the five colonies. It's a matter of simple logistics."

"Warfare and trade. What else do you see as being impossible?"

"What is the point of attempting to control that ship? You're embarking on a fool's mission!"

"It's lucky for you that I'm so fond of you, Mihan Tokastevor. Otherwise, I wouldn't be able to put up with your constant complaints."

"You haven't answered my question."

"I will, Mihan. I will...."

## 29. The Island

When they came, there were only two of them, a man-woman team of uniformed security officers from the *Whitethrell*.

They searched the island for most of a morning, finding nothing along its beaches or in any of the boarded-up structures. As far as they could tell, it was a deserted lump of wildly overgrown rock, just one in the long inner rim of island outcroppings. Their limited detection equipment was not capable of picking up signals from the underground power plant, which we had turned down to minimum when we saw them approaching.

The man was large, a slow moving Viartan with short-cropped hair. A burn scar slashed diagonally across his left cheek. I had never seen him before, but there were many of the crew that I might never run across in my day-to-day work on board. I did know his companion: Darret-el-Mar was an anthropological surveyor; she had run ground expeditions in which I had been involved. I remembered her as particularly hard-nosed when it came to her job.

They left their inspection of the house until last and would have bypassed it altogether except for her. She was carrying out orders to find me wherever I might be and she intended to be thorough.

"Come on, Dar. There's nobody here. He's long gone. We should get back to Kalanos before nightfall!"

"It won't take long to look." She was small, olive skinned, not much more than half the man's height. Several years his senior, she was trying to effect command.

"I can't imagine why he came here in the first place. It seems dead and deserted." The young man was impatient but did not want to upset his senior officer. Perhaps he had it in mind to get her back to a more comfortable setting where they could forget their duties and respective ranks for the evening.

"The *e'Nalak* steward claimed Addiman rented the *saiak* for a few days and was headed here. That was almost two months ago. Where is the boat? Where did he take it? He could have gone anywhere. His trail just vanishes. It's strange when you consider that it was so easy to follow him this far. He didn't try to conceal his movements."

They came to the front entrance much as I had done. Was it only a twomonth ago? So much had happened to me in that time with Iilaria.

They looked at each other, silently deciding how best to get inside, then she nodded. "May as well, Jai. It's locked."

He was a man who wanted to be elsewhere and soon. I can't say that I blamed him for not taking more time and trying to find another way, although it annoyed me that I could take no physical action to stop him; I was to wait until they were inside.

With a single, quick forward thrust he kicked open the wooden door. With hands held close to their holstered standard-issue B-5s, they entered.

They must have followed my trail from Pirrit Ennis, which would not have been difficult. Apparently the ship was preparing to leave the Isuran system, the repairs finished. I had not reported back to them as is usual with extended ground-leave and they had presumed me missing. As an officer I was required to observe protocol in most matters and it was not a good idea to ignore naval routine. But Iilaria insisted on my remaining silent. It appeared that I was now officially listed as "absent and unaccounted for".

They quickly searched the small house. To them it appeared as little more than an unused vacation cabin, boarded up while the owners were about their regular business. The enormous rooms that Iilaria had projected for my benefit were that and no more, intricate visuals that could be constructed instantaneously and just as rapidly shut down. What the two investigators were seeing was yet another fabrication, a mimic of the reality that both surrounded and evaded their senses – a deserted residence, a theatrical make-piece, another illusion. Eventually, they came to the old kitchen where I waited for them.

"What in the name of Gill are you trying to pull off? Didn't you hear us out there? You've been sitting here all this time? You need a boot up your rassbone!" Anger made the scar on his face burn bright red. Darret said nothing.

To add to their confusion, I vanished.

"Dar? What is this? What is going on?"

"I don't know. But that was him. Coltenent Greghory Addiman."

"You didn't have to break in, you know. The back door was open." A small boy had entered the kitchen from behind them.

"Now who the Gill are you?" Jai spun around, his weapon drawn.

"Take it easy, Jai! He's just a child." Dar was shaken but still in control. "We're looking for the man who was just here. Do you know where he – where he is now?"

"Probably back in the box." The boy was chewing on a long craelbine stem and seemed quite at ease with the two intruders. "What do you want with him?"

"What do you mean, back in the box?"

"He's not real. He's a picture. My granfaeldam made it."

"Made it?"

"Yeah. It's her hobby. She collects all the visitors. That was my Uncle Gregh. He was here in the summer. For a threeday. Or a fourday. I can't remember."

"Three or four days? Where did he go from here?"

"Back to the Big Island. Kalanos, he said."

"So why haven't we seen you until now? We've been on your island all afternoon. Where have you been?" The woman was not at ease with the boy. "And what is your name, if I may ask?"

"Mihan. My brother and I come here every summer with our uncles. They're off on one of the boats."

"Brother?"

"That's me. I'm Osseph." Another boy entered, a blue-eyed blond, slightly taller but obviosly cast in the same mould. "We saw you down on the beach."

"Why didn't you say something? Let us know you were here?"

"Why? People come over from the other islands all the time. We thought you were here just to look around, have a picnic maybe. Lots of couples come over and ..." The boys giggled at each other.

"We were playing up here. My uncles won't let us talk to strangers, anyway."

"So you think your uncle – Greghory – went back to Kalanos. Then how is it that he – or his image, or whatever – just happened to be sitting right here when we walked in?"

"We were just fooling around with the trajector. I turned him on. Do you want to see him again? You can," the older boy offered.

"Yes. We do."

Osseph went into an adjacent room and came back with a small black device and several white cubes, each about the size of a thumbnail. There was a row of flashing lights on one side of the box and inset keys along the top. He inserted one of the cubes and pressed a switch. A haziness appeared at the table where the image had been before, gradually resolving itself into the solid volumes of a seated man. It spoke to them in rasping, almost incoherent grunts.

*"Bays? e-Masengi nibberi Tordek? Bays?"*

"What is he saying?"

"We never know. The recording's no good. We keep trying to get him to say something but he can't."

"You mean he always talks this nonsense?"

"It could be Viranti. Most of the other holograms are the same. They're boring, actually."

"Let me see one of the cubes," Dar asked, adding nervously, "May I?"

"I guess." Osseph handed her one with irregular markings across its face. "You can have that one. It's no good any more."

"Er...thanks." She was not sure what to do with the offering and dropped it into her vest pocket.

"I think we're wasting our time here, Dar. Let's get back to the main island." Jai looked to the woman officer for some sign of acknowledgement.

"No, wait a moment. I'm curious about this holo. Can he move around? Walk?"

"No. The recording was made right here. It was after the noon meal. I know that for sure because Osseph wouldn't help with the cleaning up. I had to do it all."

"Not so. I had to fix the boat that afternoon," insisted Osseph.

"It was already fixed, you ragger. You just didn't want to hang around when there was work to do."

"It's all right, boys. We would simply like to know where the real Greghory has gone. He's overdue and we've had to come looking for him. He hasn't reported in for a long while and there could be something wrong," Darret explained.

"So you *are* off that cruiser! We thought so." Mihan was obviously excited about the two spacers.

"No, *I* thought so. You said they were New Foster

Militia." Osseph gave the impression that he had recognized their uniforms as offworld.

"Is it fun on a big ship like that?" Mihan asked.

"Fun? I don't know about fun," Jai answered. "It's our job. I suppose it would be fun for someone who had never been out there. He could tell you more about that than we could." He pointed to my seated projection.

"He told us a few stories about other planets. It wasn't that interesting." Osseph seemed beyond such things.

"I really liked him," said Mihan. "I'd like to do what he does. He ran away from home so he could join the space navy. He said that he was over a hundred years old. Does being on the ship make you live forever?" He could not conceal his eagerness to hear more about space travel.

"I was twenty when I joined up," said the young man. "I was in a military college on Viarta. My parents farmed on a commune. They thought it would be a better life for me than staying at home. They're probably dead. I'll never see them or my sisters again. That's all I know. You have to give up everything when you go out there."

"What about you?" Mihan touched Dar's hand and she jumped back as a bolt of static discharged through her. "Sorry. It's the heat, I think. You build up a charge walking around on the floor."

"That's all right. You startled me!" She forced a smile for the younger boy.

"I'm an archaeologist. I study remains and artifacts. There aren't many sites where we've found them but we know there were once other races. Millions of years ago. And light years away. Nothing much left now, though." Darret seemed reluctant to talk about it and fell quiet once more.

"I wish you'd tell us what it's like," Mihan begged.

"I'm sorry. We have to go. Jai, can you fix the broken latch on the door?"

"I'll put it together."

"Funny, it wasn't broken this morning," Osseph said.

"That guy kicked it," explained Mihan.

Jai left us, the two boys, Darret and my shadow-self. The woman seemed thoroughly disoriented and kept glancing towards me as if I were about to say something that would resolve her distress. She wasn't sure about me, about what she had been told. In her mind was some lurking suspicion that it was all fabrication. She might have sensed the truth of her dilemma but had no way of grappling with it.

"Are you boys here alone, then?"

"No. There's two more of our friends down at the boat house. Iily and her twin brother. And our uncles will get back later tonight."

"You do your own cooking? There doesn't seem to be much of a kitchen here."

"There are supplies on the boat. We keep everything like that down there. It's more comfortable, too. And people can't break into it."

"Listen, we're sorry about the door! Jai will fix it! But we had no idea there was anyone here. If you had at least yelled, or said something sooner. Or answered when we knocked. But the place seemed empty. The whole island! And like I said, we were here all afternoon. You could have shown yourselves sooner."

"Don't get angry with us!" It was by way of a command from Osseph. His voice had the subtle assurance of someone much older and it amplified Dar's distress. "We don't know where *he* is. If we did, maybe

289

we'd tell you. But if either one of my uncles were here they'd probably have thrown you off the island by now."

"All right, all right. I've apologized. Jai, how's the door?"

"Fixed. It was just a wood catch on the inside. Good as new."

"Then we should be going." Suddenly she seemed unable to handle the situation. There was no identifiable danger, but she did not want a confrontation with these two youngsters. Her intuition was to leave while they still had the opportunity. "We're not going to get anything out of this – persona. It seems to be rather a limited toy the boys have here."

"It gives me a weird feeling in my gut," said Jai.

"It's just an elaborate holomaph," said Dar. "There are a few on the ship that can do almost the same. Or could, with the right input."

"Mentioning the ship, we should ..."

"Right. Let's get going. We can report in from the *e-Nalak*. Dead end. The man's gone. We'll try to pick up his trail again tomorrow."

They excused themselves from the boys. "Tell your uncles we were here. They might know something that would help."

"Call in the morning if you want," Osseph suggested. "The hook-up's usually on at midday. From the *e-Nalak* visary."

"All right. And thank you for the demonstration."

I had disappeared again. Moments later as the two officers made their way down to the secluded bay where their boat was anchored, the boys flickered out of existence as well.

As they headed out across the quiet swells rolling in from the Sea of Dreams, the young man, Jai, looked back at Iilaria's island.

He wasn't certain if his mind tricked him or if it was a reflected shadow-image from the water – he thought he saw a dark-haired woman standing on the high stone bluffs. He imagined she wore a pale, shimmering gown that blew about her in the mild breeze, accentuating the elusiveness of the vision. He didn't mention it then as Dar appeared to have seen nothing. He didn't want to be ordered to turn the craft about.

Nor did he mention it in his report that night. But his dreams were some of the most intense he could remember. In his firmly implanted memory-mirage, the woman beckoned to him through the mysterious channels of his subconscious. There was little he could do but follow as she directed the formation of new memory sequences deep within the wells of his psyche. He had unknowingly joined the enormous family of Iilaria's forces.

In the early morning he awoke thinking that he might be suffering from ground-syndrome. Dar turned over beside him in half-sleep and told him to be still.

They had been looking for Naval Coltenent Greghory Newton Addiman, VNTS, Second Officer, Linguistic Cryptology and Translations. Although they had not located him in person and declared him "missing and thus de-assigned due to unknown circumstances", they had unwittingly found something else. He was with them in a way they would never have thought possible.

Dar carried him back with her aboard ship. She was compelled to try the cube she had been given. The modified replication transferred itself from the ship's visary to the on-board matrix system that it was so familiar with.

They had in fact found him, just as he had found them.

## 30. Matrix

"You'll have to learn to put up with Mihan, brother dear. He tries to be my conscience! Whenever I want to initiate some new policy, he always offers his opinion. Then I generally do the opposite!"

"I can see why he reacts the way he does, Iily. You're enough to drive a person mad."

"You males are all alike. Stubborn and difficult."

"And women? Quite beyond reason!"

"I'm flattered that you finally acknowledge I'm a woman, still."

"I never really doubted it. It just took me a little while to get used to the differences."

"So what do you think of all this now that you're with me again?"

"I don't really know. I'm not sure what to expect."

"Expect? You have to stop being so serious. You now have the freedom to do anything you choose! And for the next million or so years you can indulge yourself in becoming anything you wish!"

"As you certainly indulge yourself!"

"Mihan was worried about how you would react. Was he right after all? You're not sure of your new status?"

"Perhaps it would help if I understood what I am to be sure of. It seems that you have been leading me along some devious path."

"I have been trying to open a door for you."

"I said I'd try to see it through."

"That is all I ask."

"Doesn't it get ... rather boring?"

"I have been in matrix for a lifetime – I've lost count of the years – and I haven't had a single moment of boredom. Think about it. With this island and its mass of micromolecular templates, we can generate any sequence of events we please, any reality that seems interesting...."

"You are far too complicated for me, Iily. You remind me of our stepfather. I could never argue with him either."

"I understand that, Gregh. It is going to take time for you to adjust to this level of existence. It has its own determinants. Even its own language. There is such a vast difference between what you were and what you will be in a year or so that I can't adequately describe it. It will take understanding, but I'll be here to guide you."

"What about the others? How did they manage this transition?"

"So far there are only twenty-six of us. I have my two daughters, Lily's father, our Uncle Max, Mihan of course, and others you'll meet. Some of them prefer to remain out of matrix for periods of time. We have a system of clocking and monitoring –"

"How did they survive?"

"Very well for the most part. There were only one or two that didn't restructure completely. Osseph may be one of these – we call them spinners."

"Osseph? What will become of him?"

"With a few modifications he might stabilize. At least, the one you seem to prefer. The young Osseph."

"And all those cubes and references in your visary –"

"Our visary."

"All right, our visary. How many others can you access?"

"Hundreds. Tens of hundreds. All of the individuals who plan and organize the day-to-day operation of New Foster."

"It is an empire then. You have surpassed Osseph himself!"

"Perhaps so. But if you can lecture me on the generalities of astrophysics as you did so recently in my garden courtyard, then I can likewise tell you a thing or two about the unfairness of human relationships and what it takes to run a government like New Foster's. I need to show a strong hand."

"Dare I say it? You are the new dictator?"

"There is so much that you do not comprehend, Greghory. If you see me only as a dictator, then I have failed. What I do is set patterns, suggest priorities, encourage sensible behaviour. Osseph had no vision other than his myopic desire to destroy the Quatrec because he thought it controlled him. He had no understanding of the broader picture. He had no desire to improve the planet by carefully regulated hard work.

"If you want to call it an empire that I have here, very well. And yes, I am still in control of everything from the Council Chambers in both Denique and Materossen to the reconstruction and reclamation of the Territories. But my mandate is nothing more or less than the colony's continued existence."

"I – perhaps I misjudged –"

"Perhaps. And don't forget Mihan. He's the one who designed you. He took the old SRM theories and rewrote them. You would do well to reacquaint yourselves."

"The two of you sound to be at odds most of the time."

"Of course we are! That is the nature of our relationship! But neither could we do without each other!"

"I meant to ask him about the power supply. What happens if it fails? Wouldn't we all just vanish?"

"Of course not! Even if the system failed it wouldn't affect our modules. They could be reactivated by simply reinstating the grid running the island. But it couldn't happen – we're connected to a much wider system. Isurus itself would have to be destroyed before we were."

"Is this why you want my ship? To get beyond Isurus? To guarantee a beachhead somewhere else?"

"In a manner of speaking, yes. But this is where you come in."

"Me? Your plan for me is not finished, is it?"

"Never. What would you say, for example, if I told you that one day you could find yourself in charge of the Viartan Navy? The space fleet? What directives would you give?"

"That's easy. I'd build more ships. I'd go twice as far. Even a tentime! I'd – why? What are you suggesting?"

"You know I have no desire to go out there myself. But with your interests and experience – and you are one of them, after all...."

"Is that what this has been about?"

"Not at first, no. But when I knew you were coming down and I saw that massive piece of hardware floating in orbit above our heads –"

"You commandeered me!"

"The problem with Mihan is that he limits his vision to the immediacy of the technical."

"You abducted me!"

"You on the other hand will have no difficulty in understanding possibilities. Of inventing possibilities."

"You seduced me!"

"You and I are very much alike, you know. But I'm the only one who ever knew that."

"You gambled on my coming back."

"You could run your new ship right across the galaxy!"

"New ship?"

*"Imagine what you might find!"*

*"Something else, similar to us, coming in the other direction?"*

*"That is one possibility. So you see why it is essential that we control your* Whitethrell*? We will build our own vessel; that's where Mihan comes in. It will have to be a vastly improved piece of equipment that doesn't necessarily depend on a human crew. But for now,* Whitethrell *is our best chance!"*

*"The gene banks – we could start colonies."*

*"We have to think it all through very thoroughly, of course."*

*"I'm beginning to understand why you are always such a nag."*

*"Meanwhile, would you care for a picnic on the beach?"*

*"Only if you'll show me how you do the sound effects."*

*"Race you there...."*

## 31. Beginnings

Our language is not of words: thought flows ever cyclic, like a storm wind rushing in whiplash fury. There is no stopping it. The singular identity has vanished.

She describes herself as a new life force. She is that and far more. No human mind ever comprehended so much on a purely intuitive plane. She is the future, or will be when she is ready.

Part of it is loneliness – she was the first of her kind in this corner of the galaxy.

All she wants now is to search out others like herself.

## 32. Kalanos Separ: Epilogue

The lung fever has finally abated. I sit in the *Perrellon e'Nalak* messalliary sipping warm callafe. The quiet of autumn approaches and the other islands are obscured by early morning lowdrift. My ship has broken orbit and most of the population on New Foster's night side watched its brilliant, pulsating departure.

I will miss the long track of space, the landfall of strange planets, the endless search for unknown wonder. But I would miss this ancient beauty far more. I am home to stay.

I can resume my old identity; there will be no more hiding, no security officers searching. Iilaria concealed me well and I have stayed out of sight according to her plan. I have at least a month before I start at her university.

My naval career ends in obscurity, but as she said, my life is just begun. If I am to be master of my own destiny I had best get used to it, she thinks.

A message has arrived at the Palace from Lily. She seems curious to see me again as long as it is well away from my sister's island. She claims she wants to know everything about my past, my travels, my reactions to this much-changed world. I remember starting such a conversation with her once before I was ill.

She neglected to mention when we first met that her name was an abbreviation of her great-grandfaeldam's. It was so obvious and I hadn't recalled it: Iilaria, Iily, Lily.

I will be travelling the ocean once more, meeting Lily in Denique; it is only a twoday further on. We have no definite plans. Iilaria has offered me the

*Solyon*. We will cruise the Sea of Dreams, speaking of lives past, present and future.

*The two of us are little more than blobs of white no matter what angle the hologram is viewed from. I used to think I could make out my sister's small, rounded face, her intense dark eyes, peering over the carriage's high rim. Of me there is nothing but an indistinct patch that might have been swaddling or a pillow.*

*Was I there at all? For all I could see, I might not have existed when the image was scanned.*